IN THE SHADOW OF
THE ENEMY

IN THE SHADOW OF
THE ENEMY

Tania Bayard

This first world edition published 2018
in Great Britain and 2019 in the USA by
SEVERN HOUSE PUBLISHERS LTD of
Eardley House, 4 Uxbridge Street, London W8 7SY.
Trade paperback edition first published
in Great Britain and the USA 2019 by
SEVERN HOUSE PUBLISHERS LTD.

British Library Cataloguing in Publication Data
A CIP catalogue record for this title is available from the British Library.

ISBN-13: 978-0-7278-8843-3 (cased)
ISBN-13: 978-1-84751-967-2 (trade paper)
ISBN-13: 978-1-4483-0177-5 (e-book)

Typeset by Palimpsest Book Production Ltd.,
Falkirk, Stirlingshire, Scotland.

ACKNOWLEDGMENTS

Thanks to R. C. Famiglietti for advice concerning the court of Charles the Sixth; Sara Porter at Severn House for editorial assistance; Josh Getzler, my agent, for constant support; and my husband, Robert M. Cammarota, for loving encouragement, invaluable suggestions, and skillful editing.

PROLOGUE

When the stench of dead bodies became too strong, the king left Roosebeke and went to Courtrai to refresh himself. The town made no defense. The burgers, their wives, and all the other men, women, and children fled to the cellars and churches. There was widespread pillage, and when the king himself entered on the first of December, all those who had hidden were found and slain.

The French hated the Flemish in Courtrai because in the year one thousand three hundred and two there had been a great battle in which Count Robert Artois and all the flower of France had been killed. When the king learned about a chapel in the church of Notre Dame where were displayed five hundred pairs of golden spurs taken from the Frenchmen who had fallen in that battle, he announced that the townspeople would pay dearly, and when he left, he set the town on fire, so it would ever after be known that the King of France had been there.

Froissart, *Chroniques*, Livre II, 1376–1385

Courtrai, Flanders, 1 December 1382

As soon as the terrified citizens heard the French breaking down the gates of the city, they made haste to hide. Some fled to cellars and attics, others barricaded themselves behind the closed shutters of their shops, many sought refuge in churches and monasteries. A few even tried to conceal themselves in large chests and barrels.

Then came the pillage. The soldiers hacked their way into the houses and carted off gold coins, silver spoons, diamond rings, emerald necklaces, crystal beakers, enameled pitchers, porcelain bowls, fine linen tablecloths, priceless tapestries. They stormed into the churches and despoiled the golden chalices, silver patens, and ivory crosses. They toppled statues of the saints, smashed the altar-pieces, trod on the priests' embroidered vestments. The streets were littered with broken crockery, shards of glass, and remnants of bedding and clothes. All the wealth of the city and its citizens was plundered or destroyed.

At last, King Charles the Sixth entered, sitting tall on a big white stallion. He was only fourteen, but, at that time, strong, confident, and seemingly invincible. In a few years he would be known throughout Europe as the king who had lost his reason, but there was no sign of his madness then; all anyone could see was a proud youth exulting because his troops had won a great victory over the Flemish.

The king stayed in the city for several days. Some said he told his troops not to harm the citizens, but it makes no difference whether this is true, for as soon as he left, the killing began. The soldiers hunted out the people in their hiding places, dragged them into the streets, slit their throats, cut off their heads, impaled them on swords and spears. Those who tried to run away found themselves trapped in narrow alleyways or cul-de-sacs where they were mercilessly slaughtered. No one was spared, not even the little children, the sick and infirm, the old, the pregnant, the feeble. The air swelled in a cacophony of screaming and wailing. Women cried out for mercy as they were raped. Dogs howled as they were crushed under the feet of the soldiers. Horses reared and plunged, trampling soldiers and victims alike. The city was awash in blood and dismembered bodies.

Finally, the soldiers lit torches and set fires that would reduce the city to rubble. But before they left, they carried out one more shocking act; they ransacked the church of Notre Dame and stole what the citizens of Courtrai prized most: five hundred pairs of golden spurs stripped from the feet of dead French knights at the Battle of Courtrai eighty years earlier, treasured symbols of a great Flemish victory over the French that had been hung in the vaults of a chapel where they were celebrated every year with a magnificent ceremony.

A Frenchman who had not taken part in the massacre stood at the portal of the church and watched as a group of soldiers climbed up to the vaults, tore down the golden spurs, and flung them into the eager hands of their comrades waiting below. Two of the spurs fell close to this man. He picked them up and hurried away. As he was about to mount his horse, he noticed two children, a boy and a girl, huddled together near a burning house. The children were beautiful, and he knew the marauding soldiers would take them to be raped or sold into slavery. He lifted the boy and threw him onto the horse's back. Then he took the little girl in his arms, swung her up into the saddle, and galloped off.

The terrified girl struggled and nearly slipped from his arms. The man whispered, 'Do not be afraid. I am a friend.' The child looked into his face and relaxed.

But the boy, seated behind the man, lashed out with his fists and shouted, 'Damn you and your king to Hell!'

ONE

On the twenty-ninth of January they assembled at the royal
Hôtel Saint-Pol for the marriage celebration . . . There were
various masquerades, and they danced to the sound of musical
instruments until the middle of the night . . . Then, while the
young lords thought only of amusing themselves, someone
threw a spark at those taking part in the masquerade.
Immediately, the clothes of the dancers went up in flames.

The Monk of Saint-Denis,
Chronique du Religieux de Saint-Denis,
contenant le règne de Charles VI de 1380 à 1422

Paris, late February 1393

She was surrounded by burning men, hairy savages who
shrieked and writhed and tore at their blazing costumes. Naked
flesh peeled away. Twisted bodies fell to the floor and curled
up in agony. Friends rushed to help them; the flames seared their
hands, and they recoiled, crying in pain. A little white dog howled
as sparks reached out and transformed him into a glowing ember.

Musicians high in the air dropped vielles, trumpets, pipes, and a
bagpipe that squealed as it fell. The king's brother stood at the
door holding lighted torches. Another torch flew through the air,
landed at her feet, and threw off sparks that ignited her gown. She
plunged into a large vat of water. The water turned to blood, churned,
and spewed her out, along with a naked man who hurled bloody
platters and goblets. Flaming knives and spoons spun around her
head, setting her hair on fire. The burning men, now reduced to
red-hot skeletons, lurched toward her, and she ran to a woman
dressed in silver and crawled under the train of her gown, only to
be pushed out by a madman wearing a large jeweled crown. She
tried to pull the train back over her head, but it slithered away.
The fiery skeletons pounced. She screamed.

'*Cristina!*'

She sat up, trembling.

'You had a nightmare.' Francesca bent down and picked up the twisted bedcovers lying on the floor. 'Tell me about it.'

She shook her head. She'd never told her mother, or anyone else, that she'd seen the masquerade, and she wasn't about to do so now. But in the nightmare, it had all come back. The king and his friends, dressed as hairy savages, mocking the bride, set on fire by sparks from a lighted torch; the man who jumped into a vat of water; the little white dog that got too close; the musicians looking down from their balcony; the king cowering under the train of the Duchess of Berry's gown. Only one thing was different – the lighted torch lying on the floor; the only torches she remembered seeing that night were those in the hands of the king's brother, the Duke of Orléans.

The burning men were gone, and she could speak calmly. But her mother was shaking.

'I'm sorry I frightened you, Mama.'

'It wasn't you. I've just come from a procession. Everyone walked so fast, it was hard to keep up.'

Christine knew all about the processions, and she despised them. The king had gone mad, and day after day people marched through the city, crying and wailing and tearing their hair, praying for a miracle that would deliver him from the evil spirits that had taken his mind away. To her, it seemed absurd.

'Do you have to join every procession you see?'

'How else can we dispel the demons?'

Francesca saw malevolent beings everywhere, and she blamed them for the king's illness. Christine didn't believe in such things, but as she sat on her bed, still under the influence of her terrible nightmare, she couldn't help being affected by her mother's apprehensions. The shadows that moved around the room seemed ominous, the sudden gusts of wind that beat against the windows threated to tear away the oiled cloth that covered them, the burning logs in the fireplace sent off sparks that crackled and spit menacingly as they shot up the chimney. She smelled something burning and shuddered.

Francesca went to a chest, took out a little sack filled with rose petals, lavender, and rue she'd laid away with the clothes to discourage moths, and handed it to her. Christine disliked the smell

of the rue, but it was better than the stench in the air, and she held
it to her nose and breathed deeply.

'Georgette tripped on the hearth and nearly fell into the fire,'
Francesca said. 'The towel she was holding went up in flames, but
she did not get hurt. It will take more than that to deliver us from
her.' She smoothed her black dress over her ample hips.

Christine had to smile. She imagined the ways her mother thought
they might be delivered from their clumsy hired girl; perhaps she'd
be transformed into a sprite and blown away by the wind, still
wearing her rumpled dress and grimy apron. Or lifted up through
the chimney by a helpful hand from heaven.

The children pounded up the stairs and burst into the room.
Their little white dog, Goblin, pushed through their legs and
raced to Christine, who picked him up and buried her face in his
soft coat, remembering the white dog that had perished at the
masquerade.

'Georgette burned a towel,' twelve-year-old Marie said.

'We know. It is not the first time,' Francesca said.

'Were you afraid, *grand'maman*?' asked Jean, who was nine.

'After what happened at the palace . . .' Francesca hesitated and
glanced at her daughter. Christine wondered whether her mother
had guessed what her nightmare had been about.

'I know what happened at the palace,' eight-year-old Thomas
said. 'All those men burned up.'

'Why was the king there?' Marie asked. 'Isn't he supposed to
conduct himself properly and run the country?'

Christine looked at her daughter and smiled. 'I'm sure if you
were in charge, Marie, there wouldn't be any masquerades.'

Five-year-old Lisabetta, Christine's niece, tiptoed over and
touched Christine's hand to get her attention. 'There won't be any
more fires, will there?' She pushed out her lower lip and seemed
about to cry.

'Of course not,' Jean said. A lock of brown hair fell over his eyes
and Christine felt a pang of sadness. Tall, thin, and serious, he
looked exactly like his father, who'd been dead for several years.

'It happened because of the evil spirits at the palace,' Francesca
said. 'You must not go there any more, Christine.'

'Don't start that again, Mama. You know I need the work.' She
looked around the room. 'Only now I don't have any work.'

'Were you not copying a book about a saint for the queen?'

'The queen wanted to give it to the bride, her favorite lady-in-waiting. I don't think Catherine de Fastavarin will care to have it now, after the tragedy at her wedding ball. And the queen has probably forgotten about it.'

'Then what about those?' Francesca said, pointing to a stack of manuscript pages on Christine's desk.

'Why would anyone be interested in a book of instructions on housekeeping and morals?' Christine asked. 'It was only a whim that prompted the old Duchess of Orléans to ask me to make a copy for the queen's ladies. They certainly won't bother to read it now that the duchess is dead,' she sighed. 'She promised to pay me well. After what's happened, there won't be any payment, that's for sure.'

'You told me there are recipes there,' Francesca said. 'Now you can keep them, and we can try some.'

Christine had to laugh. 'Most of them are complicated. Not like your simple Italian cooking.'

'Nothing is too complicated for me,' Francesca sniffed. 'But the French use too many sauces.' She pointed her finger at her daughter and announced, 'I will try one, *Cristina*. Pick out something.'

'I prefer your Italian recipes, *grand'maman*,' Thomas said. 'And you can teach me all the Italian names. Then when you take me back to Italy I'll be able to talk to everybody.'

'Nobody's going back to Italy,' Christine said. 'But I'll try to find a recipe for you, Mama.'

'Good. Now we will go down and see if Georgette has recovered from her fright.'

They trooped out of the room. Christine set Goblin on the floor and laughed as she watched him run to catch up with them, his crooked tail waving and his ears flopping like little rags.

When they'd gone, she got up, dressed, and pondered her situation. For many years she and her family had been safe from any kind of want, for her father, the renowned Italian physician and astrologer Thomas de Pizan, had been an adviser to the present monarch's father, King Charles the Fifth. As a child, after her family had moved from Italy to Paris, she'd even lived at the palace. But then the old king died, and everything changed. The present king, Charles the Sixth, was only twelve at the time, too young to govern, and his uncles took over. These men, greedy and power-hungry, had little use for learned men like Thomas de Pizan, who lost much of his influence at the court and died several years later. Christine and her family were secure for a while, because her husband, Étienne, was well established as one of the royal secretaries. But then he died, and it was left to Christine to support her family. Using what she'd learned from her husband, she'd become a scribe. Francesca had objected, telling her that a woman should attend to her cooking and sewing, but she'd ignored this useless advice and found enough work to provide for their needs. Until now. She'd been counting on the money the Duchess of Orléans had promised to pay her for copying the manuscript on her desk.

She picked up the pages and leafed through them. The duchess hadn't said who the author was, but it was obvious he was well-to-do, and he seemed kindly enough, for he'd gone to the trouble of writing this tome for his fifteen-year-old bride, evidently an orphan who needed to learn how to manage his household. Christine pictured him sitting at his desk in a comfortable room, his young wife leaning over his shoulder as he wrote that he liked to see her dance and sing and tend the plants in her garden. Perhaps it was springtime and she had just come in bringing a bouquet of primroses and violets. He told her when to sow seeds and set out plants, and how to harvest and preserve herbs and vegetables. Or perhaps it was winter, and the couple sat in a tapestried room, close to a large fireplace where logs blazed and the flames threw light onto a crowd of embroidered ladies who seemed to glide around the room. The husband told his wife how she should care for him, especially whenever he came home from a journey, wet and cold and expecting to find his house in order and his every need attended to.

These were pretty images, and the man's instructions were appropriate for an elderly man who'd taken a young, inexperienced bride. But there were many pages devoted to religious instruction, decorum, and humility. Apparently the young woman needed an inordinate amount of guidance in these areas, especially concerning the requirement that wives obey their husbands in everything. Christine questioned that, but she told herself it was none of her business and vowed to find out who the author was and return his manuscript before she could brood on it further. She turned to the pages of recipes, found something simple for her mother to make, and hurried downstairs to tell her about it.

But she couldn't stop thinking about the wife whose behavior needed so much correction.

TWO

When the news of the king's illness spread throughout the kingdom, all true French people cried as though an only son had died, so much was the well-being of France attached to his health.

The Monk of Saint-Denis,
*Chronique du Religieux de Saint-Denis,
contenant le règne de Charles VI de 1380 à 1422*

T he kitchen smelled of ashes, and the children danced around Georgette as she swept them into a corner. When Thomas began to taunt the hired girl with a silly poem about a servant who'd fallen down a well, Christine stamped her foot and cried, 'Stop that.'

Francesca, sitting at the table cutting carrots and cabbages to use in soup, tried not to smile.

'You are as bad as Thomas,' Christine said.

'There is no point in scolding him.' Francesca put down her knife, went to her youngest grandson, and gave him a hug.

Lisabetta picked up some of the ashes and smeared them on her face. 'I'll be like the burned men,' she announced.

Jean frowned at her and wiped the ashes off with his finger.

Christine sat on a stool next to the fireplace and drew Lisabetta onto her lap. As she hugged her, she thought of another child, the little prince she'd known when she'd lived at the palace. He'd been a happy, fun-loving boy, and when his father died and he became king, he'd seemed so strong and capable, even taking part in an important battle in Flanders when he was only fourteen, riding proudly with his troops, vanquishing the Flemish at Roosebeke, and laying siege to the city of Courtrai so his soldiers could bring home the golden spurs stolen from the French after their disastrous defeat there eighty years earlier. The people of France loved him then, and they still did. But everything had changed. He'd been struck down by an illness that had shattered his mind, and all of his subjects suffered because of it. To make matters worse, he'd participated in the lewd masquerade, and for many people that meant he'd become a fool as well as a madman. She'd seen for herself how much he'd changed when, a few days earlier, she'd found him walking in the palace gardens with his brother, wan and nervous, biting his finger-nails down to the quick. Her heart ached for him.

Lisabetta jumped off her lap and ran to join Thomas, who was scampering around the room, pretending he was on fire. When the boy came close to Christine, she reached out, caught him in her arms, and held him tightly.

'I've got a recipe for you, Mama,' she said. 'I know you're going to buy fish at the market today, so you can make this simple soup. The old man writes that all you have to do is bray some almonds, boil them with powdered ginger and saffron, and pour the mixture over the fish after you've fried it. We'll have it for supper.'

'But you told me not to buy saffron, *Cristina*,' Francesca said.

'That's true, I did.' Christine frowned. 'Make it without the saffron.'

'The soup won't be any good without the saffron,' Thomas wailed. 'Why can't we have the saffron?'

'Saffron is expensive, and we have to be careful with expenses,' Christine said. 'I don't have any work.'

'Why do you not go to the old man who wrote the manuscript on your desk and see if he will pay you for the copy?' Francesca asked.

'I'd have to find him first. The duchess never told me anything about him. I don't even know his name.'

'I do,' said Georgette, who'd stopped her sweeping and stood resting her chin on the top of the broom handle as she followed every word of the conversation. 'I know his name.'

'What?' Christine cried. She jumped up from the stool, letting go of Thomas. 'How is that possible?'

'You're talking about those pages you brought home the day before the masquerade at the marriage ball, aren't you?' Georgette said.

Christine, so amazed she didn't know what to say, nodded.

'Well, I know who wrote them. My brother told me.'

'*Mon Dieu!* Who is he?'

'His name is Martin du Bois. He lives near here, in a big house on the corner of the rue des Rosiers and the rue des Escouffles.'

'How does Colin know?'

'He knows a boy who lives with him. The boy's sister is married to the old man. He wrote something for her, and he told her she could have it after he loaned it to the Duchess of Orléans for a while. That must be what you brought home.'

Georgette thought for a moment. 'Oh, something else,' she giggled. 'Colin says the wife told her husband that for all she cared the duchess could keep the silly book.'

'I can't believe she said that!' Christine exclaimed, although when she thought of the pages devoted to a wife's duty to obey her husband, she wasn't so sure.

'Well, I'm only telling you what Colin told me,' Georgette said as she started sweeping again. 'Colin always finds out about things.'

How true, Christine thought, remembering her own dealings with Georgette's brother, who ran errands for the queen and seemed to have his nose into everything. She said, 'I hope Colin knows what he's talking about, because I'm going to visit this man and return the manuscript. If it's not the right person, it will be very embarrassing.'

'You won't find him,' Georgette said. 'He's disappeared.'

'Disappeared? What are you talking about?'

'Martin du Bois is gone. No one knows where, not even his wife.'

Christine had to sit down again. 'Come over here, Georgette.'

Georgette set the broom against the wall, wiped her hands on her grimy apron, and stood in front of Christine, who asked, 'What other interesting bits of information do you have about this man?'

'Nothing. Just that he's gone.'

'He left his wife all alone?' Francesca asked.

'Well, she's not exactly alone. There are servants.'

'But the poor young woman must be frightened!' Francesca said.

Georgette snickered. 'According to Colin, she's not too upset.'

'I don't believe everything Colin says.' Christine stood up. 'I'll go to Martin du Bois's house right now and find out what all this means. I need to return his manuscript, and this gives me a good excuse.'

'But you promised to help me with the mending today!' Francesca said.

Christine groaned. 'So I did. I'll go tomorrow.'

'I will go with you,' her mother said.

THREE

Ha! Painful fortune, how you have taken me from high to low.

Christine de Pizan, *Ballade* VII, c. 1402

T he next morning, Colin appeared with a message: Christine was wanted at the palace. She hoped it was the queen, asking her to finish the wedding gift for the lady-in-waiting.

'I thought we were going to see Martin du Bois,' Francesca said.

'The queen has summoned me. That's more important,' Christine said, and she was surprised when her mother didn't object; usually when she said she was going to work at the palace, Francesca besieged her with a litany of worries about the evil influences there.

Colin waited for her, leaning against the door jamb, playing with a little knife. Christine thought how different he was from his sister. Georgette was fifteen, thick-set and clumsy, while Colin, a year younger, was thin and agile, and he seemed to be everywhere and to know everything that went on. Christine suspected that was why the queen used him to deliver messages; no doubt he reported back a great deal of information.

She got her cloak and went out into the street. Colin followed, and she knew he was hoping she would buy him a meat pasty or a crispy wafer from one of the vendors who hawked their wares on the rue Saint-Antoine, the broad paved street leading to the palace. When a snaggletooth crone approached and held out a basket filled with fragrant honey cakes, she bought two and gave one to the boy.

It was a sunny day, warm for February, and throngs of people were out taking advantage of the spring-like weather. A group of boys ran around making obscene gestures, trying to re-enact the fire at the palace, mimicking the burning men, screaming in pretended pain. Colin laughed, called out to the revelers, and would have spoken to them, but Christine pulled him away. She didn't need any more reminders of the tragic masquerade.

Colin looked around, and when he didn't see any more pastry

vendors, announced that he had to go on another errand and left. Christine walked on, upset – not with Colin, for she was used to his ways – but with herself because she'd forgotten to ask him if he knew where Martin du Bois had gone.

To distract herself, she thought of happier, more secure times, when there had been no need for her to do anything but keep house and raise her children. Now fortune had dealt her a cruel blow, and nothing was secure.

Unlike her mother, she didn't believe in ghosts, but she felt her husband's presence, even though he'd died several years earlier while on a mission to another part of the country with the king. His body hadn't been brought back to her, so she could picture him as he'd been when he was alive.

Concentrate on your work, he said.

'What work?' she asked.

She arrived at the palace, crossed the courtyard, and was accosted by a stocky little boy in a red jacket and a red cap who grabbed her hand and dragged her over to the big central fountain. 'Talk to the lion!' he ordered, pointing to the stone beast sitting at the top of a pillar in the middle of the fountain's basin.

'Not today, Renaut,' she said, laughing. The boy had never forgotten the first time he'd seen her, when she'd slipped on the icy cobblestones and sworn at the stone lion as though it was its fault. She took the boy's hand and led him to the palace entrance, where a large man holding a mace stood guard. The *portier*, whose name was Simon, smiled at her and hugged the boy, a child of seven whom he and his wife had adopted and who was now his constant companion.

'The queen has summoned me,' Christine said.

'Not the queen,' Simon said, pointing his mace at a man who was coming through the courtyard, a man she was embarrassed to meet because several weeks earlier she'd been convinced he'd committed a horrible crime. But here he was – Henri Le Picart, a small man with a little black beard wearing a hooded black cape with an ermine collar. He frowned when he saw her, bowed slightly, and with no further greeting said, 'Follow me.'

She stayed where she was. Why did he think he could order her around like that?

Simon said, 'You'd better go with him. He has a surprise for you.'

Reluctantly, she followed Henri into the palace. He strode through the great gallery, nodding to the guards standing silently at their posts but ignoring her as she trailed after him. He led the way along wide corridors, up narrow staircases, and through numerous winding passageways. At first she didn't know where they were going, but when they came to a sparsely furnished room with bare walls, thin rugs, and a bench in front of a small fireplace, tears came to her eyes. This was where the Duchess of Orléans had lived, and where the formidable old woman had given her the housekeeping manuscript to copy. A few weeks earlier, the duchess had died in the plain wooden bed that stood against the wall, and Christine had been one of the last people to speak with her. In the short time she'd known her, she'd learned that the ascetic duchess was not the tyrant she seemed, and she'd become fond of her.

Henri sat down on a high-backed chair in front of a huge desk decorated with inlaid panels and carved scrolls. Out of place in the unadorned room, the desk and the chair had obviously been brought from another part of the palace for his use. Henri was a complicated man, and Christine didn't know much about him except that he'd been a friend of her father's and that he dabbled in alchemy and magic and had made a great deal of money. His plain black cape was deceptive, for under it he wore an elaborately pleated red *houppelande* with ermine trim, and his fingers sparkled with jeweled rings. He was not a man to tolerate austerity. Christine disliked him intensely, but she had to admit to herself that the elegant desk suited him.

Since Henri sat on the only chair in the room, Christine went to the fireplace and sat on the bench, fuming at the man's rudeness. Henri didn't seem to notice. He said, 'The duchess was a friend of mine. Before she died, she asked me to take care of some business for her. She gave you a manuscript to copy, didn't she?'

Christine resisted the temptation to say, *If you know about it, why do you ask?*

Among the papers lying on the desktop was a leather purse. Henri picked it up and held it out to her. 'She asked me to give you this. She wanted to make sure you did not go without payment for your work.' He pushed the chair back from the desk and gazed at her. 'She admired you, you know, for risking your life to save an innocent woman.'

She felt herself blushing. The woman he was referring to had

been accused of poisoning her husband and would have died at
the stake if she hadn't tracked down the real culprit. She was
embarrassed, because she'd mistakenly thought the murderer
was Henri. And she was humiliated, too, because she'd confronted
the murderer by herself and had escaped certain death only because
Henri had come to her rescue. She thought she detected a sympathetic look on his face, but she didn't trust him, and she felt, as
usual in his presence, irritated and out-of-sorts. Now her annoyance
increased because she had to stand and go to the desk to receive
the purse.

'I haven't done much work on the manuscript,' she said.

'That is of no consequence. The duchess was a just woman.'

Christine noticed, as she had the night he'd come to her rescue,
that in spite of his disconcerting manner, his voice was not unkind.
He watched as she opened the purse and looked inside. A wave of
gratitude to the duchess swept over her. There were enough coins
to support her family for a long time.

'I need to return the manuscript to the man who wrote it,' she said.

'Just take the money.'

'I can't do that. The duchess didn't tell me anything about him, but
our hired girl thinks it was a man named Martin du Bois. Is that true?'

'It is.'

'Is it also true that Martin du Bois has disappeared?'

Henri nodded.

How does he know? she wondered. 'Is he a friend of yours? Do
you have any idea where he is?'

'You don't need to know. Just keep the manuscript. I understand
it contains a lot of information on how to run a household and a
good quantity of recipes. Just the thing for a woman.'

'Do you think that's all women are good for?'

Henri laughed.

She turned, stalked out of the room, and made her way through
all the corridors and passages until she arrived at the great gallery,
shaking with anger. She tried to calm herself by studying the
noblemen and commoners milling about in the vast space, but this
didn't do much to change her mood, for everyone seemed dispirited,
as though a shadow hovered over them. *It's the fire*, she thought.
We're all affected by the memory of it. She seemed to hear screams
and smell smoke, though the masquerade had taken place in another
part of the palace.

The crowd drew back as a handsome man wearing a green velvet cape lined with ermine and a beaver hat ornamented with peacock feathers strode in. It was the king's brother, Louis, the Duke of Orléans. People began to whisper angrily, and Christine knew why; everyone thought the fire was the duke's fault because he'd brought lighted torches into a room where there were men dressed in flammable costumes.

The duke passed by without glancing left or right. He looked unconcerned, but Christine knew he was suffering. He was an arrogant, proud man, prone to spells of remorse, when he would go to the church of the Celestine monks, near the palace, and pray for forgiveness, and for his soul. She'd heard he'd vowed to have a new chapel built there, to atone for the tragedy.

She could understand his anguish, for she'd seen him standing at the door to the room where the masquerade took place, holding lighted torches, watching in horror as four men burned to death. Suddenly she was back in her nightmare. The duke held two torches. There was another torch on the floor at her feet.

Where had the third torch come from?

FOUR

The bagpipe bewitches people. When people dance to the sounds of this bestial instrument, they seem to be out of their minds.

Eustache Deschamps (c. 1340–1404), *Ballade 923*

Since it was a spring-like day Christine decided to take a walk in the palace gardens. To reach them, she passed through cloisters and courtyards she knew well from her childhood. When she came to the royal kitchen, housed in its own building close to the palace, she peered through the open door, hoping to see the master cook, who'd become a friend. But instead of the slender well-dressed man, renowned for his culinary expertise, who'd always been glad to dip a long-handled spoon into a pot and let her taste one of his savory dishes, she saw a stout, red-faced curmudgeon threatening two sweaty kitchen boys with a chopping knife. When he saw her looking in, he brandished the knife at her, too. She moved away quickly.

All the animals and birds that lived on the palace grounds were awake: dogs in their kennels snuffling at the enclosures, eager to go on a hunt; doves cooing in their huge outdoor cages; horses impatiently pawing the floors of their stables. She heard the king's lions roaring on the other side of the royal enclave, and she remembered a night not long ago when they'd been out of their stockade and she'd thought they might attack her. She decided to visit them, hoping to catch a glimpse of the lion-keeper's assistant, a strange young woman who lived with the beasts and never spoke. She walked through pleasances and orchards, came to the lions' stockade, and looked through a space between the palings. She knew the lions were inside, watched over by their mysterious keeper, but she saw nothing and heard nothing.

She walked slowly back through the gardens, thinking of the days when she'd played there with the king and his brother. She remembered how Charles had loved anything having to do with weapons and fighting, and how Louis had cared more for games of mental agility, such as chess. She thought of the brothers as they were now, Charles so confused and unpredictable, Louis downcast and racked by guilt. She'd had her differences with Louis recently, but that didn't take away from her fond memories of him as a child.

She stopped to watch a man on a tall ladder prune a grape vine, and she idly picked up a few of the branches that fell to the ground at her feet, remembering she'd once learned how to weave such things into baskets. A bird called from one of the Hôtel Saint-Pol's famous cherry trees, and she stood for a moment, listening. Then she continued on, past gardeners trimming hedges, sweeping paths, and preparing the ground for spring planting. The scent of newly turned earth filled the air.

She came to a low wall. A bench had been placed there, and on it sat a man, slumped over, his eyes closed. His hands were bandaged, all his hair was gone, and an ugly red gash climbed up the back of his neck. It was Jean de Nantouillet, the man who'd jumped into a vat of water to save himself from the flames at the masquerade. She knew him because he'd been a friend of her husband's.

Not wanting to startle him, she coughed softly. He raised his head and looked at her with red, swollen eyes protruding from a face covered with burn marks. He didn't seem to recognize her, and she had to remind him that she was Étienne de Castel's widow.

'Those were good days with Étienne, long gone now,' Jean moaned. He covered his face with his bandaged hands.

'Étienne would have been distressed to see you like this,' she said.

He leaned back against the wall and closed his eyes. 'Étienne would never have been as foolish as I was. I can't believe I agreed to take part in the masquerade. I suppose it was because I got caught up in the king's enthusiasm. I didn't realize how weak his mind is these days.'

A little bird pecked the ground at their feet. Christine watched one of the cats the cooks kept in the kitchen to catch mice creep toward it.

'How did the masquerade come about? Can you talk about it?' she asked.

The man seemed surprised she'd asked, but he sat up and began to speak, hesitantly at first, then in bitter words that came pouring out.

'It was Huguet de Guisay's idea. Perhaps Étienne told you about Huguet, how he was always thinking up amusing things to do. Things that were clever, and cruel. When he heard the queen's favorite lady-in-waiting was going to be married, he went around the palace mocking her because it was to be her third husband. "There's going to be a ball to celebrate, and we should turn it into a masquerade and dress up like wild men of the forest," he said. He couldn't wait to get the king involved in his scheme, and the king was eager to do it because Huguet said it would be fun to terrify the guests, and also because Huguet gave him to understand that the noise of a masquerade could drive away evil spirits. "Perhaps the devils that torment you will depart and you will have some peace," he told the king.'

'Foolish superstition,' Christine said.

'I know. But once the king had agreed, the rest of us, Huguet's chosen accomplices, couldn't refuse to join in. As I look back on it now, it seems we were all bewitched.'

Jean closed his eyes and leaned back against the wall. The cat was about to spring at the bird. Christine still held one of the grape branches she'd picked up earlier, and she threw it. The bird flew away, and the cat looked at her accusingly, its green eyes glistening, and slunk back toward the kitchen.

Speaking as though in a dream, Jean said, 'The night of the ball, we gathered in a separate room to put on our costumes. Six of us, sporting like children. We'd feasted well, and there'd been no lack of wine. I remember how we laughed and called to each other as our squires slipped linen coats covered with pitch over our clothes. The king couldn't stand still, and when the squire sewing him into his coat accidentally stuck him with a needle, he just laughed, he was so excited. The squires pulled the coats tight, and then they brought in bags of flax and pushed long strands of it into the pitch. It made us sneeze! The king laughed so much we were afraid he was having another of his attacks. But before we went into the room where the ball was held, he calmed down enough to tell Yvain de Foix to make sure no one brought lighted torches in while we were there.

'Of course, I couldn't know how I looked in my own costume, but I was shocked when I saw my companions. Huguet de Guisay, so homely to begin with, didn't look much worse than usual, but I was astonished at the transformation in the others. They frightened me, for they really seemed to be hairy wild men.

'Haincelin Coq, the king's fool, pranced around, mocking us and making jokes, and we all laughed like fools ourselves. We raced into the ballroom, throwing our arms up in the air and shouting insults at each other and at the people watching us. Someone must have told the musicians to play the loudest, fastest music possible, and the screeching vielles, the blaring pipes and trumpets, and a shrieking bagpipe sent us into a frenzy. We danced such a wild dance, it was really indecent. The king, shouting hysterically, bounded over to the dais where the ladies sat, and shocked them with obscene gestures. Most of the ladies recoiled in disgust, but the young Duchess of Berry leaned toward him, trying to discover who was encased in the hairy costume.

'And then it happened. A lighted torch came from nowhere and we were enveloped in flames.'

He started to weep. Christine cringed as she watched the tears roll over the burn marks on his ravaged face.

'I felt searing pain, and I threw myself to the floor. Then I saw a large vat of water at the side of the room. I jumped up, ran to it, and dived in. I can still feel the water surging around me, and hear the hiss of the flames as they were extinguished. When I leapt out of the vat, my clothes were burned off my body, but I was too stunned to feel any embarrassment. All I knew was that four of my friends were lying on the floor, and there were flames everywhere. The Count of Joigny was already dead. The others were still alive, tearing at their bodies and screaming. Those screams still ring in my ears. I couldn't see the king. It was only later that I learned he'd been saved by the Duchess of Berry.'

'I'm surprised you remember anything,' Christine said.

'Oh yes, I remember all that. And the Duke of Orléans standing at the side of the room, holding torches. It is said that one of them was what set us on fire.'

Christine looked at the ground. The sun had been briefly hidden behind a passing cloud. Now it came out again, and as it did so, its rays struck the grape branch she'd thrown at the cat. The smooth bark glistened, and she thought of the flaming torch she'd seen on the floor in her nightmare.

She wondered again, *Where had that torch come from?*

FIVE

Thirty-two sous parisis *for having furred and trimmed two cotes-hardies for mistress Alips, the queen's dwarf, the 12th day of August 1387.*

Archives Nationales, Paris, KK 18, fol. 214v

She went back to the palace, musing about the fire. Everyone believed it had been started by a spark from one of the Duke of Orléans's torches. Was it possible another torch had been responsible? Had she just dreamed the torch lying on the floor at her feet? She decided to return to the place where she'd stood that night and try to remember.

Finding her way back wouldn't be easy. On the afternoon of the wedding ball, she'd been working in the little room in the queen's chambers where she did her copying, and she'd fallen asleep. When she'd awaked, it was dark, and the queen and her ladies had gone to the festivities. She'd heard the music in the distance, and she'd followed the sounds, wandering through unfamiliar passages to a balustrade overlooking the room where the celebration was taking place. She wasn't sure she could find the spot again, so she decided to go back to where she'd started that night and continue from there.

She crept cautiously past the queen's chambers and walked in what she hoped was the right direction, trying to imagine the sounds of the music that had drawn her along. The passageways were shadowy, even on a sunny day, and she sensed someone following her, but when she looked around, she saw no one.

When she finally came to the balustrade, she looked down at the floor below and tried to remember exactly what she'd observed that night. Once again, she saw the men in their moments of agony, and the anguished people who watched them helplessly. She saw Jean de Nantouillet jump into the water vat, and the little white dog consumed by flames. Then she looked up and saw the musicians on their balcony, their mouths agape.

'Did you see me up there that night?' a voice came out of nowhere. Christine started, looked around, and saw no one. She felt a gentle tug on her skirt, and she looked down to find the queen's dwarf.

Astonished, she asked the little woman, 'Were you on the balcony?'

'I was.'

Christine gazed at the dwarf. She'd seen her in the queen's chambers, but although she'd heard her sing, she'd never heard her speak. The queen seemed to be very fond of her, even dressing her in clothes mirroring her own. That day, she wore a blue *cotte* and a green surcoat trimmed with embroidery at the neck and lined with miniver, everything tailored to fit her small body perfectly.

Does she have a name? Christine wondered.

'Alips,' the dwarf said.

Christine felt her cheeks get hot.

'It's all right,' Alips said, reaching up to touch Christine's hand. 'Most people react like that. They don't think we have names. We're used to it.'

'How did you get up there?' Christine asked, and then felt ashamed of herself for having alluded to the little woman's stature.

Alips laughed. 'I often go there at banquets and balls. The steps are steep, but I manage, holding my skirt above my knees and heaving myself over them. The musicians play as loud as they can when they see me coming, and the sounds hurt my ears. Especially the bagpipes. But I need to get away from the dancing. When there's dancing, I get stepped on.'

'What happened on the night of the masquerade?'

'Someone up there threw the torch that started the fire.'

Christine stood aghast. 'One of the musicians?'

'Oh, no. I know all those musicians, and none of them would have done it. It was someone else, someone hiding in the shadows. I didn't realize he was there until he stepped out and threw the torch.'

'Do you know who it was?'

'No. He ran away before I could get a good look at him.'

'Who else have you told about this?'

'Only the queen. That's why I've come to find you. The queen wants to see you.'

Christine was tired, she hadn't had dinner, and she'd been planning to go home. But her curiosity about the dwarf's surprising revelation was overwhelming. She followed her through all the confusing passages and corridors back to the queen's chambers, struggling to keep up because the dwarf walked faster than she did, in spite of her short legs.

Queen Isabeau sat on her day bed with her head in her hands. She wore a loose blue chemise, and her long black hair flowed unbound over her shoulders. Christine was shocked; she'd never expected to see her in anything other than a gown of the finest velvet or silk, her hair arranged in elaborate *cornes* over her ears and topped by a jeweled circlet. Her ladies-in-waiting were not with her, and she was alone except for her animals and birds, which seemed as dejected as she did; five little goldfinches quiet in their green and white cage, a squirrel with a pearl-studded collar hiding behind one of the big cushions on which the queen's ladies usually sat, and a monkey in a fur-lined robe, squatting on a seat in front of the closed shutters of a window, his head down and his paws folded over his stomach. Isabeau's sleek white greyhound, usually alert and ready to spring at anyone who approached his mistress, sat quietly with his head in her lap, every now and then showing the whites of his eyes as he raised them to look at her questioningly.

Alips said, 'Here is Christine, *Madame*.' She crossed the room and clambered onto the seat in front of the window. The monkey moved close to her and put a paw on her shoulder, seeming to understand that all was not well.

The queen was short, a little plump, and she had dimpled red cheeks that were at that moment covered with tears. She looked like a child, though Christine knew it would be a mistake to think this denoted innocence. She felt a surge of sympathy. Isabeau had been brought to France from her native Bavaria to be married to the king when she was fifteen, and now, at twenty-two, she'd borne five children, two of whom had died, and her husband was not in his right mind. She had few friends in France. *She must be very lonely*, Christine thought. People were always criticizing her, especially for her difficulty with the language. Christine had discovered that although she still made mistakes, she actually knew French fairly well; she simply had trouble with the pronunciation and spoke with such a thick German accent, people had a hard time understanding her.

She started to kneel, but the queen motioned for her to rise. 'I must speak with you,' she said.

She stood and waited. There was no fire in the large fireplace that usually kept the room too warm. She wrapped her cloak tightly around her, glad no chambermaid had come to take it.

The queen said, 'The king has great danger.'

'What danger?'

'Someone tries to kill him.'

Christine shuddered. 'Why do you think that, *Madame*?'

'The fire at the wedding ball. It was the king who was meant to die.'

'What proof do you have of this?'

'What I feel in my bones. So many bad happenings. Someone causes them.'

'Who?'

'I know not. The doctors' medicines are bad; the sorcerers and magicians make him worse. But they are not the ones. Someone is here among us, putting an evil shadow over us. I have felt it since the night of the unwise masquerade.'

'Surely you must suspect someone,' Christine said.

'I know not all that goes on here. People hide things from me. When they speak, they are not honest. Alips only is my eyes and ears.'

The dwarf climbed down from the window seat and came over to the day bed. The queen reached down and put her arm around her.

Christine wondered why Isabeau's ladies-in-waiting weren't there. She'd never seen her without them, babbling to each other and eager to please her.

'What has Alips told you?'

'About the musicians' balcony. The torch. The Duke of Orléans is not to blame.'

'Perhaps Alips only *thought* she saw someone throw a torch from the musicians' balcony.'

The dwarf started to say something, but the queen interrupted. 'Alips sees things clearly,' she said.

Christine looked around the room. In spite of all the lavish furnishings – the red and gold coverlet on the queen's day bed, the gold-trimmed chairs, the tapestries embroidered with golden fleurs-de-lis, the crystal goblets glittering on a sideboard, the carpets so soft and thick one's feet sank into them as into the moss of a forest floor – it seemed a desolate place without the queen's ladies and all the curious people who were usually there to entertain her. She missed the Spanish minstrel named Gracieuse Allegre who sat in a corner, composing a song and accompanying herself on her lute, and the queen's fools, Jeannine and Guillaume, who struck exaggerated poses and made mimicking gestures. Jeannine rarely spoke, but Guillaume, who didn't seem to mind being the only male in a group of women, never stopped chattering. He wore a cap and liked to watch people's expressions when he removed it, for he was completely bald. Christine imagined he'd been added to the queen's entourage to make up for Jeannine's silence, as well as for the silence of a mute named Collette, who was always smiling in spite of her affliction. Sometimes the queen had in her company a goddaughter, a little dark-skinned Saracen girl who was cared for by the nuns at a nearby priory, and the pretty young daughters of two of her favorite *huissiers*.

Without her usual companions, the queen was sad and lost. *Is Alips the only person she can trust?* Christine asked herself. *Are her other attendants not here because she suspects one of them of having evil intentions toward the king?*

Her unspoken question was answered when the queen said, 'The person who tries to kill the king is among us here, in my chambers. I feel this.' Isabeau had been slumped over on the day bed. Now she sat up straight. 'I want that you discover who it is.'

'How can I do that, *Madame*?'

'I have asked you to copy a book, a wedding gift for Catherine de Fastavarin. I know it is not yet finished. I want that you spend time here until it is. And you will listen and observe all that goes on around me.'

Christine couldn't refuse a request from the queen. And at least she would have the money the queen paid for the copy work. She said, 'If it is your wish, *Madame*.'

'You have saved Alix de Clairy. Now you must do the same for the king.'

True, I saved a young woman from burning at the stake, Christine thought. *But that was different. And I had a lot of help.*

'I will do what I can,' she said.

'That is good. You may go now. Soon I will send for you.'

Christine made her obeisance and left. In the hallway, Alips joined her.

'Do you feel danger as the queen does?' Christine asked the dwarf.

'Yes. Someone deliberately set the men on fire. Perhaps the intended victim was the king, or perhaps all the masqueraders. Perhaps the whole palace, and everyone in it, was meant to go up in flames.'

'What a horrible thought!'

'Of course. There is a monster here.'

By the time Christine left Alips, it was dusk. As she walked through the shadowy corridors and galleries of the Hôtel Saint-Pol, she thought of what the dwarf had said, and she breathed a sigh of relief when she arrived at the palace entrance.

'You shouldn't walk home alone,' Simon the *portier* said. 'Colin will go with you.'

As usual, Colin was nearby. He started his prattle as soon as they were out in the street.

'Lots of thieves and murderers around,' he said. 'And witches, sorcerers, and the *loup-garou.*'

She thought of her mother. The *loup-garou* was a werewolf that was supposed to come out after dark in search of children to eat. If that didn't satisfy him, he'd find dead men and drink their blood. Francesca believed all this.

A strong wind propelled them down the street. Christine pulled her cloak close around her and wished Colin would stop talking. When they got to her house, her mother was waiting at the door. Christine knew the boy hoped to have a conversation about evil beings lurking in the shadows, but she told him to go back to the palace. He turned away, looking disappointed.

'I have warned you about being out after dark,' Francesca said.

'I know. But I'm safely home now, so please get me something to eat.'

Francesca took a deep breath. 'I have a surprise for you,' she said as she led the way into the kitchen. There Christine was astonished to see the children arguing with a girl who sat at the table holding Goblin in her lap. The little dog struggled to get away, but the stranger held him tightly.

'Let him go!' Thomas cried. 'He doesn't like you.'

Christine couldn't believe Thomas was being so rude. But she saw why when Jean and Marie walked over to the girl and tried to lift the dog out of her arms.

'He likes me better than you,' the girl said. She tightened her grip on Goblin, flounced over to the fireplace, and plunked herself down on a stool.

Christine asked, 'What's going on, Mama? Who is this person?'

Francesca coughed nervously and said, 'This is Klara, Martin du Bois's wife.'

SIX

There is nothing more unbecoming in a woman than an uncomely and ill-tempered manner.

Christine de Pizan,
Le Livre des Trois Vertus, 1405

As Christine looked at the young stranger, any fantasies she'd had about a meek little wife sitting at her husband's side while he wrote a book instructing her on housekeeping and proper behavior vanished. Klara was a bit chubby, with curly blond hair, pink cheeks, a dimpled chin, and a petulant expression that kept her from being pretty. Christine wondered whether she had dimples in her cheeks as well as her chin, but she suspected it would be hard to find out because the girl didn't look as though she ever smiled.

She drew her mother back into the hall and asked, 'What have you done?'

Francesca fiddled with the strings of her apron. 'I felt sorry for the poor little wife, all alone.'

'So you went to Martin du Bois's house and took her away. Wasn't there anyone there to stop you?'

'There was a woman with her, a beguine named Agnes. I've seen her before. She lives at the beguinage on the rue de l'Ave-Maria. Martin must have hired her to look after his wife.'

'What did the beguine say when you showed up?'

Francesca looked at the floor and said in a small voice, 'She said she'd had enough of the girl.'

'Did she tell you why?'

'Only that the girl is unhappy. She hates Paris. Martin brought her and her brother back from Courtrai after the city was destroyed. They miss their home.'

'The sack of Courtrai! That was eleven years ago!'

'I know. Martin was there. The king's soldiers were taking Flemish children away to be raped or sold as slaves. He saw these two standing alone, crying for their parents, and he felt sorry for them, so he brought them to Paris. Klara was five, and her brother Willem was eight. Martin raised them, and last year he married Klara, when she was fifteen.'

'Where is the brother?'

'Agnes says he ran away several years ago. According to her, Willem raged all the time about how the French had killed his family and burned down his city. Klara was too young to remember much about what had happened, but her brother talked about it constantly.'

Christine put her hands on her hips and glared at her mother. 'What did Klara say to you? Did she just meekly follow you out of her house?'

'She did not seem to care. I had the feeling she was glad to go.'

'What are we going to do with her? Surely we can't keep her here.'

'You are going to find Martin du Bois, are you not? As soon as you do that, we can take her back.' Francesca untied and then retied the strings of her apron. Then she patted them into place, as if to say, 'That settles that.'

One by one, the children crept into the hall. 'Is she going to stay here?' Thomas asked.

'She'll have to learn some manners,' Christine said.

Then Klara appeared, still holding Goblin, who was licking her face. 'You see? He likes me.'

'Apparently,' Christine said. 'But he belongs to my children, so why don't you give him back now?'

Thomas stepped forward and Klara, pouting, handed him the dog.

'Is supper ready, Mama?' Christine asked. 'I've had nothing to eat all day.'

'It was ready a long time ago,' Francesca said. They all went into the kitchen, where Georgette was stirring a pot of soup over the fire. The trestle table had been prepared, and Marie hurried to set out bowls and spoons. Thomas, still holding Goblin, stood in the doorway, making faces at Klara.

'Enough, Thomas,' Christine said. She took the boy's arm and pushed him down on the bench by the table. Then the other children sat, too, without leaving a place for Klara. Christine frowned at them.

'Does she really have to eat with us?' Jean asked.

'Of course she does,' Christine said. 'She's our guest.'

'Don't guests have to be polite?' Marie asked.

'They do. And I'm sure Klara will be polite if you are.'

They all moved around and made a place for the girl, who stomped over and sat down. Georgette brought the pot and ladled soup into the bowls, spilling some onto the table. She looked at Francesca to see whether she'd noticed and tried to wipe it up with her apron. Francesca groaned.

Christine said, 'You're welcome here, Klara.'

'Are these your children?' the girl asked.

'And my niece, Lisabetta, who lives with us because her father is in Italy,' Christine replied, putting her arm around the little girl.

'What's he doing in Italy?' Klara asked.

'He's gone there to take care of some business. Italy was our home once, before we moved here so my father could work for the king's father.'

'Your king came and destroyed my city!'

Christine was taken aback by Klara's outburst. How much did the girl remember? She said, 'The king was only fourteen then, so he may not have been entirely responsible for what happened.'

'He was. My brother told me how he came riding in on a big white horse and let his soldiers kill everyone. That's when my mother and father died.'

Lisabetta gave a little cry, and Christine pulled her close. 'It's all right. Your father will be coming back to us soon.'

'*My* mother and father are never coming back,' Klara said.

'Do you remember them well?' Christine asked.

'Not very. I was only five when your king came and destroyed my city. My brother Willem remembers them. He saw them die. He says the soldiers cut their heads off.'

Jean and Marie gasped. Thomas, who usually loved to hear about gore and slaughter, choked on his soup. Lisabetta started to weep.

Christine decided it was time to change the subject. 'Do you know, Klara, my mother found the recipe for the soup we're eating in the housekeeping manual your husband wrote for you?' It wasn't true, and she hoped Francesca wouldn't contradict her.

'How do you know about the book?'

'I have it upstairs on my desk. The Duchess of Orléans asked me to make a copy.'

'You can keep it if you like.'

'Your husband wrote that you asked him to write it. He wrote that you told him you wanted to learn how to please him.'

'He likes to think that. But I don't want to be a housekeeper. That's what servants are for.'

'But you should be able to tell them what to do!' Francesca exclaimed.

'Well, I don't have to worry about that now,' Klara said. 'Martin's not there, and most of the servants have left.'

'I don't blame them,' Thomas said under his breath. Christine gave him a kick.

'Do you know where your husband is?' Christine asked.

'No, I don't.'

'And I'll bet she doesn't care, either,' Thomas said.

Francesca went to Klara and put her arms around her. The girl tried to pull away, and then she leaned against Francesca and started to cry. Christine got up and gently pulled Klara to her feet. 'Come with me,' she said. She lit a taper and took the girl upstairs to Francesca's room. 'You can sleep here tonight, with my mother.'

A shutter had blown open, and Klara went over and tried to peer out into the night through the oiled cloth covering the window. Christine had the feeling she'd climb out and escape if she could. She marveled at how childish she was. Many young women her age were married and perfectly capable of caring for a husband and his household. She herself had been married at sixteen, and she'd never acted as Klara did.

By the light from the fireplace she could see that the girl was very tired, and she drew her over to the bed and made her sit down. 'You can sleep soon,' she said. 'But first we have to talk.'

Klara turned away, but Christine put her hand under her chin and turned her head so she was facing her. A log shifted in the fireplace, and shadows leapt around the room.

'Your husband left, Klara. Did he tell you where he was going?'

'Martin never tells me anything.'

'Didn't he tell you *why* he left?'

Klara gazed at the floor. Just as Christine had resigned herself to the fact that there was no use in questioning her further, she said, 'He said something about the king.'

'Exactly what did he say?'

'Just something about the king being in danger. He said it under his breath. He didn't mean for me to hear.'

Christine thought about what she'd learned from the dwarf. Someone at the palace wanted to kill the king. Was it possible that Martin du Bois knew who it was? Or could it be Martin du Bois himself?

'When did you hear your husband say this, Klara?'

Klara lay down on the bed and turned her back to Christine. 'The night he left.'

'And when was that?'

'The night those men burned up at the palace.'

SEVEN

The Duke of Berry, whose first wife had died, wanted to marry the daughter of the Count of Boulogne. The king had a good laugh about this, because the Duke of Berry was quite old. He said, 'Uncle, what will you do with such a young girl? She is only twelve, and you are sixty.' To this his uncle replied, 'Then I will spare her for three or four years, until she is full grown.' To which the king replied, 'Actually, it is she who will not spare you.'

Froissart, *Chroniques*, Livre III, 1386–1388

First thing the next morning, Christine looked through Martin du Bois's manuscript. The old man had enlivened his practical advice with references to people he knew, and she thought perhaps one of those people might be able to tell her where he'd gone.

The Duke of Berry was mentioned several times, so she decided to ask Klara about him.

She found the girl in the kitchen, sitting on a stool in front of the fire, watching Georgette sweep.

'You forgot that,' Klara said, pointing to a piece of onion under the table. 'And those,' inclining her foot toward some crumbs. Georgette laughed and swept everything in her direction.

Christine went to the girl, took her arm, and lifted her off the stool.

'This is not your house, Klara, and Georgette is not your servant. It's no wonder your husband thought you should have a book on how to behave.'

'Oh, leave her alone,' Georgette said. 'She isn't bothering me. Not much anyway.'

'I'm surprised at you, Georgette,' Christine said. 'You shouldn't let yourself be treated like that.'

'I'm sure she doesn't really mean it. She's just frightened.'

Georgette has more patience than I do, Christine thought. She looked at Klara, who seemed about to cry, and regretted her harsh words. She eased the girl back down onto the stool.

'Listen, Klara. I have to find your husband. Perhaps you can help. Do you know why he mentions the Duke of Berry in the manuscript he wrote for you?'

'No. Martin never talks to me about his friends.'

Christine sighed. The girl didn't seem to know anything. Or want to know.

Francesca appeared, and Christine suddenly realized she hadn't seen the children. 'Where's everyone?' she asked.

'Outside. I asked them to stay here and keep Klara company, but they ran out.' Francesca went to Klara and put her arms around her.

'I have to go and see the Duke of Berry,' Christine said. 'He's mentioned a number of times in her husband's manuscript. Perhaps he'll be able to tell me where the man is, and then we can take her home.' *And find out whether Martin du Bois had anything to do with the fire at the palace*, she thought.

'Poor child,' Francesca said. 'I can't imagine how she was raised, without a mother or father or any other relatives besides her brother.'

Klara looked up and said, 'Martin has always been kind to me. But I don't want to be married to him.'

Christine and her mother looked at each other. What were they going to do with this young woman who seemed so confused about who she was and what she was supposed to do?

'My mother says there was someone with you, Klara. A beguine.'

'I don't like her.'

Christine whispered to Francesca, 'This isn't helping me find her husband. I'm going to talk to the duke.'

'I am going to early mass at the cathedral. You can walk with me part of the way.'

'The children will be at school, and someone has to stay with Klara,' Christine said.

'Do you think we can leave her here with Georgette?'

'Georgette has enough to do without having to worry about her. You brought her here. You figure out what to do with her.'

'I could take her with me to the cathedral.'

'I don't think that would be wise,' Christine said as she watched Klara playing with Goblin. She knew from reading Martin du Bois's manuscript that he'd instructed Klara about the importance of prayer and what to do at mass, but she didn't think Klara had paid much attention. She said to her mother, 'She might get bored and run away.'

Klara solved the problem for them. 'You got me up too early. I'm going back to bed, and I'm going to stay there all morning.' She marched up the stairs.

'Good,' Christine said, and she accompanied her mother out the door.

The weather was warm and sunny, and puffy white clouds sailed across a blue sky as they walked to the place de Grève, the open space beside the Seine where wine boats docked. Christine slowed her steps to accommodate her mother, who walked with a limp she'd acquired when she'd fallen from a horse in an Alpine pass on the way from Italy to Paris. By the time they got to the Grève, the first wine boats of the morning were in. A wine crier approached, holding out a bowl and inviting them to taste. They ignored him and continued on to the Planche-Mibray, the footbridge over the Seine to the Île. There Christine left Francesca on the rue de la Juiverie, crossed over the Petit Pont, and walked down the other bank of the river, watching the swells on the water sparkle in the sun and listening to linnets and sparrows welcoming the possibility of spring from the tops of willow trees. Beside her, horses towing river barges trudged along a path, and the cries of the men leading the horses and the shouts of the bargemen rang in her ears. Beyond, she saw fishermen sitting silently on the river bank, gazing hopefully into the water.

The Duke of Berry's grand Parisian residence, the Hôtel de Nesle, sat on the edge of the Seine, facing an even grander palace, the Louvre, across the river. Christine had met the duke at the Hôtel Saint-Pol, but she had never been to this imposing mansion. There were no other visitors or petitioners in the reception hall, and a page led her immediately along a wide corridor to one of the duke's apartments, a huge space with a high vaulted ceiling and stained-glass windows through which the early morning sun streamed, throwing rainbow colors onto the polished wood floor and touching crystal goblets on tall sideboards with flashes of red, green, and blue. The brightness nearly blinded her as she stepped in from the shadowy corridor.

The duke sat at a desk, turning the pages of a large illuminated manuscript, and on the other side of the room a woman whom Christine knew to be his young wife, Jeanne of Boulogne, perched on a cushioned window seat, watching him. Since the duke didn't look up when she was announced, Christine stood in the doorway and studied the pair, marveling at how different they were. The duke, short and squat with a pug nose and small eyes set in a fat, wrinkled face, appeared to be between fifty and sixty, while his wife was only sixteen and looked even younger. Christine knew how much hilarity the duke had caused at the court four years earlier when he'd announced that he intended to marry a twelve-year-old girl. Now as she looked at the pair, she sensed the old man had met his match. To be sure, everything about him was overpowering – his magnificent bright-green *houppelande* with its long, flowing ermine-lined sleeves and wide ermine collar, the rubies and diamonds sparkling on his fingers, the sickly sweet odor of the cloves, nutmeg, and galingale coming from his pomaded hair. But the demeanor of his young wife was more impressive. Jeanne of Boulogne, modestly dressed in a simple blue kirtle, had a quiet reserve and a determined manner that had manifested itself the night of the tragic fire, when she'd thrown the train of her gown over the king and saved him from a horrible death.

The page had announced her, but the duke seemed not to have noticed, so Christine went in and knelt beside his desk, being careful not to step on a small lap dog sleeping on the floor. The duke looked up from his manuscript and said, 'I remember your father. And you, when you were a little girl, at the palace.'

'Yes, *Monseigneur*. A long time ago.'

The duke turned a page in his manuscript. 'What brings you here?'

'A man has disappeared. His name is Martin du Bois. Since he may have been in your service, I thought you might be able to tell me where he has gone.' Her knees began to hurt, and she shifted her weight from one leg to the other. The little lap dog stood up and wagged his tail.

'Du Bois? So many people work for me. I don't recall him. Why does he interest you?'

'He disappeared the night of the wedding ball at the palace, *Monseigneur*. His young wife is left alone, and I think it's important to find her husband.'

'I was not at the wedding ball. My wife was.' The duke glanced over at the young woman sitting quietly by the window. 'Perhaps she knows something about this man.' He went back to his manuscript, then looked down at Christine, surprised to find her still there. She was grateful when Jeanne of Boulogne called across the room, 'Please rise and come over here.' She stood and went to the duchess, who motioned for her to sit beside her, and as she sank down onto the soft cushions, the little dog, who'd trotted after her, jumped into her lap. He had silky fur and delicate features, and to Christine he seemed more like a toy than a real dog, not nearly as appealing as Goblin with his crooked tail and ragged ears.

The duchess reached into a sack lying on the seat beside her, took out a tiny biscuit and gave it to the dog, which ate it in one gulp. She said, 'You must excuse the duke. He waited more than a year for the illuminators to finish that manuscript. It was delivered to him this morning, and he can't keep his eyes off it.'

Christine nodded, wishing the duke had offered to let her have a look.

The duchess took her hand and said, 'I know a lot about you. I was so glad when you saved Alix de Clairy. I did not know her well, but I liked her. You did a courageous thing.'

'Thank you, *Madame*.'

The duchess had blond hair, small blue eyes, and a rather large nose, but her manner was so charming and gracious, she seemed beautiful. 'What did you say was the name of the man you're asking about?'

'Martin du Bois.'

'Was he at the wedding ball?'

Christine thought about what Klara had told her, that her husband had muttered something about the king being in danger, the night he'd disappeared. But that didn't prove he'd been at the ball. She said, 'I'm not sure.'

'Of course you know all about what happened that night,' Jeanne said.

'Yes. I know you saved the king.'

'If only I could have saved the others.' Tears formed in Jeanne's eyes. 'Especially Yvain de Foix.'

Christine knew something of Jeanne of Boulogne's history. From the age of three she'd been raised in the household of a powerful count, Gaston de Foix. Yvain, the count's bastard son, had probably been like a big brother to her, and it must have been unbearable to see him burning to death. And yet, she'd had the presence of mind to save the king.

Christine said, 'I am so sorry about Yvain, and the others who died.'

Jeanne wiped away her tears. 'The tragedy affects us all.'

'The king's brother thinks the fire was his fault,' Christine said.

'I don't think it was,' Jeanne said.

'Why do you say that?'

'Because I saw the Duke of Orléans holding two torches, and yet there was a third torch lying on the floor. That must have been the one that set the men on fire.'

So there really had been a third torch! It wasn't just something she'd seen in her nightmare. Christine looked over at the duke, to see whether he'd heard. He was engrossed in his new plaything. She was certain the young woman hadn't told her husband what she'd just told her.

'I've tried and tried to think whose the other torch could have been,' the duchess continued. 'Someone wanted those men to die. Or perhaps just Yvain.' There were tears in her eyes again.

'I'm sure you were close to Yvain,' Christine said.

'He was kind to me, when I lived in his father's house. The count died recently, as I'm sure you know, and Yvain had been here in Paris ever since because the king had taken a liking to him.'

Christine had seen Yvain at the palace, a handsome young man with an open, pleasant manner that had won him many friends. It was no wonder the king had been reluctant to let him leave.

'Yvain was a bastard,' the duchess said. 'But his father loved him and wanted to leave his estates to him.'

Christine knew that because Yvain had been illegitimate, a cousin, the Viscount of Castelbon, claimed everything should go to him. She'd heard the viscount had come to Paris to make sure the king didn't decide to give it to Yvain instead. *He won't have to worry about that now*, she mused, and she wondered whether the duchess had the same idea.

The duchess was looking over at her husband. He hadn't raised his plump face from the manuscript. 'Someone threw that torch at the dancers,' she said, in such a low voice that Christine could hardly hear.

It could have been meant for Yvain de Foix, Christine thought. But the queen was convinced it was intended for the king. And what Klara had heard her husband say indicated that he thought so, too. Or perhaps he didn't just think so. Perhaps Martin du Bois knew the torch was going to be thrown at the king because he was the one who was going to throw it. She was about to share this thought with the duchess, but she changed her mind. All she said was, 'You're right. There was a third torch. Other people saw it.'

The duchess clapped her hands. 'You see! The Duke of Orléans *is* innocent. It pains me to see him going around the court suffering with remorse for something he didn't do.' She glanced over at her husband again and lowered her voice. 'If only we could find out who threw that torch!'

Before Christine could say anything, the duke looked up and asked, 'What are you two whispering about over there?'

The duchess said, 'We're talking about Martin du Bois, the man who disappeared the night of the marriage ball. You told Christine you don't remember him. Has some recollection of him come to your mind now?'

'No, it hasn't.' The duke went back to his manuscript.

The duchess turned to Christine again and asked, 'Why are you so anxious to find this man?'

'My mother felt sorry for his young wife and brought her home to stay with us. I'd like to find her husband so she can go back to her own home.'

'Do you think this man had anything to do with the fire?'

'He disappeared that night without telling his wife where he was going.' She had another thought. Perhaps there was some connection between Martin du Bois, the Viscount of Castelbon, and a plot to kill the king.

'Tell me about his wife,' the duchess said.

'She's sixteen, an orphan Martin du Bois rescued when the city of Courtrai was sacked.' She remembered that Jeanne herself was sixteen, and thought how different she was from Klara.

'My husband was in Courtrai with the king,' the duchess said.

'Martin du Bois may have been there with him.'

'Then the duke should certainly have some memory of him. He's engrossed in his new manuscript now, but later he may be persuaded to think more seriously about this.'

Christine had the feeling this young woman would be able to persuade her husband to do almost anything. 'Thank you, *Madame*,' she said. 'If the duke remembers something, please send word to me. I live just outside the old city wall, on the street that goes past the King of Sicily's palace. A messenger will easily find me; tell him to look for the house just beyond the first three market gardens.'

Christine rose, curtsied to the young duchess, and started to do so to the duke, but he dismissed her with a wave of his hand.

Out in the street, she had sobering thoughts. She was no closer to finding Martin du Bois than before. And what would she do if she discovered that the Viscount of Castelbon had been trying to kill the king? How would she, a commoner, go about accusing a nobleman of such a thing? It seemed she'd taken on an impossible task. But she thought of the queen's distress, Alips's suspicions, the shadow they felt over everything at the palace, and she knew she had to accomplish it.

EIGHT

Even Jesus Christ was willing to associate with prostitutes while turning them away from sin.

Christine de Pizan,
Le Livre des Trois Vertus, 1405

Christine walked slowly up the bank of the Seine, and crossed the river on the Grand Pont, where the sounds of hammering in goldsmiths' shops and the shouts of early travelers hurrying into money-changers' establishments rang in her ears. She was so lost in thought she paid no attention to anything until a man carrying a basket covered with a white cloth approached. She bought one of his pork pasties, then nearly dropped it as she was jostled by a procession of weeping men and women who swept past, trailing after two barefoot priests carrying a large wax effigy of the king. She knew the grotesque figure would be stationed in front of a statue of the Virgin in one of the city's churches, and the priests would throw themselves onto the cold stone floor and beseech the Blessed Mother to deliver the real king from his terrible affliction. The mock king bobbed up and down over the heads of the people in the crowd, a hideous imitation of the beloved monarch who'd lost his reason.

On the other side of the river, as she walked with her head down, she bumped into a tall woman with flaming red hair who wore a crimson cloak and carried a large emerald-green purse decorated with embroidered dragons and lizards.

'Pay attention to where you're going, Lady Christine,' the woman said, laughing. 'If you keep looking at the ground, you'll walk into the river.'

Christine sat down on the edge of a water trough near the Châtelet, the fortress-like prison that cast a pall over that part of the city. 'You're right, Marion,' she said.

The beggars and other vagrants who loitered around the trough looked on, dumbfounded to see a short, proper-looking lady in a plain blue *cotte* and simple white headdress talking to a tall prostitute in her extravagant clothes. Some of them edged closer, all ears to find out what these two women could have to say to each other. Christine was used to people wondering about her friendship with Marion. Her mother, especially, took a dim view of the association. She'd promised Francesca that since Marion was an expert embroiderer she would try to get her to take up that profession instead of prostitution, but lately she'd given up worrying about it. She liked Marion, who'd helped her save Alix de Clairy.

'Why do you look so downcast on such a beautiful day?' Marion asked, sitting beside her and looking up at the people who surrounded them. One man put out his hand, hoping for a coin, while others merely stood with their mouths open. One particularly ragged fellow in a torn brown jerkin and muddy boots snuck away when he saw Christine frowning at him.

Marion stood up and went to the back of the crowd where a

woman in a red, green, and yellow skirt and a huge turban stood staring at Christine.

'That's my friend,' Marion said. 'Do you want to meet her?'

The woman pranced away, and Marion laughed.

'We have to speak quietly,' Christine said as Marion sat down beside her again.

Marion tossed her head. 'What's the big secret?'

'To begin with, my mother brought home a disagreeable young woman whose husband has disappeared. She seems destined to stay with us forever unless I can find him.'

'Lost husbands aren't easy to find.'

'I'm not sure his wife wants him to be found. She's very discontented with him. I think it's because he's much older than she is.'

Some of the beggars moved closer. Christine waved them away.

'Lots of young women are married to older men.'

'I know. I've just been to see the Duchess of Berry, and if anyone should be unhappy with her husband, it's that young lady. But she doesn't complain. In the case of the young woman my mother brought home, it's the husband who should be discontented with *her*.'

'Why?'

'I told you, she's very disagreeable. But that's not the point. I have to find her husband.'

'So you can get rid of her.'

'It's more than that.' She leaned over and said in a low voice, 'Just before he vanished, his wife heard him mutter something about the king's life being in danger.'

'Who is this man?'

'His name is Martin du Bois.' Christine pulled Marion closer. 'There's more. The queen thinks someone is trying to kill the king.'

'God's teeth,' Marion cried.

'Keep your voice down, or I won't tell you anything more.'

'What makes her think that?' Marion asked in a whisper.

'Remember the fire at the palace and the four men who burned to death?'

'How could anyone forget?'

'Everyone thinks the fire was started by the Duke of Orléans. Some say it was a spark from a torch he was holding. Others say he threw the torch at the dancers. But the duke swears he didn't do it, and I believe him. He's ambitious, but I don't think he's capable of such evil.'

'I don't either. I know he'd like to be king, but to kill his own brother? And in such a horrible way? Not possible.'

'In any case, when I thought about it, I realized he was holding two torches while the men were burning. If he came in with two and he was still holding them both, he can't have thrown one at the dancers. And besides, I saw a third torch on the floor.'

Marion jumped up and pommeled the air with her fists. 'I knew it! I knew you were there!'

Christine grabbed Marion's hand and pulled her back down on the edge of the trough. 'I'm sorry I never told you. It was just by accident that I saw those men burning. I've been too upset to talk about it.'

Marion looked at Christine with pity in her eyes. 'I understand. It must have been horrible!'

'It was. I have nightmares.'

'So if there was a third torch, where did it come from?'

'That's what we have to find out.' Christine looked at the people standing around and whispered, 'There's more.'

Marion leaned closer. Several beggars moved closer, too. Marion stood up, and they scurried away.

'Someone told me she saw a lighted torch flung from the musicians' balcony.'

'Who told you that?'

'The queen's dwarf. She was up on the balcony. She told the queen about it, and the queen thinks the torch was meant for the king. She's convinced the person who threw it is still at the palace, and he's determined to kill the king. She's asked me to find out who it is.'

Marion let out a whistle of surprise. Then she said, 'I suppose you're the right person to ask since you've already found one murderer. But I think if anyone threw a torch, he meant it for Huguet de Guisay. Lots of people wanted to kill Huguet. He had no respect for anyone. He called commoners dogs, and he was really cruel to his servants. He used to stand on their backs, dig into them with his spurs, and cry "Bark, dog!" Huguet de Guisay was the perfect target for a flaming torch.'

'The Duchess of Berry thinks it was meant for Yvain de Foix.'

'She told you that?'

'Not exactly. But she implied that the Viscount of Castelbon was lucky Yvain died when he did. Nevertheless, the queen believes it's the king who was supposed to die, and I think she's right, because of what the abandoned wife heard her husband say.'

'So what are you going to do?'

'The dwarf told me she's sure it wasn't one of the musicians. But perhaps they saw something. I'm going to go and speak to them.'

'You can't do that. You're a lady. When they see you coming, they'll run like hell.'

'So what should I do?'

Marion stood up, adjusted her crimson cloak, and squared her shoulders.

'Let me go and talk to them,' she said.

NINE

Don't let your maidservants lie, play unlawful games, swear foully, or speak words that suggest villainy or that are lewd or coarse, like some vulgar people who curse 'the bloody bad fevers, the bloody bad work, the bloody bad day.'

From a book of moral and practical advice
for a young wife, Paris, 1393

C hristine walked home, rejoicing because Marion had offered to help her. Marion lived by her own rules, and her ways were unconventional, but she'd provided the key to the identity of a murderess at the palace a few weeks earlier, and Christine hoped she would work a similar miracle again.

But her heart sank when she came to the door of her house. She heard angry voices coming from the kitchen, and when she went in, she found Klara having another battle with the children. Thomas held Goblin, Klara tried to get the dog away from him, and Lisabetta crouched on the floor, crying loudly. Marie and Jean sat at the table, their hands over their ears.

'He's our dog. You can't have him,' Thomas screamed at Klara.

Georgette, who'd been stirring a pot of soup over the fire, shook her spoon at the boy. 'Can't you share the poor dog?'

'No,' Thomas shouted.

'The Devil take you,' Klara shouted back at him.

Georgette said, 'This young lady doesn't know where her husband is. Don't any of you feel the least bit sorry for her?'

'No,' the children cried in unison.

'You're all bloody fools,' Georgette said.

Just then, Francesca came into the room. 'I have told you before, Georgette, I will have no talk like that in this house.'

Thomas pointed at Klara. 'She said something bad, too!'

'*Basta, Tommaso!*' Francesca said. Then she whispered to Christine, 'This has been going on all morning.'

'What shall we do?' Christine whispered back.

'Did you find out anything about her husband from the Duke of Berry?'

'No. He doesn't even remember him.'

Klara had stopped trying to get Goblin away from Thomas, and she sat down at the table. Her blond hair was disheveled, and her cheeks were blotched and stained with tears. Marie and Jean turned away from her in disgust.

'She's torn the sleeve of her kirtle,' Christine said.

'She needs other clothes,' Francesca said. 'We should go to her house and get some.'

'I suppose you're right. Let's do it this afternoon, right after we've had dinner.'

Francesca called to Georgette, 'Get the table ready. And you can help her, Klara.'

Klara wiped her nose on her sleeve and went to stand beside Georgette, who'd taken the pot off the fire and was ladling soup into bowls.

The children seated themselves at the table, and Klara carried the bowls to them, plunking them down so hard that soup splashed onto the tablecloth.

Thomas ate a spoonful, put his spoon down, and said, 'This is terrible.' He looked at Klara. 'It must be one of your husband's recipes.'

Francesca slapped him gently. 'This is your favorite soup, *Tommaso*. So be quiet and leave Klara alone.'

After that, the children were subdued, and they ate peacefully, not looking at Klara, who hardly ate a drop. Then Francesca got up and said, 'We are going to go to Klara's house and get her some clothes.'

'That means she's going to be here for a while,' Thomas whispered to Jean.

'You'd better come with us, Klara,' Christine said. 'You can tell us what to take. And you come, too, Jean. You can help carry everything.'

Klara made a face. 'I'd rather not go there.'

'You can't stay here forever,' Francesca said. 'Once your husband comes back, you'll go home. Don't you want that?'

'No.'

'Well, you will go back, and there is nothing you can do about it,' Francesca said as she took Klara's arm and steered her into the hall to get her cloak.

Just a week before, the market gardens near Christine's house had been covered with frost, but now everything was coming to life under a late-winter sun. A few tender green shoots poked up through the barren earth, and there were even some early snowdrops and crocuses, if one looked closely. Klara marched along, looking at the ground, but not noticing the flowers. When they came to the magnificent mansion known as the King of Sicily's palace, Jean asked her, 'Wouldn't you like to live there?' She barely glanced at it.

So far, they'd been the only people on the street, but on the other side of the old city wall, they had to press through throngs of people hurrying in and out of shops or simply ambling along enjoying the spring-like day. Mules laden with bulging sacks plodded past, horsemen in fur-lined cloaks and big beaver hats with tall peacock feathers flopping from side to side shouted warnings as they galloped toward the palace, street vendors cried their wares, and beggars pleaded with outstretched hands. Christine bought some wafers, Francesca pressed deniers into the hands of the beggars, and Jean gaped at the horsemen and their mounts. Klara paid no attention to anything.

They made their way down the rue des Rosiers to the rue des Escouffles and found Martin du Bois's house, a mansion several stories high with gabled windows and a large arched doorway. On one side of the house, there was a large kitchen garden, and on the other, a stable and a washhouse. *The man certainly isn't lacking for money*, Christine thought.

Klara held back as they approached the door. 'I hope that woman is not here.'

'She means the beguine,' Francesca whispered to Christine. 'I wonder why she dislikes her so much.'

No one stood guard at the door, which was not locked, and they stepped into a hall with a large fireplace. There was no fire, and the place seemed deserted, until a slim maid appeared at the end of the hall. 'Denise,' Klara called out, and the girl approached warily. 'Where's the beguine?'

'She left,' the girl said.

Klara smiled. 'Good.'

'Where have you been?'

'With these people. I need clothes. Come upstairs and help us find some.'

They all traipsed up a wide staircase and into a room full of chests and coffers. Klara dove into one of the chests and started throwing out gowns and underclothes. Francesca pushed her aside and began lifting the garments out carefully, examining them, and deciding which ones should be packed. Denise hurried to fold them and stuff them into a large sack.

Christine snuck away so she could look around, hoping to learn something about Martin du Bois. What she found was an ordinary Parisian house, with the living and dining quarters and several bedrooms on the second floor. The furnishings were those of a man who liked things plain and neat: chests, coffers, and benches without the elaborate carvings many people prized, rush mats to cover the floor, tapestries embroidered with simple designs. She wandered to the end of a gallery and found a small study with a large desk, a chair, a fireplace, and shelves overflowing with books. Martin du Bois was well read.

The room had an unpleasant smell, and she shuddered when she looked at the bare floorboards and realized what it was. There had been a fire. A spark from the fireplace must have fallen on a rush mat and burned through it, charring the wood underneath. The flames had been extinguished quickly, for nothing else had suffered, but she could imagine how frantic Martin du Bois had been to put them out. A house fire in the city could quickly reduce a person's home to ashes.

On another part of the floor a large rust-colored stain spread from one side of the room to the other. She'd seen a similar stain in her own house, one day when Georgette had come back from the market with a bowl of pig's blood for black pudding and spilled it on the wooden floor of the hallway. Someone had bled profusely in this room. Was it someone who'd been wounded? Or murdered? She remembered what Klara had heard her husband say about the king, just before he disappeared. Many troubling thoughts came to her mind.

Wondering what Klara knew, she went back to her room, where she heard a cry of surprise from Jean, who'd opened a coffer and found it filled with a profusion of jeweled brooches, buckles, and rings.

'I don't know what she's got to complain about if her husband gives her all these,' he said. He dove into the coffer, rifled through its contents, and pulled something out. 'What would she do with this?'

Christine looked at what he held in his hand and asked herself the same question. The object was bent and encrusted with grime, but completely recognizable. It was a golden spur.

'Put it back, Jean, before Klara sees,' she said.

But Klara had seen. She ran over and grabbed the spur. 'That's mine. Leave it alone.' She thrust it into the sack with her clothes.

Francesca was still examining the contents of the chest and handing things to Denise to pack, so Christine went to help her. As she sorted through kirtles, chemises, surcoats, and undergarments, she thought about the spur and wondered why Klara had hidden it in a coffer with her jewelry. But she was more concerned with what she'd seen in the husband's study, and she asked herself, *Who is Martin du Bois, and what terrible things have gone on in his house?*

TEN

When a puffer starts to blow and the bagpipe begins to whine,
a large crowd gathers round. There's more to this than joy;
they leap about as though demented, flinging their hands and
legs and feet about with no sense or reason or restraint.

Eustache Deschamps (c. 1340–1404), *Ballade 923*

Marion, her hair bound with glittering beads and carrying her emerald-green purse with its embroidered dragons and lizards, strode down the rue Saint-Martin toward the rue aus Jugléeurs, the street where many of the musicians and instrument-makers of Paris lived and worked. Her brothel was in another part of the city, but she lived in a rented room not far from the rue Saint-Martin, and she was well known in the neighborhood.

She pushed her way through the crowds, stopping every now and then to gaze at the jewelry, goblets, candlesticks, knives, hats, belts, shoes, and linens displayed on counters in front of shop windows. When she came to a bronze-worker's establishment, she couldn't resist going in to ask about a brooch she saw outside. The proprietor took the brooch from the window and held it up so she could see its decoration – two dragons with their long necks entwined. She dug into her embroidered purse, brought out some coins, and was about to hand them to the man when she noticed on the counter a bronze key ring decorated with a little sculpted figure of a jester. She thought of Francesca. She knew Christine's mother didn't like her, though she'd become less hostile lately, and she thought she'd give her the key ring as a way to make peace with her. She bought it and the brooch and stuffed them into her purse.

Then she continued down the rue Saint-Martin, looking about carefully. She came to a tavern, hesitated, entered, and surveyed the customers seated at long wooden tables with beakers of wine before them. A tall, thin man with a hooked nose sat with two companions at the back of the room, and when he saw her, he called out, 'Come join us, Marion.'

She wound her way over, her crimson cloak brushing against the tables, nearly sweeping several beakers to the floor, and sat down beside him.

'Hello, Denisot. Introduce me to your friends.'

'So nice of you to join us musicians, Marion. This is Thibaut, who plays the pipes, and Philippot, who drives people mad with his bagpipes.'

Philippot, large and red-faced, laughed and clapped Denisot on the back. 'I don't suppose *you* drive anyone mad, blasting away on your trumpet?'

'It's not the same,' Denisot said.

Marion took a sip of Denisot's wine. 'Of course, if you play like that, anyone standing nearby might find the music a bit loud, no matter which instrument it is,' she mused.

'I suppose so,' Denisot admitted. 'But most of the time we have to play loud, so we can be heard above the noise of the crowds.'

'Even when you're up on the musicians' balcony at the palace?'

Denisot clapped his hands and called for more wine. 'Up there, no one's close enough to be bothered. It's just us, so we play however we want.'

'But what if someone else was up there with you? Would you all be concentrating on your playing so much that you wouldn't notice?' She took another drink of Denisot's wine.

Thibaut, a skinny man who looked like a frightened rabbit, shifted uneasily on the bench. Philippot rubbed his hands on his ample thighs.

'What's this got to do with anything?' Denisot asked.

'One thinks about such things, you know.'

'Think about something else, Marion.'

'Actually, I'm thinking about the night of the masquerade ball. I suppose you were all there?'

'So what if we were?' Philippot asked.

'Perhaps you can tell me something about what happened that night.'

The three men looked at each other.

'You don't need to be afraid,' Marion said. 'I know you didn't do it. But there were other people besides you musicians on the balcony. One of those people threw a lighted torch at the masqueraders.'

Thibaut started to shake, and Philippot put his arms around him to quiet him.

'It's nothing to do with us,' Denisot said. 'Is anyone accusing us?'

'No one thinks you had anything to do with the fire,' Marion said. 'But someone wants to know if any of you saw a stranger up there.'

'This is none of your business,' Denisot said.

'I'm making it my business,' Marion said. 'Four men burned to death, and the king could have died, too.'

Philippot and Thibault got up from the table. 'Time for us to go,' Philippot said, and they scurried away.

'They didn't see anything,' Denisot said.

'Did you?'

'No. And even if we did see something, we wouldn't talk about it.'

'And no one else will, either? Is that what you're saying?'

'Look, Marion. I don't know who has put you up to asking these questions, but you'd better be careful. People have died.'

'And more people may die. Even the king.'

'I don't understand.'

'It's true, Denisot. And I need to know what you saw.'

Denisot took a drink of wine and looked at Marion for a long time. Finally, he said, 'There were several men playing vielles. One of them, Bernart le Brun, stood behind us for a moment fixing a broken string on his instrument. He might have seen something.'

'Where can I find Bernart le Brun?'

'I haven't seen him for a while. I know he lives on the rue aus Jugléeurs. But be careful, Marion. This could be a dangerous business.'

Marion made her way back through the room, ignoring the drinkers saluting her with raised beakers, left the tavern, and made her way slowly down to the rue aus Jugléeurs. Tall buildings leaned precariously over the narrow street, children ran in and out of the houses, and through open doors she could see steep staircases and dark interiors. Many instrument-makers lived there, and she heard the sounds of trumpets, pipes, shawms, even a bagpipe. But other people had shops there, too – an apothecary, a shield-maker, a dressmaker, and a garlic-seller. A woman sitting in front of the dressmaker's shop looked her up and down and motioned for her to come over so she could talk to her.

'That's a beautiful purse you have. Who did the embroidery?'

'I did.'

'You could make a good living from work like that.'

Marion laughed. 'So a friend of mine is always telling me.'

'Will you sell it to me?'

'Not today.'

The woman shrugged and went back to her sewing.

Next to the garlic-seller's shop stood an empty house with a door that swung back and forth, creaking on rusty hinges. She hurried past. A man holding a trumpet came toward her, and she asked him, 'Do you know where Bernart le Brun lives?'

'At the end of the street.'

She walked to the last house and knocked on the door. A woman in a short-sleeved *cotte* and a dirty apron opened it. Marion said, 'I'm looking for Bernart le Brun.'

'He's not here.' The woman started to close the door. Marion put her foot out and held it open.

'Please, can you tell me where he is?'

The woman kicked her foot aside and slammed the door.

Marion turned and started back down the narrow street, hoping to find someone who could tell her where Bernart le Brun might be. As she passed the empty house, a horseman charged by on a black stallion, coming so close she jumped back and fell against the creaky door. It swung open and she tumbled into a dark hallway, landing on her hands and knees. Stunned, she remained there for a moment, feeling pain where her hands had scraped against the rough floorboards, and listening to the rasping of her breath. She reached out blindly for something to hold on to so she could pull herself to her feet. But instead of a wall or a banister or a piece of furniture, she touched rough cloth, and then cold flesh. There was someone beside her, someone who was not moving.

She jumped up and ran out into the street, screaming.

ELEVEN

Dear Sister, I beg you, in order to preserve your husband's love and good will, be loving, amiable, and sweet with him. Keep peace with him, and remember the country proverb that says there are three things that drive a good man from his home: a house with a bad roof, a smoking chimney, and a quarrelsome woman.

From a book of moral and practical advice
for a young wife, Paris, 1393

When Christine went into the kitchen the next morning, she found Georgette kneeling on the hearth, grumbling to herself as she tried to light the fire.

'You don't have the proper kindling,' said Klara, who sat on a stool, holding Goblin.

'Perhaps Klara learned something from her husband's manuscript after all,' Christine said to her mother. 'There's a passage where he tells her how to prepare wood for starting a fire.' She looked around. 'Where are the children?'

'They're outside, plotting how to get Goblin away from her.' Francesca chuckled.

'That's not amusing, Mama. They should know better. Klara, too. She's sixteen and married. Isn't she at all worried about her husband?'

Francesca shook her head. 'It does not seem so.'

'I'm sure she gives him a lot of trouble. He points out many times in his manuscript that wives should be loving and peaceful with their husbands. Do you see any signs that Klara is loving and peaceful?'

'None whatsoever. The poor man.'

'Some of this may be his fault, you know.'

'It is the woman who must keep peace in the family.'

'Men have to do their part. A wife can't be blamed for everything that goes wrong.'

'I did not say that.' Francesca picked up a bellows and went to help Georgette with the fire.

'But I know what you were thinking,' Christine called after her.

Francesca worked the bellows, sparks caught, and flames leapt up. She turned to Klara, handed her the bellows, and said, 'You should learn how to use this. I am sure your husband expects you to keep his house warm.'

'I don't have to do that,' Klara said.

Francesca looked at Christine, who'd come over to stand beside her. 'Did you not just tell me that her husband gives her instructions for making a fire?'

'I did.'

Francesca turned back to Klara, 'If your husband expects you to do something, you must do it. Always obey your husband, and you will keep peace with him. That is what I did, when my husband was alive.'

Christine started to laugh. 'That's not true, Mama. You didn't keep peace with Papa.'

'How can you say that?'

'You argued with him all the time, especially when he was teaching me to read and write. You told him girls didn't need to learn about such things.'

Francesca shrugged.

'Don't pretend you don't remember. You're lucky he didn't give in. If he had, I wouldn't know how to do anything but keep the fire going and cook and sew. Then where would we be?'

Francesca sat on the bench by the fireplace, drew her daughter down beside her, and put her arms around her. 'Perhaps I was wrong. I am sorry.'

Christine hugged her mother. 'We shouldn't be arguing. We should be deciding what to do about Klara.'

'Perhaps her husband is dead. Will we have to keep her here forever?'

'That's what I'm afraid of.'

'Then you had better find Martin du Bois. Have you asked Georgette if her brother has told her where he is?'

'Come over here, Georgette,' Christine called out to the girl, who was about to hang a cauldron of water on the pothook.

'I know what you're going to ask me,' Georgette said. She set the pot on the floor, wiped her hands on her apron, and shuffled toward them. 'But I can't tell you anything. Colin's never said anything about Martin du Bois. All I know is, he's talked to Klara's brother Willem.'

'What do you know about Willem?'

'Nothing more than what I've already told you.'

Georgette went back to the fire, picked up the cauldron, and hoisted it onto the pothook, spilling water on the floor, and on herself, in the process. She took off her wet apron and used it to dab at her dress and wipe up the floor.

'What are we going to do?' Francesca asked.

'She's the only help we can afford,' Christine said.

'I mean about Klara.'

'Marion says she can help with her.'

Francesca jumped up and shook her finger at her daughter. 'She's a prostitute! We will not let her anywhere near Klara!'

'I thought perhaps you'd made your peace with her,' Christine said.

Just then there was a knock at the door, and when Christine answered it, she found Marion, who cried, 'I have to talk to you! About the musicians.'

'Come in, but don't say anything to my mother.'

They went into the kitchen where, at the sight of Marion with her crimson cloak, flaming red hair, and glittering beads, Klara sprang up from the stool and dropped Goblin, who landed on the floor with a thud.

'It's all right, Klara,' Christine said. 'This is my friend Marion.'

'And who is this little lady?' Marion asked.

'This is Klara, whose husband has disappeared.'

Marion stepped over to Klara. 'I'm happy to meet you,' she said.

Klara backed away, almost falling over the stool.

'Haven't you ever met a prostitute before?'

Francesca gasped and the children giggled. 'Don't talk to her like that, Marion,' Christine said.

Marion laughed. She went to Francesca, took the key ring she'd bought on the rue Saint-Martin out of her embroidered purse, and handed it to her.

'I know you keep your cupboards, spice chests, and the door to your house locked at all times, so I thought this might be useful.' Then, under her breath, 'Of course, locking the door won't keep out the evil spirits you're always worried about.'

Christine was relieved to see that her mother accepted the gift graciously. Then Marion stepped over to Klara, reached into her purse again, and brought out the bronze brooch.

'This would look nice with that pretty dress you're wearing.'

Klara couldn't back away any more; she was already up against the wall. She reached out for the brooch, took it gingerly, and inspected the dragon decoration.

'Thank you,' she whispered.

Marion turned to Christine. 'I have to talk to you.'

Francesca put her hand on Christine's arm and squeezed it.

'It's all right, Mama,' Christine said. She took Marion into the hall.

'You can't keep everything from her,' Marion said.

'I have to. If she finds out about what the queen has asked me to do, she'll be beside herself with worry, and she'll try to stop me.'

'She's got enough to do, with that little lady in there.'

'I don't know what to do about Klara. The only one who seems to get along with her is Georgette.'

'What's wrong with her?'

'I told you. She thinks her husband is too old. She doesn't want to learn how to keep house and care for him. He hired a beguine to help her, and that seems to have made it worse; she hates her.'

'I can straighten her out.'

'How?'

Marion laughed. 'If I can help Loyse, I can help anyone.'

'What are you talking about? The only Loyse I know is the lion-keeper's helper.'

'That's who I mean.'

Christine stared at Marion. She, like everyone else, thought Loyse was mad. The girl dressed in rags, never combed her hair, never spoke, and never left the lions' stockade.

'You think Loyse doesn't know what goes on around here,' Marion continued. 'But she does.'

'Does Loyse talk to you?'

'Not exactly. But I'll take you to see her, and you'll find out how wrong everyone's been about her. Meanwhile, let me spend some time with Klara.'

'We'll see. But you came to tell me something. What is it?'

'Some of the musicians who played the night of the masquerade told me one of the vielle players, Bernart le Brun, might have seen something, so I went to his house on the rue aus Jugléeurs to talk to him.'

Marion's voice rose as she began to recount her terrible experience. Christine put her finger to her lips and nodded toward the kitchen, where her mother might be listening.

Marion lowered her voice and rushed on with her story. 'His wife said he wasn't home, so I went out to ask about him. I walked down the street, a horseman came by, I jumped out of the way, and I fell through the door of an empty house. I reached out in the dark, and I touched him. He was dead.'

'Great God! But how did you know who it was?'

'I didn't, until the sergeants from the Châtelet came and carried him out into the street where I could get a good look at him. They said he'd been poisoned, but I suspected that already, because he was covered with vomit.'

'So he must have seen the person who threw the torch! And he got himself killed because of it.' Christine thought of Alips, who'd seen that person, too. 'Did the sergeants from the Châtelet say anything else?'

'They wouldn't tell me anything. At least they didn't accuse me of murdering him.'

'We know more about why he was poisoned than they do. But what can we do about it?'

'Perhaps his wife knows something. I'm sure she won't talk to me, though. If you go there, maybe she'll talk to you.'

'That's a good idea. We'll go together. Meet me first thing tomorrow morning at the corner of the rue Saint-Martin and the rue aus Jugléeurs. If I'm not there then, come the next morning.'

Francesca stood in the doorway, her hands on her hips. 'What are you two talking about?'

'Marion thinks she can help us with Klara,' Christine said.

'Make a *prostituta* out of her?'

'That is not amusing,' Christine said. She took her mother by the shoulders, turned her around, and gently pushed her back into the kitchen.

TWELVE

The doctor, Guillaume de Harselly, said to the king's brother and his uncles, 'He is better now, but his mind is still weak. Don't tire him with affairs of state. Let him relax with amusements and sports.'

Froissart, *Chroniques*, Livre IV, 1389–1400

The next morning, Colin came and announced that Christine was wanted at the palace. Marion would not find her at the corner of the rue Saint-Martin and the rue aus Jugléeurs as they had planned. But Marion was patient; she'd be there again.

'You have to finish the manuscript you're copying,' Colin said.

How does he know? Christine asked herself. The boy was a snoop. She reflected that this might be a good thing; he might be able to find out where Martin du Bois had gone. She'd talk to him about it on the way to the palace.

On the rue Saint-Antoine, Colin looked around for the pasty and wafer vendors. But they weren't there, which was surprising on a warm day. They soon saw why. A group of people stood near the cemetery of the church of Saint-Pol, looking at the ground and talking excitedly. Colin ran over and pushed his way through the crowd. Christine followed him.

Evergreen trees grew at one side of the cemetery, and a caretaker had discovered a woman lying unconscious under one of them. She wore only a white chemise and her face was covered with dried blood. The caretaker knelt beside her. '*Dieu!* She must have been here since last night.' He touched her cheek. 'But she's still alive! It's a miracle. If the weather hadn't been so warm, she'd have died.'

Several people bent down to get a closer look. 'She's been hit on the head,' said an old man. To demonstrate, he lifted his cane and brought it down hard on the ground. '*Merde!*' exclaimed the man beside him as he jumped out of the way. Then an old crone tried to pull the injured woman's chemise down so her legs would be covered. 'To make her decent,' she said.

One of the wafer vendors stepped up and shook his fist at them. 'Don't just stand there talking! Take her to a doctor.' A man ran to get a large plank lying beside the road. Strong hands lifted the injured woman onto it and started to carry her away.

'She might die,' Colin said, looking worried.

'Perhaps not,' Christine said. 'I wonder who she is. Have you ever seen her before?' The boy didn't answer. Instead, he ran after the men carrying the litter.

Christine wanted to call him back, but he was out of sight. She was not surprised he'd gone to find out what would happen to the woman – Colin pried into everything – but she was irritated that he'd disappeared before she'd had a chance to talk to him about Martin du Bois.

At the palace, she stood in the doorway to the queen's chambers and was relieved to see that Isabeau, reclining on her day bed in a blue velvet *houppelande* with ermine-lined sleeves, a wide pearl-studded belt, and a circlet of jewels that sparkled whenever she turned her head, was dressed like royalty again. She appeared to have recovered from her gloom, for she was playing with her grey-hound and smiling at her ladies-in-waiting, who sat on big cushions by the bed, wearing gowns nearly as elegant as hers. Christine looked down at her own plain blue surcoat and sighed.

A chambermaid brought in the little Saracen girl. The queen lifted the child onto the bed, and they laughed when the monkey scuttled over, hid behind a cushion, and reached out a paw to pat the greyhound's head. Guillaume the fool ran to them and danced around, making comments about the dog's cold nose. 'Just like a maid's knee,' he said, looking at the chambermaid.

The queen motioned for Christine to come to her. As she approached the bed, Guillaume made a little bow and said, 'Welcome, fair scribe.' He sprinted to the other side of the room, his bald head shining, and said to Gracieuse the minstrel, who sat with her lute on her lap, 'Give us sweet sounds for the scribe.' Gracieuse picked up her lute and started to play, whereupon

Guillaume seized Jeannine the fool's hands and swung her around in a wild dance.

The queen watched him and smiled. 'So much dancing. He will again have holes in his shoes, and I will again have to buy him new ones.'

Christine knelt. Isabeau looked at her hopefully. 'Are you here to do what I ask?'

'I will try, *Madame*.'

Isabeau motioned for her to rise. 'At least you will accomplish something for Catherine. She is distressed. The book will cheer her.'

I wonder, Christine said to herself as she went to the room where she did her work. The book she was copying was a *Life of Saint Catherine of Alexandria*, a martyr who'd suffered a horrible death, and she didn't think Catherine de Fastavarin, still tormented by thoughts of the tragic fire, would be in a hurry to read it.

Through the open door she could see into the room where the queen and her ladies sat, and as she waited for the manuscript to be brought to her, she watched a page come in, kneel before the queen, and present her with a leather pouch resting on a little red velvet pillow. The ladies-in-waiting crowded around as she opened the pouch and removed something that Christine, whose view was blocked by voluminous gowns and massive jeweled circlets, couldn't see. When Guillaume and Jeannine ran over to find out what all the excitement was about, curiosity got the better of her, and she joined them.

The queen had in her hands a set of playing cards. First she showed them to the little girl sitting beside her on the bed, and then she held them up, one by one, so her ladies could admire them. Each card had a picture of an implement of war, set against a gold background. Battle axes, swords, shields, spurs, and helmets appeared, and finally one that was different; a deer with a gilded collar shaped like a crown.

Christine felt a tug on her sleeve and looked down to find Alips, who said, 'She had them made as a present for the king.'

'I'm sure the king will like them,' Christine said. 'He loves anything having to do with battles. But I'm puzzled about the deer.'

'The king has special affection for deer. Someone told him that in the forest of Senlis they'd found a deer that had been there since ancient times. They said words proving this were inscribed on a collar around its neck. The king thinks this has special meaning for his own reign.'

'And they call us fools,' Guillaume said. He bounded to the other side of the room and did a few somersaults.

'Whose idea was it to give the king playing cards?' Christine asked Alips.

'The doctor. He says the king should have things to amuse him.'

Better than dressing up like a savage and disgracing himself, Christine thought.

'Playing cards are an innocent amusement,' Alips said.

Christine went back to the room where she did her work, musing about the dwarf and wondering how she always knew what she was thinking. As she waited for the manuscript, Alips came to her side again. 'Just look at them,' she said, gesturing toward the ladies-in-waiting, who were bending down to see the cards. 'Their big hairdos are bumping into each other.'

Christine had to laugh. The hairdos really were ridiculous. To construct them, chambermaids twisted long strands of their mistresses' hair around balls of cloth, fastened them with jeweled pins, arranged them over their ears like horns, and topped them with padded circlets studded with jewels. The results were so large and so ungainly that Francesca, who took note of everything that went on at the court, wondered how the ladies could get through the palace doorways.

Suddenly the ladies drew back and made hurried curtseys as a large woman in a dark red *houppelande* trimmed with miniver strode into the room with a jangle of gold bracelets and necklaces. It was the Duchess of Burgundy, the wife of one of the king's uncles, the Duke of Burgundy. She made a brief show of kneeling before the queen, then rose to her full height and glared down her long nose at the playing cards. 'What are those?' she demanded to know.

The queen clutched the cards to her breast and glared back at her. 'For the king.'

'She will try to get the cards away from her,' Alips whispered to Christine.

'Those things are evil. The king must not have them.' The duchess reached out for the cards. The queen tightened her grip on them, and her godchild started to cry.

'I will talk to my husband about this,' the duchess declared.

'It is on the duke's order that these have been made for my husband,' Isabeau said. 'The doctor has told Charles's uncles that they must provide him with amusements, to calm him and steady his mind.'

'We will see about that.' The duchess called for her maid, and stalked from the room, the skirts of her red *houppelande* swishing and her gold bracelets and necklaces jingling and clinking. The queen's ladies knelt as she passed, and they all kept their heads down, except for a slender blond woman, much younger than the others, who looked directly at the duchess and smiled. The duchess smiled back; it was the only time Christine had ever seen her without a frown on her face.

THIRTEEN

The Duchess of Borgoyne, who was a cruel lady, had the queen under her control, and no one could speak with the queen unless she approved.

Froissart, *Chroniques*, Livre IV, 1389–1400

The ladies came back and crowded around the queen, talking excitedly, the long fur-lined sleeves of their gowns swirling around them and the jewels in their hairdos sparkling.

'Why do they burden themselves with those hairdos?' Christine asked Alips. 'They look as though they have bowls of fruit on their heads.'

'They're just copying the queen.'

'Do you think she tells them to?'

'She doesn't have to. She knows they will follow her lead.'

Alips sat down on the floor by Christine's feet. 'The queen understands her ladies very well. I don't think they understand *her*, though. Except for Catherine de Fastavarin. She understands her because they grew up together in Bavaria, and they speak German to each other. But Catherine is so distraught about the fire, she doesn't come here now. I've heard she's hardly able to get out of bed these days. It must not be pleasant for her new husband.'

I'm sure the queen misses Catherine sorely, Christine thought. The other ladies, wives of knights and court officials, had been chosen for her, and most of them were older than she was. They were handsomely rewarded for attending to her every need, from her clothes and hair to her jewels and her books, and they seemed more like paid companions than friends. She watched them intently, wondering whether there was one among them who wanted the king to die.

Jeanne de la Tour, the oldest, who was quite frail, began to shake and had to sit down on one of the big cushions. Marguerite de Germonville, a large, bossy woman, hovered over her, telling her in a loud voice to take a potion of valerian and lavender for the tremor in her hands. 'And chamomile,' added Madame de Malicorne, a stout personage who was in charge of the queen's children. She held the queen's year-old son and dangled a diamond bracelet in front of his eyes.

'The queen gave her that bracelet yesterday,' Alips said. 'The others are envious. She's a great favorite, and they think she's haughty. She's actually very kind. She laughs at the things I tell the queen.'

Catherine de Villiers, a little bird-like woman who cared for the queen's many books, came in bringing the manuscript Christine was copying. She hurried to the room where Christine waited, nodded to Alips, who had risen so she could pass, went to the desk, and slowly removed the book from its linen case. As she placed it in front of Christine, she cautioned her to treat it with care. Christine was not offended. She knew the woman loved books as much as she did, for she'd often seen her sitting with Isabeau as they read together from one of the volumes the queen had in her own collection or from something they'd borrowed from the king's library, which was even more extensive than the queen's.

Catherine went out and joined the other ladies, who were examining the playing cards again. Madame de Malicorne placed the baby in the queen's arms, picked up the cards, and turned them over and over in her hands, so engrossed, she forgot the others were waiting for a chance to examine them.

'Let someone else have a look,' Marguerite de Germonville said. At the sound of her booming voice, the Saracen girl clutched the queen's hand, and the baby started to cry. Madame de Malicorne laughed and handed Marguerite the cards. When it was Jeanne de la Tour's turn, she held them carefully in her trembling hands, but almost dropped them when the queen's greyhound brushed against her. The woman who'd smiled at the duchess earlier laughed.

'That's Symonne du Mesnil,' Alips said. 'She acts that way

because she drinks too much wine at dinner. Everyone wonders why she has to lie down for the rest of the afternoon.'

Christine was shocked. The women chosen to be the queen's ladies-in-waiting were supposed to be models of decorum. 'How do you know?'

'I know most everything about those ladies. Except for Symonne. She hasn't been here long. The Duchess of Burgundy brought her.'

'There used to be more of them around the queen. Where are the others?'

'The duchess sent them away. She'll get rid of all the rest, too, if she has her way. She wants to be the only one who can speak with the queen.'

'Why?'

'The king's uncles are running the government now, because the king is ill. The Duke of Berry doesn't take much interest, but the Duke of Burgundy is hungry for power. He told his wife to make sure no one else has influence with the queen, especially any of her ladies who were married to the king's advisers.'

Christine opened the manuscript to the page where she'd left off her copying, cringing when she saw the illumination there, a naked Saint Catherine, her hands folded in prayer, standing inside a spiked wheel, waiting to be torn to pieces.

Alips stood on her toes, trying to see, so Christine turned the manuscript in her direction. The dwarf looked at the picture and said, 'I know what happened next. The wheel broke apart before the spikes got to her. In order to kill her, they had to cut off her head.' She looked up at Christine. 'I listened when Catherine and the queen were reading.' She laughed. 'The Duchess of Burgundy saw me, and she got mad.'

'Do you think the duchess will have you dismissed, Alips?' Christine asked.

'She might. I know Catherine de Fastavarin talked to her about it. But for now, she doesn't think I'm important enough to bother with.'

'You seem important to the queen.'

'I suppose it's because we're both strangers here.'

'Weren't you born in Paris?'

'I don't know. I don't remember my parents. They may have given me away, or perhaps I was stolen. All I know is, I was raised by an old woman who sold rags. She never told me where I came from.'

Christine started to say something, but Alips interrupted her. 'You're wondering how I got here, to the palace.'

'I'd like to hear about it.'

'I ran away because a man molested me. I fell into a ditch, and the husband of one of the queen's ladies found me. He gave me to his wife, the Countess of Eu. Do you remember her?'

'Yes. She's dead now.'

'She was a jolly, good-natured lady, and she found me amusing. She thought I'd be good for the queen, and she brought me to her.'

Alips watched the queen sitting on the bed playing with her baby and her godchild. 'She looked very different the day I first saw her,' she said. 'She was pregnant, her hair was disheveled, and her cheeks were covered with tears. She was terrified because there was a thunderstorm. Every time she heard a clap of thunder or saw a flash of lightning she started up and cried out.

'Catherine de Fastavarin was with her, and she looked at me with malice. I knew right away she was one of those people who hate dwarfs, fearing we will bring them misfortune. The Countess of Eu paid no attention to her. She said to the queen, "I've brought someone to cheer you, *Madame*."

'The queen stopped crying and pushed her hair away from her face so she could get a good look at me. Catherine leaned close to her and hissed into her ear some words in German; I didn't have to be told she was advising the queen to send me away. The belief that dwarfs can bring any kind of luck, good or bad, is nonsense, of course. I could sense the queen knew that. I remembered something the old rag-picker had told me, and I said, slowly, because I wasn't sure how well the queen understood our language, 'When I was a baby, someone put me on the ground, and while I was lying there a man came and stepped over me. He didn't know that unless he then stepped backwards over me I would never grow tall. That is why I am a dwarf, *Madame*.'

'At that point, the Countess of Eu must have had second thoughts about bringing you to the queen!' Christine exclaimed.

'She looked aghast. I grinned at her.'

'What did the queen do?'

'She laughed and laughed. She reached down, took my hand, and drew me close. Catherine spoke to her angrily, but she waved her away.

'Ever since, I've been the queen's friend. She accepts me, even though Catherine de Fastavarin doesn't. The other ladies-in-waiting don't know what to make of me.'

It was a mild day, and the windows were open, letting in a soft breeze and the sound of birds chirping on the roofs of the palace. Christine wondered whether any of the ladies-in-waiting would rather be outside than in the over-warm room with the queen, imprisoned in cumbersome gowns. The dwarf wore a heavy gown, too, and Christine thought she might feel weighed down by it.

Alips said, 'When I was young, I wore rags, and I was often cold, because we lived in a shack; in the winter, the wind blew right through the walls. But in the summer, it was worse, because the stench of sewers permeated everything. Here, I'm never cold, and if I'm hot in the summer, the queen lets me cool off in her beautiful bathtub.'

Christine remembered seeing that tub, when she was a child. Made of polished wood and entered through a trellised door, it was one of the marvels at the Hôtel Saint-Pol. She wondered how many other people were allowed to use it.

The queen's greyhound trotted over and sat down beside the dwarf, who said, 'There were always dogs around the shack where we lived. They were covered with fleas, and they stank of the garbage they ate and the filth they rolled in.' She put her arm around the greyhound and buried her face in his clean white coat.

Two chambermaids bearing silver salvers heaped high with sweets approached the queen. She gathered up the playing cards and put them carefully back in the pouch they'd come in.

'She doesn't want them dirtied by sticky hands,' Alips said. 'She's careful of her treasures.'

Isabeau gave her godchild a candied cherry, took a candied almond for herself, and told the maids to pass the sweets to her ladies. Gracieuse the minstrel strummed softly on her lute and sang something in Spanish.

Alips laughed. 'She's made up a song about marzipan.'

'You understand it?'

'She's taught me a little of her language.'

Collette, the mute girl, couldn't hear the music, but she tapped her foot nevertheless. Jeannine the fool laughed, and Guillaume swung her around in an awkward dance that ended when they fell to the floor in a tangle and lay there shrieking with laughter. The daughters of the queen's *huissiers* came in and nearly tripped over them. The queen's monkey ran around, hooting and squealing, the greyhound dashed over to see what was going on, and the goldfinches chattered loudly in their cage. The only one who didn't take part in the fun was an old woman wearing a wimple with a large, high gorget who stood quietly, watching.

'That's Jeannine's mother,' Alips said. 'She's come to visit her.'

Christine tried to go back to her copying, but after a while she gave up. It was more interesting to watch the fools, the mute, the Spanish minstrel, the pretty daughters of the queen's *huissiers*, and the Saracen girl, who sat giggling on the bed, playing handy-dandy with the queen, who'd given her one of her rings.

The ladies-in-waiting were perched soberly on their big cushions, paying no attention to all the commotion, and Alips said, 'They don't have much fun, just sitting around like that all day.'

Christine asked, 'You would have known if it had been one of them on the musicians' balcony the night of the masquerade, wouldn't you, Alips?'

'Of course,' the dwarf said. 'The hairdo alone would have given her away. But I'm sure the person who threw the torch was only an accomplice. Anyone in this room could have bribed him to do it.'

'Do you know who it is?'

'I have my suspicions.'

FOURTEEN

At some point in his life, the king was afflicted with a strange and incurable malady that often deprived him of his reason.

The Monk of Saint-Denis,
*Chronique du Religieux de Saint-Denis,
contenant le règne de Charles VI de 1380 à 1422*

C hristine remembered she hadn't told the dwarf about Bernart le Brun.

'You said you know the musicians who played at the masquerade, Alips. What about a vielle player named Bernart le Brun?'

'I like Bernart. He doesn't start playing extra-loud when he sees me coming up the stairs to their balcony. Sometimes he even helps me up.'

Christine took a deep breath and said, 'Bernart is dead.'

Alips gasped.

'He was poisoned.'

'Who would poison Bernart? He was a good man. His poor wife. She was devoted to him. She used to sneak up to the balcony to listen while he was playing.'

'Perhaps Bernart saw who threw the torch,' Christine said. 'That may be why he's dead.' She looked at her small companion and added cautiously, 'The person who threw the torch must have seen you, too.'

'I'm sure he didn't. Most people don't. And I was in the shadows.'

Christine marveled at how little the dwarf worried about her own safety. Then she remembered her conversation with the Duchess of Berry. 'Do you know anything about the Viscount of Castelbon?'

'Only that he was here in Paris, making sure he inherited Gaston de Foix's estates. It seems he feared the king might decide to give everything to Yvain de Foix. But he doesn't have to worry about that now. Yvain is dead.'

'I was speaking with the Duchess of Berry, and she intimated that he might have had something to do with the fire, because Yvain was one of the masqueraders.'

'I don't think so,' Alips said. 'There is no doubt in my mind that the king was the intended victim.'

Suddenly, the Duchess of Burgundy strode into the other room, her gold necklaces and bracelets clattering, and there was a great stir as the ladies struggled to rise from the big cushions. Guillaume the fool dashed over, removed his cap, and said to the duchess, 'Shall I speak or hold my tongue, *Madame*?'

'Be quiet, fool.' The duchess turned her back on him.

Alips laughed. 'He asked her that because he's dying to say what everyone knows but no one dares to say out loud; the duchess is a liar. She goes around announcing that she was the one who saved the king from the fire. She says the Duchess of Berry only tried to help later.'

'But everyone saw what the Duchess of Berry did! The Duchess of Burgundy had nothing to do with it!'

'We all know that. But only Guillaume would be brash enough

to announce it to the world.' Alips lowered her voice. 'The Duchess of Burgundy is devious.'

'How do you know?'

'I heard her talking to the Duchess of Berry about something that happened last summer, before the king went mad.'

Christine sighed, remembering the time when the king was well. Those days seemed so far away.

Alips said, 'All the terrible things that have happened began when the Duke of Brittany sent his cousin to kill the king's constable.' Alips had been speaking quietly, but she lowered her voice even more. 'I heard the Duchess of Berry tell the Duchess of Burgundy that she overheard someone tell her husband what was going to happen. She assumed her husband would relay the information to the king so he would prevent it, but the duke did nothing, and the constable was nearly killed. The Duchess of Berry feels guilty because she thinks she should have gone to the king herself.'

'What did the Duchess of Burgundy say when the Duchess of Berry told her this?'

'She told her she was right not to repeat her husband's conversations. Except to her.'

Christine could picture the two women, the innocent Duchess of Berry with the crafty Duchess of Burgundy towering over her.

'The Duchess of Berry thinks that if the constable hadn't been attacked, the king wouldn't have gone out to get revenge on the Duke of Brittany, and he wouldn't have gone mad,' Alips continued.

'It's true that the king went mad while he was on his way to Brittany. But no one knows what caused his mind to shatter, not even his doctors,' Christine said.

The greyhound wandered in and went to Alips, who put her arm around his neck. Then the monkey ambled in and leapt onto the greyhound's back. The dog stood up, trotted over to the queen, and tried to shake the monkey off, sending the Saracen girl into gales of laughter.

'Do you think the Duke of Berry wanted the constable to be killed?' Christine asked.

'It's possible,' Alips said. 'But I'm sure he wouldn't have wished for such a thing if he could have foreseen the consequences. It must be horrible to have to defer to a nephew who's unfit to rule and who embarrasses you with his foolish actions.'

The greyhound, who'd managed to free himself from the monkey, came back, and Alips stroked his ears. 'But I'm sure the uncles knew long before his attack of madness last summer that Charles is not fit to be king. I noticed something was wrong from the first moment I saw him.'

'When was that?'

'Soon after I was brought to the palace, seven years ago. He was standing in a courtyard talking with some of his knights. I was close to him, and I could see that even though he smiled and joked with everyone, he had a strange look in his eyes. He appeared not to be in full control of his senses. Ever since then, I've felt a sort of kinship with him, as though we both suffer, I with a twisted body, he with a twisted mind.'

Christine looked down at her small companion and felt a pang of guilt. She hadn't thought about how the dwarf must suffer because she did not have a beautiful body like many of the women around her.

Alips smiled. 'Being beautiful is not the most important thing in the world. I'd rather be as I am than have a mind as disturbed as the king's.'

'I suppose we all should have seen it,' Christine said. 'He's been acting strangely for a long time.' She thought of something that had happened several years earlier, when the queen made her ceremonial entry into Paris. The streets were draped with crimson, green, and gold, the fronts of the houses were covered from top to bottom with magnificent tapestries, the fountains overflowed with milk and wine, and in the midst of this wondrous spectacle, the king did something truly shocking. He disguised himself as an onlooker and, together with the queen's *maître d'hôtel*, galloped into the crowd on a big black stallion, shouting and scattering people in every direction. The king's officers drove the horse back, but not before many people were knocked down and bruised. The king himself was nearly beaten by his own bodyguards, who had not been forewarned of what he'd planned to do. The king found this hilarious, but everyone else was horrified.

Alips said, 'I used to see him at jousting matches. The fiercer the games became, the more excited he grew, until he seemed to lose control of himself. And at balls, I'd go up to the musicians' balcony and watch him dancing, lurching around like a disjointed puppet and becoming so wild, he frightened me.'

Christine couldn't help thinking that the king's uncles would not be unhappy if they were secretly relieved of their burdensome nephew.

'Did anyone else hear what the Duchess of Berry told the Duchess of Burgundy?' she asked.

'I don't know. Perhaps that monk, the one from the abbey of Saint Denis who's always around, watching and listening because he's writing the history of the king's reign.'

'Brother Michel? He's a friend of mine. My mother, too. Sometimes he comes to our house and they discuss superstitions. He always arrives just in time for dinner.'

Alips smiled. 'I was curious about him, so I got up my courage and asked him about his chronicle. To my surprise, he was happy someone took an interest in it.'

'You could do worse than make a friend of Brother Michel. He knows everyone and everything. Did you know that he helped me save Alix de Clairy?'

'Of course. You could ask him to help you again. When he comes to your house for dinner.'

Christine laughed. She wondered whether Alips ever regretted not having had a mother to cook her a good dinner. Perhaps the old rag-picker had cared for her that way, but she didn't want to ask.

The duchess was standing by the queen, who sat on the day bed showing her goddaughter the playing cards. The duchess picked up one of the cards and turned it over in her hands. 'I'm sure these cost you a large sum.' She looked at the dark-skinned child and sniffed. 'You shouldn't let her touch them.'

'Hateful woman,' Alips whispered.

FIFTEEN

Purchased from Guillaume Testart for the month of February: anise, candied walnuts, rose sugar, marzipan, madrean, crystalized ginger, comfit of pine nuts, and sugared almonds.

Compte de l'Hôtel de la Reine, Isabeau de Bavière, 1401

Christine left the palace knowing she would have to return the next day; she'd spent a long time talking to Alips, and she'd made little progress on the copy of the manuscript. As she left the courtyard, she saw the Duke of Burgundy, sitting tall on a big black stallion, ride up to the king's residence, accompanied by the Duke of Berry, bouncing along on a slender horse too small for its bulky passenger.

Neither of the dukes paid any attention to her, and she continued on her way, musing about them and the way their hold on power waxed and waned. For a long time after the old king had died, they'd been in control of the government, for Charles the Sixth was not at that time old enough to rule by himself. But when Charles was twenty, he decided he was going to take over, and he dismissed his uncles. Everyone thought this was a good idea – everyone except the uncles.

Francesca laughed about it for days. 'Those greedy uncles are so angry, people think they will explode. I wish they would.'

The uncles were even angrier when Charles chose his own advisers – a constable they hated and a group of commoners they mockingly called *marmousets*, a reference to little sculptures of misshapen men and other grotesque creatures that decorated the capitals of columns and piers in the churches. Then the king had his first attack of madness. The uncles took control again, the *marmousets* were deposed, some even imprisoned. And, as she'd learned from Alips, the queen's ladies-in-waiting who were wives of *marmousets* were also dismissed.

Would the uncles really try to kill the king? Christine asked herself. That would relieve them of the shame of having to serve a monarch, their own nephew, who was mad. She couldn't imagine the Duke of Berry attempting murder. The power-hungry Duke of Burgundy was a more likely suspect. But if the king died, the king's brother, the Duke of Orléans, would be regent until the dauphin came of age, and the Duke of Burgundy would have less power under him than under Charles, who was more easily influenced, especially when he was suffering from one of his 'absences,' as his bouts of madness were called.

She was so preoccupied with these thoughts, she almost walked past her house. Francesca, who was waiting at the door, called out to her, and she turned to find her mother waving her arms frantically.

'What's wrong? Christine asked.

'Klara,' Francesca wailed. 'She does nothing but cause trouble. Only Georgette gets along with her, because she lets herself be ordered around.'

'I wonder what Georgette sees in the girl.'

'Did not your friend Marion say she could do something with her?'

Christine laughed. 'Surely you aren't hoping Marion will come here again.'

'I almost wish she would. I would send Klara off with her and hope neither of them ever comes back.'

'You're the one who brought Klara home.'

'Do you think I am happy about it?'

In the kitchen, Marie, Jean, and Thomas sat at the table, while Lisabetta crouched on the floor, holding Goblin. Klara stood next to Georgette, who was washing the dishes. 'You should be careful,' Klara said. 'There's water on your dress.'

Georgette laughed and flicked her hand, sending drops of water onto Klara's hair.

'As if that one knows anything about washing dishes,' Thomas sneered.

'*Enfant pourri,*' Klara retorted.

'I'm not a spoiled child,' Thomas said, and he began to cry. Christine put her arms around him, looked at Klara, and said, 'This has to stop.'

'She started it,' Jean said. He pulled his mother down on the bench beside him. 'Where have you been?'

'With the queen.'

Klara, who was dabbing at her hair with a dishtowel, said, 'I've never seen the queen. What does she look like?'

'She's pretty. Not very tall, not too thin. She has black hair, probably because her mother was Italian.'

Her children had never shown much interest in what went on at the palace, but all of a sudden they wanted to know everything.

'What does the queen do all day?' Jean asked.

'First she has to get dressed and have her hair arranged,' Francesca said. 'That must take hours.'

'I'm sure you're right,' Christine said. 'Did you know, she has a special chair to sit on while her hair is combed? It's covered with red velvet, and it has silk fringes and gilded nails.'

'And then that ridiculous hairdo has to be constructed,' Francesca said. 'I wonder what holds it all together.'

'Lots and lots of pins,' Christine said, laughing. 'Of course, they aren't like your pins, Mama. Some of the queen's pins have jewels on them.'

'And the circlet she puts on top,' Francesca continued. 'With all that padding and all those diamonds and rubies and emeralds, it must weigh her head down.'

'I'm sure she wears beautiful clothes,' Klara said.

'She does. All her ladies, too. They have gold-embroidered *houppelandes* made of the finest silk and velvet. The sleeves are lined with expensive furs, like ermine and miniver, and they're so long, they reach the floor.'

'I like your plain white headdress. And your old blue gown,' Jean said.

'You make me feel like a pauper,' Christine said, thinking that was what she might really become.

'After she gets dressed?' Thomas asked impatiently.

'I'm sure she spends time alone with her children. But when I see her, she's sitting on her day bed, with her ladies-in-waiting perched all around her on big cushions. There are other people, too – two fools, a minstrel from Spain, and a mute. Sometimes a little Saracen girl visits; she's the queen's goddaughter. There are two young girls, daughters of some of the queen's *huissiers*. And a dwarf. The queen is very fond of the dwarf.'

'Dwarfs bring bad luck,' Francesca said.

'That's one of your more foolish superstitions, Mama. If you could meet the dwarf, you'd be ashamed of yourself for saying that.'

Francesca sat down on the bench beside her daughter. 'You have some strange friends, *Cristina.*'

'I'll tell you what else the queen has in her room,' Christine said to the children. 'Goldfinches in a big green and white cage, a greyhound, a squirrel wearing a pearl-studded collar, and a monkey in a fur-lined robe. With the queen's ladies-in-waiting chattering, the goldfinches chirping, the minstrel singing, the monkey hooting along with the music, and the fools laughing and dancing, it's a noisy crowd. The greyhound gets so excited, he runs around barking at everyone.'

'Naughty dog,' Lisabetta said to Goblin. He licked her face.

The fire was smoking, and since it was a warm evening, Francesca went into the hall and opened the door, to let in some fresh air. Christine said, 'At the palace, it's hard to breathe. The windows are usually closed, and the air is filled with candle smoke. And it's smelly, because of all the perfume the queen and her ladies wear. I don't mind the rosewater and lavender, but there's a special scent from the Orient that stings my nostrils. It's delivered to the queen in little silver phials, and she uses it a lot.'

'Stinky,' Thomas said, holding his nose.

'But you'd be happy there, Thomas, because the queen loves sweets. They're brought to her on fancy silver salvers, and she and her ladies nibble on them all day.'

'What else do they do?' Klara wanted to know.

'The queen likes to read. She has a lot of books. So does the king.'

'Ugh. Books,' said Thomas, who hated school.

'They aren't all dull, Thomas. Some of them have exciting stories about kings and knights and heroes. There's even one about a magician.'

'I wish *I* could read them,' said Jean.

'What do the queen and her ladies talk about?' Marie asked.

'Right now they're excited about a set of playing cards the queen had made for the king. They have pictures of battle axes, swords, shields, things like that. And a deer.'

'What's a deer got to do with battle axes and swords?' Thomas asked.

'Someone told the king they'd seen a deer with a golden collar around its neck. The king thinks it's a sign meant for him.'

'A good sign,' Francesca said.

'You and your signs! The king's belief in this deer only proves he's not in his right mind.'

'Signs are important. The king did not observe the signs, and demons took his mind away.'

'This has nothing to do with signs,' Christine said. 'The doctor said the king needs amusements, and the playing cards might help.'

Thomas jumped up and down. 'Playing cards are boring. The king should play hopscotch. Or tag. Or hide-and-seek.' He ran around the room, tripped on the hearth, and fell.

Jean looked down at his brother and laughed. 'Serves you right.'

Marie shook her finger at Thomas and said, 'The king isn't supposed to play games. He's supposed to sit on his throne and rule.'

Thomas stood up. 'Tell us more about the queen's pets. Does she have horses?'

'Yes,' Christine said. 'She's a good rider. The king gave her a beautiful palfrey and a special velvet saddle bordered with gold to go with it.'

'What's it like at the palace, after the fire?' Jean asked.

'The king's brother walks around brooding all the time,' she said. *And there's a shadow over everyone*, she thought, but she didn't say anything to her family about that.

'I hope you do not feel sorry for the duke,' Francesca said. 'He was rude to you when you were trying to find out who poisoned that knight.'

'I do feel sorry for him. I can't forget the good times we had together when we were children.'

'He's arrogant and vain,' Marie said. 'He should feel guilty.'

'Have a little compassion,' Christine said. 'Perhaps he didn't do it.'

But if not the king's brother, who? she asked herself.

When Christine returned to the palace the next day, the Duke of Orléans was standing in the courtyard of the queen's residence, talking to Henri Le Picart. She didn't want to talk to either of them, and Henri, at least, sensed this, for he quickly took his leave of the duke, acknowledged her with a slight nod of his head, and walked away.

The duke looked embarrassed. *He should be*, Christine thought. He'd truly wronged her in the matter of the murder of Alix de Clairy's husband, threatening her and continuing to believe Alix was guilty even after she'd been proven innocent. She was tempted to snub him, but she couldn't; he was royalty.

The duke approached her, looking wretched even though he wore an elegant purple jacket and red hat topped with a large peacock feather. He said, 'We've had our misunderstandings, Christine, and I apologize. Besides, I want to tell you, as I tell everyone, I accept blame for the fire at the wedding ball. To make amends, I will have a chapel built in the church of the Celestines, and prayers of atonement are to be said there daily.' Tears ran down his cheeks.

'I understand, *Monseigneur*.' She pitied him, and in spite of the way he'd treated her in the past, she longed to tell him she didn't believe he'd been responsible for the tragic fire. But she couldn't do that until she knew who the real culprit was, so she simply made her obeisance and walked away.

Then she saw Brother Michel from the abbey of Saint Denis

hurrying toward her, his black habit swirling around his feet. Without greeting her, he said, 'I want to talk to you, Christine, but not here.'

Wondering why he couldn't talk in the courtyard, she followed him to the palace gardens, where they sat on a bench under the twisted branches of an apple tree. The sun beamed down, and she turned her face to it, imagining she could smell the lilies and roses that would soon be blooming there. She closed her eyes and forgot her problems.

Her moment of peace was short-lived. 'I know you are copying a manuscript for the queen,' the monk said, his voice stern.

She opened her eyes. His pale blue eyes blinked furiously, and the fierce expression on his round face alarmed her.

'These are perilous times at the palace, Christine. Very perilous. Do your copying, but otherwise do not come here.' He waved his hand, as if to shoo her away.

She thought perhaps he was worried because he knew there was a murderer lurking about. 'Do you think the king is in danger?' she asked.

'The king is always in danger. His doctors are doing him great harm.'

'I thought he had a famous physician treating him.'

'Guillaume de Harselly did as much as he could. But he is old, and he had to go home. There are other doctors now, and to my mind, they are all quacks. They claim they have miraculous cures, such as incisions bored into his skull and potions made of powdered pearls. It's all useless, and it could be dangerous.'

'But they aren't trying to kill him, are they?'

'Of course not! They truly believe their cures will work.'

'But what if someone really *is* trying to kill the king?'

'I suppose you mean the king's brother.'

'Do you believe Louis started the fire at the masquerade?'

'He says he didn't do it on purpose, but, yes, it was his fault.'

'I'm not sure it was. The queen's dwarf says she saw someone throw a lighted torch from the musicians' balcony. It might have been meant for the king.'

He slapped his hand on the bench and said angrily, 'Alips has a vivid imagination. Give no credence to what she says.'

She was shocked. Her usually mild-mannered friend was glaring at her, and she had to look away.

On another side of the garden, she saw an elegantly dressed

woman strolling along a path. It was Valentina Visconti, the Duke of Orléans's wife. Michel was watching her, too, and he said, 'There is an example of what I mean when I say there are many dangers here at the court. The Duchess of Burgundy has started a rumor that Valentina is a sorceress. She's telling people Valentina cast a spell on the king, causing him to lose his mind.'

'Who would believe such a thing!'

'Not many people, I hope. But Valentina's family has a propensity for evil doings. That doesn't mean Valentina is that way.'

He shifted on the bench and tucked his hands into the wide sleeves of his habit. 'The duchess's false accusation about Valentina is just one example of how grievous things are here, now that the king is ill. There are many dangers, Christine, many dangers.' He shifted on the bench, looked at her intently, and said in a harsh voice, 'You must extricate yourself from the court, and especially from the queen.'

'Why?'

'Don't you see how the Duchess of Burgundy watches over her? The duchess craves power, and she will make trouble for anyone she thinks might thwart her. If she sees you are friendly with the queen, she will suspect you of plotting something against her. She might even start a rumor like the one about Valentina, because you come from Italy, too. You will be in a perilous position, a very perilous position indeed if the Duchess of Burgundy becomes your enemy.'

He took his hands out of the sleeves of his habit and waved them in her face. 'You must warn Alips about this, too. Tell her to stop spying on people!'

She didn't know what to say. The monk had helped her save Alix de Clairy, arranging for an audience with the king and encouraging her to keep looking for the real murderer even when everything seemed hopeless. Now he was frightening her. She had wanted to ask him about the Viscount of Castelbon, but she didn't dare. She nodded, said she was late for the queen, and left him sitting under the apple tree, fingering his prayer beads.

SIXTEEN

All reasonable people should cast away from themselves the sin of envy.

Christine de Pizan,
Le Livre des Trois Vertus, 1405

S he found the queen surrounded by her ladies, who were arguing about something.

'What has happened?' she asked Alips.

'The playing cards the queen was planning to give the king have disappeared. They are accusing each other of having lost them.'

Marguerite de Germonville turned to Jeanne de la Tour, pointed a finger at her, and said, 'You nearly dropped them once. Perhaps now you have misplaced them.'

Jeanne de la Tour recoiled at the sound of Marguerite's loud voice, but she tossed her head indignantly and shuffled away. Then Marguerite bore down on Catherine de Villiers. 'Perhaps they are hidden among the queen's books.' To which Catherine replied, 'Playing cards are nothing like books. Place your accusations elsewhere.'

Symonne du Mesnil sidled up to Madame de Malicorne. Her voice wavered as she said, 'I'm sure you were the last to have them.'

'She must have had wine this morning,' Alips whispered.

Guillaume the fool skipped over and said, 'She should drink with the ducks.'

'He means Symonne should drink water, not wine,' the dwarf said.

Marguerite de Germonville, Jeanne de la Tour, and Catherine de Villiers agreed that Madame de Malicorne was the last to have the cards. 'They accuse her because they are blinded by envy,' Alips whispered. 'They think the queen likes her best.'

The queen's ladies should be above such pettiness, Christine thought.

Madame de Malicorne looked at Symonne du Mesnil scornfully.

'I think it was you who had them. Perhaps you have hidden them somewhere.' She held the queen's baby, and she shifted him from one arm to the other, which made him cry. Guillaume took off his cap and made faces at the little prince, who stopped crying, reached out, and touched his bald head.

The fool said to the women, 'Stop looking, and they will be found.' He darted away and ran around the room, pretending to look for the lost cards under the big cushions, behind the tapestries, in the crystal goblets standing on a sideboard. Then he sat on the floor, held up his hands, and exclaimed, 'Here they are,' as though the cards had miraculously reappeared.

Christine was about to go back to her work, but the queen beckoned to her. As she knelt by the day bed, she saw that Isabeau had her hand over her mouth; she was trying to suppress a laugh.

'Rise,' the queen managed to blurt out. Then she whispered, 'Alips says someone may be hiding the cards, to play a joke. She has told me that a person who hides something is a thief, and the children of this person will be poor and they will be liars, too.' Then she became serious and said, 'Other things are more important than the cards. Have you learned anything?'

Christine looked at the ladies-in-waiting, who were still arguing.

'They know nothing,' the queen said. She leaned back against her pillows and put her hand to her forehead. 'I am very afraid for the king.'

Before she could say anything else, the Duchess of Burgundy charged into the room, the skirt of her black *houppelande* rustling and her heavy gold necklaces clattering. The ladies knelt and moved away, followed by Guillaume, who pretended to be herding them out.

Christine hurried back to her copying. After a while Alips came in.

'Where do you suppose the cards are? Do you really think someone has hidden them?' Christine asked her.

'Of course not. I just said that to make the queen laugh.'

In the other room, the Duchess of Burgundy stood over the queen. She said, 'I have heard that the playing cards have been lost. I hope you do not trouble yourself looking for them. Playing cards are evil, and the king should not have them.'

The queen looked at her defiantly. 'They *will* be found. And I *will* give them to the king. They will help him become well.'

'You are a foolish young woman. You and that Italian wife of the king's brother. Neither of you knows what is proper here in France.'

'She hates Valentina,' Alips said. 'Valentina holds a higher place at the court, and she never lets that presumptuous woman forget it.'

'I've heard she's started a rumor that Valentina is a sorceress. Does the queen know this?'

'No. And I hope no one tells her. I'm certainly not going to.'

'I'm glad,' Christine said. 'She has so much on her mind, with the king's illness and all this dissention around her.'

'It's true. The queen is deeply distressed by many things, but most especially by the king's condition. I don't think his illness is a surprise to her, though. She was aware right from the moment they were married that all was not right. I could see it. She was very upset because he was so restless and didn't often stay with her – just often enough to get her pregnant, it seemed to me. He wasn't even there when her first child was born. There were many doctors and midwives, but no one who could ease her mind.'

'Wasn't her friend Catherine de Fastavarin with her?'

'Sometimes. But the queen needed more than that. I hadn't been here long, but she knew I would say something to distract her, so she called for me. I went into the childbed chamber. She was lying under a great green canopy, surrounded by green curtains. I'd never seen anything so splendid. There were gold and green velvet draperies covering the windows and dozens of candles for light. It was so hot, beads of perspiration covered her forehead. I told her the windows had to be kept closed so no evil spirits could get in before the churching and harm the baby. She seemed relieved to know that. Then I looked at the baby and said, "You have a boy. If you want him to have curly hair, wash his head in white wine and put a bryony root in his bath water." She laughed like a little girl. "Where have you learned this?" she asked.

'I didn't want to tell her the old rag-picker who'd raised me was a witch, so I kept silent. She said, "It must have been your mother. From my mother too, I learned such things."'

'And then she lost the child,' Christine said.

Alips nodded. 'The next time I was with her, I knew something was wrong. She was out of her confinement, and she was holding the baby on her lap and gazing at him sadly. When she lifted him up for me to see, he lay listlessly in her arms. I lowered my eyes;

I couldn't bear to look at him, he was so sickly. Several weeks later, the little prince died.

'When she was pregnant again, I tried to think of things to amuse her, to keep her from worrying. I told her that if someone put salt on her head while she was sleeping, she'd know when she woke up whether she'd have a boy or a girl.'

Christine laughed. 'Did anyone do it?'

'Oh, no. But no one could stop me from talking. One day I told her not to let anyone give her fish heads to eat or her baby would have a big pointed mouth. The ladies-in-waiting, especially Catherine de Fastavarin, were so angry I thought they would burst, but the queen laughed until she cried. Then she talked to me about similar beliefs her mother had taught her, and she became sad, because her mother had died when she was eleven.'

'I've wondered about her family,' Christine said.

'She misses her father and her home in Bavaria. That's why Catherine de Fastavarin is so dear to her. But she knows what Catherine is like, and she told me not to worry about all the bad things she says about me. "I know those things are not true," she said.'

There was a disturbance in the other room. The queen's greyhound was sniffing around the duchess, who'd seated herself on one of the big cushions and was struggling to get up. Guillaume ran over and extended his hand. When the duchess waved him away, he did a backwards somersault and bumped into the dog, which nipped at his heels. Guillaume howled, pretending to be hurt. The queen stood up, grabbed the greyhound's collar, and shook it. He cowered and looked up at her guiltily.

'This is unworthy of a queen of France,' the duchess cried. She called to one of her maids, who ran over and escorted her from the room.

The queen sat on the day bed and buried her face in her hands. Her shoulders were shaking, and Christine knew she was laughing.

Alips was laughing, too. Then she looked solemn and said, 'One of these days that woman will go too far. I think she already has.'

'Is she the one you suspect of being responsible for the fire? That's a dangerous thought!'

'Don't worry. I can take care of myself,' the dwarf said.

SEVENTEEN

Any woman who has a mind is capable of accomplishing any task.

Christine de Pizan,
Le Livre de la Cité des Dames, 1404–1405

Christine decided to go again to the balustrade overlooking the room where the wedding ball had been held, hoping to remember something more about the masquerade. When she looked down, she saw Henri Le Picart studying the floor. He bent over, picked up something shiny, and stood examining it. She drew back into the shadows, hoping he hadn't seen her.

But he had. As she was leaving the palace courtyard, he came up to her. 'You're wondering what I was doing.'

She said nothing and tried to look uninterested.

Henri glanced at the entrance to the palace, saw the *portier* watching, and drew her out into the street. Then he held out his hand. In it was a golden spur, just like the one she'd seen in Klara's jewelry coffer.

'I found this on the floor of the ballroom, in a corner. The porters who cleared away the debris missed it. Are you familiar with these things?'

'Not really.'

Henri's black eyes flashed.

She didn't dare not tell him what she knew. 'Do you remember I asked you about Martin du Bois the other day?'

'Did you find him?'

'No. But I found his wife, or at least my mother did.'

'Why was your mother looking for his wife?'

'When she heard the husband had disappeared, she felt sorry for the young woman. She went to find her, and she brought her home.'

'That's very nice. But what does it have to do with the spur?'

At this, Christine was tempted to walk away. But Henri's look stopped her.

'We went to Martin's house to get some of his wife's clothes, and we found a spur she kept with her jewelry. It looked just like this one.'

'That doesn't surprise me,' Henri said.

Two noblemen in short cloaks and beaver hats came down the street. Henri slid the spur under his black cape. The men smiled and nodded to them as they passed. After they'd entered the court-yard, where they were accosted by Renaut, he took the spur out from under his cape and said, 'This is an old spur, not like the ones worn by knights today.'

'I don't know anything about spurs.'

'This spur has a single piece of metal to goad the horse. The spurs used today have spiked wheels. Does that suggest anything to you about who the owner of this spur might be?'

'There are many older knights around. It could be one of them.'

'It could, but it isn't. As I'm sure you know, when the French troops destroyed the city of Courtrai, they went into the church and took away hundreds of pairs of golden spurs the Flemish had stripped from the feet of dead French knights in a battle that took place eighty years earlier. Martin du Bois was there, and he brought back two of those spurs. I believe this is one of them. The spur you found with his wife's jewelry must be the other.'

Henri glanced around and saw coming toward them a man elegantly dressed in a red velvet jerkin, parti-colored hose, and a feathered cap. Again, he hid the spur under his cape. When the man seemed about to stop and speak with him, Henri waved him away. Then a group of men on horseback rode up to the king's residence, and they, too, acknowledged Henri, nodding and smiling as they passed. *Does he know everyone in Paris?* Christine wondered.

'What was the spur doing on the floor of the room where they had the masquerade?' she asked.

'That is the important question.'

'You're a friend of Martin du Bois, aren't you?'

'In a way. I don't think he quite trusts me.'

Christine smiled. Everyone seemed to know Henri, but surely not everyone trusted him. She certainly didn't. Nevertheless, she wanted to find out where Martin du Bois was, and she suspected Henri had the answer.

'His wife told me Martin disappeared the night of the masquerade,' she said. 'The night the king almost died.'

'There isn't necessarily a connection between the masquerade and Martin's disappearance.'

'There might be. The Duke of Orléans didn't start the fire. Somebody on the musicians' balcony threw a lighted torch.'

'How do you know?'

'The queen's dwarf saw it. Unfortunately, she doesn't know who it was.'

Henri waited for her to go on.

'And I saw a lighted torch that didn't belong to the duke lying on the floor near the burning men.'

'Surely you weren't at the ball!'

'I wasn't exactly *at* the ball, but I saw what happened. It's a long story. I'll tell you about it sometime.'

Henri was gazing at her with a peculiar gleam in his eyes. She said, 'I believe the torch on the floor was thrown at the king. Perhaps the golden spur was thrown at him, too. And Martin du Bois disappeared that night.'

'Are you suggesting that Martin threw a lighted torch from the balcony?'

'Don't you think it could have been him? After all, you just implied that the golden spur you have in your hand is his. And I saw curious things in his house.'

'What things?'

'There'd been a fire, and there were blood stains on the floor.'

Henri started to laugh. 'You're developing a nice theory to prove that Martin du Bois is a murderer. But you're wrong.'

Christine felt her face get red. 'I suppose you think my theory can't be right because I said it.'

'You must admit, women aren't good at solving problems like this.'

'Have you forgotten, I solved the mystery of who poisoned Hugues de Précy. I and my friend Marion. Both of us women.'

'And then you went running after the murderess, in the dark, all alone, and nearly got yourself killed.'

Such an infuriating man! But there was something compelling about him, and she couldn't stop herself from asking, 'Will you give some credence to my theory if I can prove that Martin du Bois was on the musicians' balcony the night of the masquerade?'

'Oh? How are you going to do that?'

'One of the musicians, Bernart le Brun, may have seen him.'

'Have you talked to Bernart?'

'No. Someone didn't want *anyone* to talk to him. He's dead. Someone poisoned him. Marion and I are going to see his wife tomorrow to find out what she knows.'

'I'd better come along.'

Christine took a step back. 'We may be women, but I think we can handle this ourselves!'

'Bernart le Brun's house is on the rue aus Jugléeurs. I'll meet you there.' Before she could object, he'd walked away, and she could do nothing but go home and seethe with anger at his audacity.

Early the next morning, she went to the corner of the rue Saint-Martin and the rue aus Jugléeurs and found Marion, just as she knew she would. And farther down the street, Henri, waiting for them.

'He's coming with us,' she said to Marion.

'What do we need him for?'

'I tried to discourage him. But perhaps it's a good thing. Bernart's wife may be more willing to talk to him than to either of us, because she's sure to be intimidated by him.'

Henri said nothing, merely walked on ahead of them, his black cape blocking their view of the street. *Rude, as always*, Christine thought as she and Marion hurried after him.

The woman sitting in front of the dressmaker's shop motioned for Marion to come over, but Marion just waved at her. As they passed the empty house, Christine asked, 'Is this where you found the body?'

'Yes. The door's nailed shut now. But look, there on the cobblestones. You can still see the vomit.'

Several people looked apprehensively at Henri, but he paid no attention, just strode up to the last house on the street and went in without knocking. Bernart le Brun's wife sat listlessly on a bench by a long work table, staring into space, paying no attention to the intruders. Strings, bows, scrolls, tuning pegs, files, chisels, knives, pots of glue, and vielles in various stages of construction covered the table, and the odor of wood shavings, varnish, and glue permeated the air. The woman had obviously been working, for she wore long oversleeves to protect her arms, and a nearly finished vielle dangled from her hand. She held the instrument so carelessly, Christine feared she would drop it. Henri took it from her and laid it carefully on the table. Then he spoke to her with more gentleness in his voice than Christine would have thought possible.

'I'm very sorry about your husband, Nicole,' he said.

The woman looked up at him and started to cry. 'Bernart went out that day, and he never came back.' She wiped her eyes with her apron.

'It's said he was poisoned. Do you know how that could have happened?'

'There's no poison here.'

'Did he eat something unusual? Did you have any guests who brought food?'

'He and I were the only ones here. He'd had a toothache for several days.'

'Oh, I know what that's like,' Henri said, putting his hand on his jaw. 'Did he take any medicine?'

'He had me go to the apothecary's shop down the street and get a potion to relieve the pain. The apothecary had to prepare it and have it delivered later. We've known him for years. There couldn't have been anything wrong with the medicine he sent.'

Henri picked up the vielle he'd laid on the table. 'This is a beautiful instrument. I'd like to buy it.'

The woman smiled for the first time. 'I'm just varnishing it. Come back another day, and you can take it.'

'Thank you. We'll leave you to finish your work.'

Christine wanted to stay and learn more about the woman and the instruments she was making, but Henri hustled them away. 'Let's find out about the person who delivered the medicine,' he said as he rushed down the street.

'I didn't know he could play the vielle,' Marion whispered to Christine as they ran to keep up.

'A man of many talents,' Christine said. 'If only he had some manners.'

Henri stomped into the apothecary's shop. A squat, bald man balanced on a ladder, arranging neatly labeled and stoppered glass bottles and jars on a shelf. He hurried to climb down when he saw Henri, who strode up to a long counter, pushed aside a large marble mortar and pestle, and leaned heavily on his elbows. The apothecary put his hand on the pestle to stop it from rattling in the mortar and looked at his scales, alembics, and crucibles to make sure they hadn't been upended by Henri's abrupt gesture.

'You sent some medicine to Bernart le Brun a few days ago. What was it?' Henri asked.

'Bernart had a toothache. He often did. His wife used to give him cloves and have him breathe steam from a pot of boiling water and sage.'

'I've tried that,' said Marion, her voice muffled because she was peering into one of the many large barrels on the floor. Henri turned and glared at her.

'He needed something stronger this time,' the apothecary continued, 'so I sent over a gargle of poppy juice, myrrh, and honey.'

Henri said, 'Do you know that Bernart died the same day?'

'Of course I know.'

'He was poisoned.'

'I hope you don't think I was responsible! There was only enough poppy juice in the gargle to make him sleepy.'

'No one suspects you. Is the boy who delivers your preparations here?'

'No. He's sick. Come to think of it, he was sick the day Bernart's wife asked for the medicine. I gave the bottle to a boy who came into the shop and asked where Bernart lived. I thought that as long as he was going there, he could deliver it.'

'Do you remember what the boy looked like?'

'No. I was so busy with customers, I hardly glanced at him.'

Henri slapped his hand on the counter, overturning one of the crucibles. He righted it and plunged out of the shop, leaving Christine and Marion to scramble after him.

They went back to Bernart's house, where his widow was varnishing the vielle Henri wanted to buy. Without any explanation, Henri asked, 'Do you remember who brought your husband's medicine from the apothecary's shop?'

'I wasn't here when the medicine was delivered. I'd gone to the market.'

'When did your husband take the medicine?'

'While I was out. When I came back I found the empty bottle on the table. Bernart wasn't here. I didn't know where he'd gone until the sergeants from the Châtelet came and told me he was dead.'

Henri turned on his heel and left. Christine wanted to give the woman some explanation, but there was no time. When she and

Marion caught up to him on the rue Saint-Martin, he turned and said, 'Your theory about Martin du Bois being the murderer was wrong, of course, Christine.'

Before she could respond, he added, 'It was the boy who brought the poison to Bernart. Bernart took it, believing it was medicine for his toothache. He became deathly ill, and he went out to get help.'

'And he got only as far as that empty house,' Marion said. 'He must have stumbled and fallen through the door, just like I did.'

'Right,' Henri said. 'The next task is to find that boy.'

'But we don't know anything about him,' Christine said. 'We don't even know what he looks like.'

'Since you two are so good at solving problems, you can figure it out,' Henri said, and he walked away, leaving them staring after him, open-mouthed.

EIGHTEEN

You'll never see a man so old that he won't gladly take a young wife.

From a book of moral and practical advice
for a young wife, Paris, 1393

'What do we do now?' Marion asked.

'I have no idea.'

They walked to Christine's house, lost in thought, and when they got there, they found Francesca standing at the door. 'Where have you been, *Cristina*?'

'Go back inside, Mama.'

'It is dinner time,' Francesca said as she stalked into the house. Christine told Marion to wait and went after her mother. In the kitchen, she said, 'Let Marion stay and eat with us.'

'I know she helped you save Alix de Clairy, but enough is enough. Should she not be at that brothel of hers?'

'I'll tell you a secret. I think Marion is selling her embroidery, which means she doesn't need money from her other profession.'

'Has she told you that?'

'No. And don't ask her. She'll tell us about it when she's ready. Let her stay for dinner.'

Francesca slammed a pot down on the table, but she didn't say no.

Christine went to get Marion and found her with Brother Michel, who was shaking his finger at her.

'I'll wear what I like, *porc de Dieu*,' Marion said.

'Doesn't she know she can be arrested for wearing that gold belt?' the monk asked Christine.

Marion folded her arms and turned her back.

Christine asked, 'What are you doing here, Michel?'

'I'm worried about you. I don't think you took seriously what I was telling you about the court.'

'You don't need to remind me. But I'm glad you're here. There's someone I want you to meet. My mother is preparing dinner; she'll be pleased to see you. You stay, too, Marion.'

Marion turned around and said, 'Your mother won't be pleased to see *me*.'

'Never mind,' Christine said. 'Go on in, Michel. I want to talk to Marion for a moment.'

Michel gave one last accusatory look at Marion's belt and went into the house.

'He warned me about the court. He told me to stay away,' Christine said. 'So don't say anything to him about what we're doing.'

'I won't. But let's go in quickly. I can't wait to see what that little lady does when she sees a monk.'

'Perhaps he can help her. But I'm not counting on it.'

'I told you, I know how to straighten her out.'

'Have you something in mind?'

'You'll see,' Marion said.

They took off their cloaks and went into the kitchen where the children, holding plates and goblets, stood waiting for Georgette to set up the trestle table. Klara sat on a stool by the fire holding Goblin.

'You could help, too, Klara,' Christine said.

'We don't have to do that at Martin's house.'

'Is that so?' Marion said. 'What a spoiled little lady you are.'

'*Putain*,' Klara said. Then she saw Michel. She let go of Goblin and started to cry.

'It looks as though she's learned a bit of humility. Perhaps she's read her husband's book,' Christine said.

'She needs to read some more,' said Marion. 'I'd like to meet that man.'

Christine said to Klara, 'This is Brother Michel.'

Klara wiped her eyes, and tried to smile.

Francesca said, 'Stay for dinner, Michel.'

Michel went into the hallway to take off his cloak. When he returned, the children crowded around him. 'You said you'd take us to see your abbey,' Jean said, remembering a promise the monk had made several weeks earlier.

'And so I will,' he assured them.

Thomas looked skeptical. 'I'll bet you don't even live there.'

Michel laughed. 'If you mean I'm always at the court instead, you're right. That's because I'm writing about the king, and I have to observe everything he does. I can't do that if I stay at the abbey all the time.'

Francesca brought a basin of water and a towel, and they washed their hands and sat down at the table. Michel said a blessing, and Georgette handed around bowls of soup.

'*Zuppa di cipolla*,' Thomas shouted.

Michel laughed. 'Still learning Italian from your grandmother, Thomas?'

'I'm getting good, too. I'll be able to talk to everybody when she takes me to Italy.'

Christine looked at her mother. 'You have to stop putting these ideas about Italy into his head!'

Klara was sniffling. Christine put her arm around her shoulder and said to Michel, 'Klara's husband has disappeared, and she's staying with us until he's found.'

'Where have you looked for him?'

'He knows the Duke of Berry, so I went to the duke and asked him if he could give me any information.'

'And what did the duke tell you?'

'He didn't even remember him.'

Michel laughed. 'I'm not surprised. The duke doesn't have much interest in anything other than his jewels and castles and illuminated manuscripts.'

'And pretty young men,' Marion muttered under her breath.

Georgette, who was taking empty soup bowls away to be washed, hurried back to the table.

'Why are you standing there with those dirty dishes?' Francesca asked her. The girl slouched away.

Christine said to Michel, 'I did have a conversation with the duke's wife.'

'Jeanne of Boulogne is a remarkable young woman,' Michel said. 'Only sixteen, but more sensible than her much older husband.'

'Why would she marry an old man?' Klara asked.

'Surely you know there are many young women married to older men,' Michel said.

'She doesn't know lots of things,' Thomas muttered.

'*Basta, Tommaso!*' Francesca said.

'Actually, the duke's brothers and the king questioned the marriage, too,' Michel said. 'At the time, the girl was only twelve.'

Klara gasped.

'And besides that, the Count of Foix, who had brought Jeanne up at his court, wanted her to marry someone else.'

'And why didn't she?' Klara asked.

'The duke got one of the king's advisers, Bureau de la Rivière, to talk to the count. The count relented, but the duke had to pay him a lot of money.'

'What did Jeanne think?'

'She doesn't seem unhappy,' Christine said. 'From what I've seen, I'm sure she really cares for her husband.'

'That's fortunate,' Michel said, 'because I don't think the duke realizes what a strong woman he has on his hands.'

'She saved the king's life,' Jean said.

'She did indeed. And now she's saved Bureau, too.'

'How?' everyone asked at once.

'After the king went mad last year, his uncles threw his advisers into prison, Bureau included. Bureau hasn't been beheaded because Jeanne reminded her husband of how he'd persuaded the Count of Foix to change his mind about the marriage.'

At the mention of beheading, Klara started to cry. Christine remembered the girl had told them her brother had seen the French soldiers in Courtrai cut off her parents' heads. She put her arms around her.

Georgette returned with bread and cheese, set them on the table, and stood behind Marion, who whispered, 'I can't tell you anything more about the Duke of Berry.'

'Go and finish washing the dishes, Georgette,' Christine said.

'Tell us about what's going on at the court, Michel,' Francesca said. She'd once had many friends there, and Christine wished her mother wouldn't dwell on this because she was aware of things her mother knew nothing about. Certain people had derided her father for having tried to cure the king with a medicine that might have caused him harm, and there were those who'd laughed at him because he'd made tin figures that were supposed to represent Englishmen and had them buried all around France in the hopes that this would make the enemy leave. She knew that Henri Le Picart had been involved in the absurd project, and this was one of the reasons why she disliked him so much.

'We're all worried about the king,' Michel said. 'After the tragedy at the palace, we were afraid he'd have another of his attacks. So far he hasn't, but it's obvious he is not well. Imagine, letting himself be drawn into the disgusting masquerade. He made a fool of himself.'

'A king isn't supposed to act like that,' Marie said.

'Were you at the masquerade?' Francesca asked Michel.

'No. But it's been described to me many times.'

'Tell us about the men who burned up,' Thomas said, bouncing up and down. Georgette, who stood close to the monk with a stack of bowls in her arms, said, 'Yes, tell us.'

'Did the Duke of Orléans start the fire?' Jean asked.

'Of course he did,' said Marie. 'Everyone says so.'

Michel said, 'You're right, Marie. It is generally accepted that it was a spark from the duke's torch. That doesn't mean he did it on purpose, although many people think he did.'

'Because he wants to be king?' Francesca asked.

'Not only that. Some people think he did it out of revenge, because last summer the king almost killed *him*.'

'I hadn't heard that,' Francesca said.

'It happened when the king went mad, on the way to fight the Duke of Brittany. I was there, and I saw it. After he'd drawn his sword and killed four of his knights, he charged toward Louis and brandished the sword at him. Louis escaped, but I could see that he was deeply affected. Imagine thinking your own brother is trying to kill you.'

'How did he do it?' Thomas asked. 'Was he sitting on his horse?' He straddled the bench and made lashing motions with his arms, upsetting a goblet of water.

'Stop that, Thomas,' Christine said. 'The whole story is terrible enough without your making a game of it.'

'The whole journey was terrible,' Michel said.

'Tell us about it,' the children cried.

'Where should I begin? The king was in a bad state, very bad. For days, he'd hardly eaten, and he had a constant fever. I heard his doctors telling his uncles not to let him ride. But he insisted, and there was nothing they could do. He was determined to go after the Duke of Brittany, no matter how hard his uncles tried to stop him. Then, on the way, something strange happened.'

'I know,' Thomas shouted. 'The madman! Did you see him?'

'I did. He jumped out of the woods and grabbed the bridle of the king's horse. "Go back," he shouted. I'll never understand why the king's soldiers let the man get away. It's almost as though everyone was glad the man had frightened the king, because even though it probably precipitated Charles's attack of madness, it did put a halt to his plan to make war on the Duke of Brittany.'

'The Duke of Berry could have prevented the whole thing,' Christine said.

'What are you talking about?' Michel asked.

'Alips overheard the Duchess of Berry tell the Duchess of Burgundy she heard someone talking to her husband, warning him there was going to be an attack on the constable. The duke didn't do anything about it.'

'I told you to tell Alips to stop listening to people's conversations!' Michel exclaimed. 'She likes to think no one knows she's listening, but she's wrong. If she heard such a conversation, she should keep quiet about it.'

'Who's Alips?' Jean asked.

'The queen's dwarf,' Michel said absently.

Francesca gasped and whispered to Christine, 'I told you, dwarfs bring bad luck!'

'You don't even know what he's talking about, Mama.'

'If Michel is angry about the dwarf, that means she's making bad things happen at the court.'

Christine sighed and turned away from her mother.

'Why wouldn't the Duke of Berry want to warn the king?' Jean asked Michel.

'He tries not to get involved in affairs at the court,' the monk said.

'But he went on the march to Brittany,' Jean said.

'He didn't want to. Neither did the Duke of Burgundy. The Duke of Berry is just lazy, but the Duke of Burgundy had other reasons, one of which was that his wife is the Duke of Brittany's cousin, and he knew he'd have to answer to her for it. We all know what a disagreeable woman she is.' He shook a finger at Christine. 'I'm warning you about her again, Christine. She's treacherous, especially for those who are close to the queen.'

Francesca let out a little cry. 'You must never go to the palace again, *Cristina*!'

'I have to go.'

'It is not safe, *Cristina*. There is evil there.'

'Perhaps an evil spell made the king's brother set those men on fire,' Thomas said.

Marion, who had been sitting quietly without entering into the conversation, suddenly asked Michel, 'Are you absolutely sure the king's brother was responsible for the fire?'

The monk looked at Christine and frowned. 'Absolutely. Anyone would be foolhardy to try to prove otherwise.'

NINETEEN

Dame Agnes the beguine is with you to teach you wise and mature conduct and to serve and instruct you.

From a book of moral and practical advice
for a young wife, Paris, 1393

As soon as Michel left, Marion turned to Klara and said, 'Come with me. I want you to meet someone.'

'What are you saying?' Francesca cried. 'She's not going anywhere with *you*!'

'Don't worry. Christine understands.'

Francesca put her hands on her hips and shouted at Christine. 'I can't believe you'd leave Klara alone with this *prostituta*!'

Christine drew her mother aside and whispered to her, 'Marion thinks she knows how to make Klara behave.'

'*Questo è totalmente assurdo!*'

'What's she saying?' Marion wanted to know.

'She says it's absurd to think you can do anything with Klara.'

'She doesn't even know what I'm going to do.'

'At least tell us where you're taking her.'

'I want her to meet someone. Not a prostitute, if that's what you're thinking.'

Klara said to Francesca, 'You can't tell me what to do. I'll go with her if I want.'

'We can't stop her,' Christine said. 'She's a married woman, capable of making up her own mind.'

Francesca threw up her hands and stormed out of the room.

Marion had Klara out the door before Christine could say anything else. But as they walked down the street away from the house, Klara dragged her feet, and Marion had to keep stopping to wait for her to catch up.

'What's wrong with you, Klara?'

'I'm not sure I want to go with you. Where are we going, anyway?'

'To the palace. You'll see why when we get there.'

But instead of turning up the rue Saint-Antoine, Marion went to the rue de l'Ave-Maria. When they came to a complex of buildings around a church, she said, 'Christine told me you had a beguine helping you. She probably lives here.'

Klara shrugged.

'Haven't you ever wondered about her?'

'All I know is that her name is Agnes. I don't like her. She has too many rules.'

'That's because she lives by those rules, as a beguine. They're like nuns, but they aren't, really. Most of them are poor women who just want to live peaceful, prayerful lives. They have to support themselves, so they go out to work, doing all kinds of jobs, including the one your husband gave Agnes, caring for an ungrateful girl like you.'

'Don't talk to me like that!'

'I talk to you like that because you *are* ungrateful and uncaring. Your husband was kind enough to hire someone to help you, and you do nothing but complain. You act the same way with the people who've taken you into their home. You don't know anything about them, and you don't even want to know.'

'I know that Christine is boring. She's always out working for the queen while her mother stays home and takes care of the children, who are rude. What else is there to know?'

'A lot.'

Marion turned up another street and entered an area with trees and shrubs. Klara stopped. 'I don't want to go in there.'

'Nonsense. You wanted to go to the palace. This is one of its orchards. There's something special here.'

'Just old trees with no leaves.'

'Of course they don't have leaves. It's not spring yet. Although actually, the leaves are just coming out. Look. Can you see them?'

'Sort of. Is that what you wanted to show me?'

'No. Follow me.'

They walked on until they came to a place where there were no trees, just a tall, sturdy stockade, much of it hidden under thick bushes and dead branches, and a large gate. They could hear something shuffling around on the other side of the enclosure.

Klara turned and started to run away, but Marion caught her arm. 'There's nothing to be afraid of. You like animals, don't you?'

'What kind of animals?'

'The king's lions.'

'Lions! They're dangerous!'

'These aren't, not unless they're provoked. I want you to meet the woman who takes care of them.'

'Why?'

'Because she needs friends. You're about the same age as she is, so you two should get along.'

'Who is she?'

'Her name is Loyse. She helps the king's lion-keeper because he says he's too old to do the job all by himself. She's good with animals, the way you are with Goblin.'

Between the palings of the stockade, they could see a shadowy figure moving around, and then, very slowly, the gate opened. Klara stepped back. 'What if the lions escape?'

'They won't. See, she's shutting the gate behind her, and the lions are safe inside.'

Klara stared at the person who approached them, a woman dressed in rags, with matted auburn hair that swirled around her head and almost completely hid her face. Marion took Klara's arm and drew her forward. 'This is Loyse,' she said.

The two young women looked at each other. Then Loyse put out her hand and gently touched Klara's cheek. Klara didn't pull away; she seemed mesmerized.

Loyse unbolted the gate and motioned for Klara to follow her. As if in a trance, Klara stepped gingerly into the lions' stockade.

'Why doesn't she talk?' Klara whispered to Marion, who was right behind her.

'I'll tell you later.'

The interior of the lions' stockade was not as dark and frightening as Klara had feared. A large trough of fresh water stood in one corner, and mounds of leaves and grass covered the ground, as though someone had tried to make comfortable places for the lions to sleep. Klara started to back away when she saw six lions standing quietly, staring at her. Loyse went up to one of them and put her arms around his neck.

'I could never do that,' Klara whispered to Marion.

'Of course you could.'

Loyse beckoned to Klara, and the girl tiptoed gingerly up to the lion. Loyse indicated that she should put her hand on his mane. The lion turned his head and leaned it against Klara's chest. 'I guess they aren't so different from Goblin,' Klara said.

Loyse grabbed another lion by his mane and pulled him forward. And then another. Soon Klara was surrounded by all six lions. She looked frightened, and then she relaxed. She stroked the lions' heads, while Loyse looked on, smiling. After a while Klara said to Marion, 'You come and pet them, too.'

'It's time to go now,' Marion said.

Klara looked disappointed, but she followed Marion out of the stockade. Loyse shut the gate after them and watched them as they made their way through the orchard back toward the street.

'Tell me about her,' Klara said excitedly. 'Why doesn't she speak?'

'Can't you guess? She's deaf. She can't hear, and so she never learned to talk. When her mother came to work at the court, she found out that the lion-keeper wanted a helper, and because she didn't know what else to do with her, she let Loyse become his assistant.'

'How did you come to know her?'

'It's a long story. All I'll tell you now is that her mother was a murderess, and the woman you find so boring tracked her down and exposed her before the wrong woman could be burned at the stake.'

'I didn't know that.'

'Of course you didn't. You're too busy feeling sorry for yourself. What's so bad about the life you've led, anyway?'

'Nothing, I suppose. Martin is kind enough. But he's too old. And I don't like living in the city. It's better when we go to Martin's house in the country.'

'House in the country? Where?'

'Somewhere outside the Temple Gate, past a village called La Courtille.'

'Do you like it there?'

'Yes. Martin's house is big, and it's on a farm with animals and gardens and orchards.'

They were passing the beguinage, and Klara looked glum. 'Agnes comes with us to the house in the village. She spoils everything.'

'I can't imagine she's as bad as you say.'

'You don't know her.'

'You don't seem to like anyone very much, Klara.'

'I don't have any friends.' Klara bent down, picked up a stone lying in the road, and tossed it up in the air. 'How is it that you're friends with Christine? You're a prostitute.'

'That's part of the long story you don't know yet. But I'll tell you a secret. Do you see this embroidered belt I'm wearing?'

'It's pretty.'

'I made it myself. I make lots of embroidered things, like belts and purses and collars. And I sell them. That's how I make most of my living now. But I haven't told Christine and her mother yet. Francesca gets so upset about my being a prostitute. I like to watch her fuss.'

'I'll bet Christine knows already,' Klara said.

Marion walked on in silence for a while, lost in thought. Then she said, 'Has anyone gone to see whether your husband is staying at his farm near La Courtille?'

'His steward, Jehan, went out there, but they told him no one had seen Martin for a while.'

'I wonder about that,' Marion said under her breath.

TWENTY

There are so many perils at the court, it's hard to stay safe.

Eustache Deschamps (c. 1340–1404), *Ballade 208*

Marion and Klara returned home to find Christine and Francesca sitting in the kitchen, looking worried. Francesca jumped up and ran to Klara. 'Are you all right?'

'Of course she's all right. What did you think I'd done to her?' Marion sniffed.

Francesca put her arm around Klara's shoulder and made her sit down on the bench. 'Tell us where you have been.'

Klara looked at Marion. 'It's a secret,' she said.

The children filed into the room and gathered around Klara. 'I'll bet she's done something naughty,' Thomas said.

'I have not! *Enfant morveux.*'

'I am not,' Thomas cried. 'And anyway, it's better to have a snotty nose than no nose at all!'

Francesca slapped him. 'I do not want to hear you say that ever again.'

Christine went to Marion and whispered, 'Whatever you did with Klara doesn't seem to have helped much.'

'But it has. Be patient, and you'll see. We have other things to think about, like the big problem Henri Le Picart left us with.'

'I know. But I'm too tired to think about it tonight. I'm going to bed.'

'No supper?' Francesca asked. Christine didn't hear; she was already at the top of the stairs.

'Where's Goblin?' Klara asked, and the dog came running to her.

'Are you planning to take him with you when you go back to your house?' Thomas asked.

'I'm sure Klara knows he is our dog,' Francesca said.

The children sat down to their supper, grumbling, and Klara flounced up the stairs, clutching Goblin to her chest.

Marion left. *We really do have to find that girl's husband*, she thought.

In the kitchen the next morning, Christine found Lisabetta watching Francesca and Georgette make an onion tart. Francesca shaped the pastry dough, and Georgette, sniffling and wiping her watering eyes with a dish towel, chopped the onions, dropping pieces onto the floor. Francesca looked at the girl and muttered something under her breath.

Georgette looked up. 'Why can't I make the dough and *you* do the chopping?'

'No,' Francesca said as she patted the dough around the inside of a ceramic tart pan she'd brought from Italy. The pan, which would be covered with a ceramic lid and buried in the live embers of the fire, was fragile, and she wasn't about to let the clumsy girl handle it.

Georgette started to protest, when there was a knock on the door. Christine went to open it and found Colin.

'The queen wants you,' he said.

She went upstairs to get her writing materials. When she came back down, she found Lisabetta and her mother in the hall waiting for her. She put on her cloak, took Lisabetta in her arms, and asked, 'Do you know what *grand'maman* is going to say?'

The little girl nodded. 'Don't go there. There are evil spirits.'

'There, Mama. She's said it, so you don't have to.'

Francesca stomped back into the kitchen.

Colin said, 'I'll walk with you,' and they went out into the street. On the rue Saint-Antoine several pastry vendors approached them. Christine bought a pork pasty from one, a sweet wafer from another, and a marzipan tart from a third, giving everything to Colin, hoping that on a full stomach he might be induced to talk about Martin du Bois. But when she questioned him, he just shrugged and walked on, ignoring her. At the palace he hurried across the courtyard and disappeared.

In the queen's chambers, Isabeau, dressed in an emerald-green *houppelande* with a pearl-studded belt and a diamond circlet, sat on her day bed. The Duchess of Burgundy, wearing a black gown with blood-red rubies at the neck, stood over her with a malevolent look on her long, severe face. The queen tried to meet her gaze, but the duchess looked so menacing, she had to turn away, and when she did, she saw Christine standing at the door. She raised her hand in greeting but seemed powerless to summon her.

Alips, who'd been standing behind a large chair, came over to Christine, followed by the greyhound, and drew her into the hallway.

'The queen wants to talk to you, but the duchess is there, so no one else can get near her, not even her ladies-in-waiting. They've all left. I was hiding, and the duchess didn't see me.'

'Brother Michel warned me about the duchess.'

'I know she's treacherous.'

'You're not afraid of her?'

'Did he tell you I should be?'

'He did. He says you shouldn't be listening to people's conversations. He was adamant about it.'

'What about your friend Marion? Did he say she should be careful, too?'

'Do you know Marion?'

'I know all about how she helped you save Alix de Clairy. I'm sure she's helping you now. I'd like to meet her.'

'I don't think she'd be welcome here.'

'She's already been here. I've seen her talking to some of the guards.'

Christine started to laugh. 'I mean, she won't be coming to see the queen, at least not if the Duchess of Burgundy has anything to say about it.'

The queen looked pale and tired, and when Madame de Malicorne appeared with her baby and placed him in her arms, she fondled the little prince listlessly. Everything in the room seemed to have been infected by the duchess's malicious demeanor. The golden fleurs-de-lis in the tapestries didn't shine, the silver bowls and crystal goblets on the sideboard had lost their sparkle, the glass in the windows admitted no colored light.

The duchess waved Madame de Malicorne away; Isabeau sighed as she watched her go.

Guillaume ran to the duchess and fell to his knees. 'Shall I speak now, *Madame*?' he asked. The duchess tried to step around him, but he shifted around to keep her from passing.

'You fool! Don't you know I could have you hanged?' she asked. He sprang to his feet, pranced to the other side of the room, and fell to the floor, shouting, 'You're right. I'm a fool. But you won't have me hanged.'

Gracieuse picked up her lute and sang something in Spanish.

'I think the song has something to do with the duchess,' Alips said. Jeannine seemed to understand. She cast sly glances at the scowling duchess and giggled.

The queen, who usually laughed at Guillaume's antics, sat morosely, looking sadly at her baby.

'You've got to help her,' Alips said.

'What can I do? Right now I can't even talk to her. The duchess is there.'

'Not for long,' the dwarf said. She grasped the greyhound's jeweled collar and whispered something in his ear. The dog ran toward the duchess, barking. She gave a little cry and put her hands over her face. The queen spoke sharply to the dog, and he sat, making soft growling sounds.

'Get that beast out of here,' the duchess commanded.

'He won't hurt you,' the queen said. The duchess was not reassured. She called to one of her ladies and swept out of the room.

The queen beckoned to Christine, who went in and knelt.

'Have you learned anything?'

'I have many questions, *Madame.*'

'You are clever. You will find the answers.' The queen rocked the baby and tickled his stomach. The little prince didn't laugh; he just looked at his mother and started to cry.

Guillaume ran over. He made faces, waved his cap, and did a few somersaults, but nothing helped. Madame de Malicorne came in and took the wailing baby away.

'Please go to your work,' the queen said to Christine. 'Come back to me later.'

Christine knelt quickly, went to the room where she did her copying, and sat at the desk. Alips followed and stood at her side.

'There's something I didn't tell her,' Christine said. 'The person who threw the torch seems to have thrown a golden spur as well.'

'How do you know?'

'Henri Le Picart told me.'

'I know who he is.'

'He found the spur on the floor of the ballroom. He thinks it's one of the golden spurs taken at the sack of Courtrai.'

'I didn't see anything like that, it all happened so fast. It makes sense, though, if the Duchess of Burgundy is responsible. She couldn't have done it herself, so she got someone else to throw the torch, perhaps someone who's angry at the king because of what he did in Courtrai. Her father is the Count of Flanders, so she has lots of Flemish connections.'

Alips had her arms around the greyhound, which had followed her. *How little she is*, Christine thought. *She's not much taller than the dog.*

'I've found out something else about the Duchess of Burgundy,' Alips said. 'Do you remember that when the king was on his way to fight the Duke of Brittany last summer, a ragged man jumped out of the woods and told him to turn back because he was betrayed?'

'I've heard the story many times.'

'The Duchess of Burgundy put the man up to it. Only it wasn't a man. It was a boy.'

'How do you know?'

'I heard the duchess tell her husband. She didn't want the king to fight the Duke of Brittany, so she got a boy to dress in rags and scare him away.'

Christine was alarmed. 'You're putting yourself in too much danger, Alips, listening to conversations you aren't supposed to hear. Especially when the people talking are the Duke of Burgundy and his wife!'

'I'm not worried.' Alips stood on her toes and whispered in Christine's ear, 'I think the madman and the boy who threw the torch are the same person.'

Catherine de Villiers stood at the door. When the dwarf looked around and saw her, she grabbed the greyhound's collar and led him from the room. Catherine turned and watched her go, a strange look on her face. Then she went in, placed the *Life of Saint Catherine* on Christine's desk, and left without a word.

Worried that Catherine had heard what Alips had said, Christine got up and started to go after the dwarf and warn her that she must keep quiet about her suspicions. But although the greyhound sat beside the queen's day bed, Alips was nowhere in sight.

Determined to finish copying the manuscript, Christine worked diligently for several hours, becoming so engrossed that in spite of her concerns about Alips she didn't notice Isabeau and her ladies leaving. When she finally looked up, the queen's chambers were deserted. There was no fire in the fireplace, the window shutters were closed, and the place was deathly quiet.

She felt a chill, and she sensed someone watching. She closed the manuscript, gathered together her writing materials, and walked quickly through the queen's rooms, thinking as she did so that someone could be hiding behind a high-backed chair, under the day bed, or in back of the sideboard with its goblets and platters. But there was only silence.

She peered into the hallway. It was empty. She stepped out, heard rustling noises, stepped back in, and laughed at herself when she realized it was only the sound of her own skirt. Then she heard footsteps on the bare wooden floor. She looked around the door. Two chambermaids carrying soiled linens came toward her. They stopped beside a large wooden chest standing on one side of the hallway, opened the heavy lid, deposited the laundry, and continued on. She was tempted to follow them, but she told herself not to give in to her fears and waited until they were out of sight before she walked slowly through shadowy passages and corridors to the safety of the great gallery and its guards.

TWENTY-ONE

*When you and Dame Agnes the beguine are in the village, she
is to order Robin, the shepherd, to care for the sheep, ewes,
and lambs; Josson, the herdsman, the oxen and bulls; Arnoul,
the cowherd, and Jehanneton, the dairymaid, the cows, heifers,
calves, sows, pigs, and piglets; Endeline, the farmer's wife,
the geese, goslings, roosters, hens, chicks, doves, and pigeons;
and the farmer's wagon man our horses, mares, and the like.*

From a book of moral and practical advice
for a young wife, Paris, 1393

M arion lived in a room near the place where the rue Saint-Honoré crossed the rue de l'Arbre Sec. When she left Klara, she went there, and before going to bed searched through a chest for her oldest clothes and her stoutest boots. The next morning, she rose early and went to the nearby house of a man who had horses for rent. She took a deep breath and pounded on his front door.

'I need a horse,' she said when the man appeared.

'What for?'

'That's my business.'

The man led her to a stable beside the house. Marion looked at the horses apprehensively.

'Do you know how to ride?' the man asked.

'Of course,' she answered.

'Of course.' He instructed a stable boy to bring out a gentle-looking brown palfrey that eyed Marion suspiciously. Marion eyed the animal back, then took off one of the many long strands of beads she wore and slid it over his head. The little horse stamped his foot but stood still as the stable boy bridled him and placed a saddle on his back.

'Just bring him home in one piece,' the man said as he led the palfrey out into the street. 'Hang on to the pommel if he goes too fast.' He helped Marion into the saddle and gave the animal a sharp slap on the rump.

Marion turned the palfrey's nose toward the rue Saint-Honoré and urged him through the crowds near the market at les Halles. They went up the rue des Lombards, where Italian bankers standing outside their counting houses turned to look in amazement at a horse bearing a tall woman with flaming red hair and a crimson cloak. As she trotted past the glassmakers' shops on the rue de Verrerie, her beaded necklaces jangled in time to the clip-clop of the palfrey's hooves, and the glass vases and pitchers on the shelves in front of the shops clinked in return. Many people knew her, and they stood gaping, poking each other in the ribs, and making crude jokes as she bounced past. Marion laughed and waved. She turned down the rue du Temple and jogged to the gate in the city wall. There the guards asked her where she was going. When she told them to La Courtille, they smirked and said she wouldn't find much to interest her there. 'You'd be surprised,' she answered as she shook the reins to make the palfrey hurry by.

Outside the wall, Marion entered a different world. All the bustle of Paris's crowded streets was gone, and she rode past open fields, vineyards, and trim cottages. The silence was strange to her, and she felt very alone. She patted the palfrey's neck for reassurance. The little animal seemed to understand, and he neighed softly in return.

Klara had said her husband's farm was past the village of La
Courtille. Marion needn't have worried about missing the house,
for it was the largest and most impressive one on the road, a stone
manor surrounded by neat fields and gardens. Men in rolled-up
breeches and broad-brimmed hats were out ploughing the fields, a
shepherd watched a large flock of sheep, and women in simple
cottes and kerchiefs turned the soil of bare gardens. They all turned
to look at her. She tossed her head, rode up to the door of the
house, and slipped off the horse's back. A stout woman in a green
woolen chemise and a long white apron appeared. Chickens and
geese that had been scratching the ground around the house ran up
to her. She shooed them away and stood in front of Marion, her
hands on her hips.

'Don't worry. I'm not here to rob you,' Marion said.

'I didn't think you were. Who are you and what do you want?'

'I'm a friend of Martin du Bois, or of his wife, at least. Is
he here?'

'We haven't seen him for a while. His steward came looking for
him. He said the master has disappeared.'

'I'm looking for him, too.'

'Why?'

'Because his wife doesn't know where he is.'

'How are you acquainted with such an innocent young lady?'

'That's a long story. And the innocent young lady, as you call
her, isn't as innocent as you think.'

'Maybe not. Insolent might be a better word.'

While they talked, a crowd of the farm's workers gathered
around. 'This woman is trying to find the master,' the woman in
the green chemise said. 'It seems his little wife wants him back.'
They all laughed.

Marion's palfrey had wandered over to the stables and was
making friends with four large, well-groomed work horses standing
patiently outside. A stable boy brought some hay and water and
stood running his hands over the palfrey's flanks. 'This is a fine
animal,' he called out. 'Is he yours?'

'Belongs to someone I know,' Marion called back. 'I hope he
didn't get his feet too muddy on the way here.'

'City folk always worry about that,' the stable boy said. 'Like
the man in a black cape who rode out here the other day. He was
looking for the master, too.'

Marion's mouth flew open in astonishment. She turned to the woman in the green chemise. 'Do you know who the man was?'

'He said his name was Henri Le Picart.'

'The swine!' Marion said. 'He didn't find him, did he?'

'No more than you will.'

Marion turned to the others. 'Do any of you know where the master might be?'

'No, we don't,' several of them said together.

'But the last time he was here, he borrowed some of my clothes,' said a young man who had just come in from the fields. 'I've no idea what he wanted them for.'

The woman in the green chemise had disappeared into the house, and now she reappeared, bringing a slice of bread, a chunk of cheese, and a beaker of wine. 'You'll be hungry on your way back,' she said.

Marion munched on the bread, drank the wine, and looked around, wondering whether Martin du Bois might be hiding somewhere. It didn't seem likely. But why had he borrowed a workman's clothes? Did Henri know? Were they friends? She got back on the palfrey, aided by two of the farmhands, who were only too glad to put their arms around her and hoist her into the saddle, and headed back to the city.

TWENTY-TWO

The duke said: Listen to me, anyone who can hear. It is all my fault. Don't accuse anyone else. It grieves me terribly, and if I had known what was going to happen, nothing on earth would have made me do what I did.

Froissart, *Chroniques*, Livre IV, 1389–1400

The Duke of Orléans had come to the Hôtel de Nesle to see his uncle, the Duke of Berry. He did that regularly in the days after the fire at the palace, and he often visited his other uncle, the Duke of Burgundy, as well. He needed to assuage his guilt, for he really believed he had caused four men to die a horrible death. The Duke of Burgundy advised him to spend more time in prayer at the church of the Celestines. The Duke of Berry told him just to forget the incident, for there was nothing to be done about it now. They'd all made a procession of repentance to the cathedral the day after the fire, walking barefoot behind the king, who rode a black stallion. After that, it was obvious the uncles thought no more about the burned men, considering them beneath their concern. They told Louis he should be thankful the king had not been killed, for then the people of Paris would have turned on them and murdered them all.

The king's brother, however, wouldn't be comforted. When a page ushered him into the room where his uncle sat, he fell to his knees, weeping. The old duke, who was looking at a manuscript he had just acquired, told him to get up and stop acting like a child. 'You know better than this,' he said. 'Go away and let me be. Or else, take a look at what I've just received.' He turned the manuscript toward his nephew so he could see an illustration of one of his many castles.

'That's fine, uncle,' said Louis, who had his own magnificent collection of manuscripts, 'but I'm not interested in that now. What use do I have for these things when four men are dead, and it's my fault?

'Then go to the Celestines and pray, nephew. I'm tired of hearing about your guilty feelings.'

Louis turned away sadly, and noticed his uncle's young wife sitting on a seat by the window, leaning against richly embroidered pillows and looking at him with pity in her eyes. 'Come here,' she said.

The young man crossed the room and sat down beside her. She took his hand. 'I understand what you're feeling. If it will help, I'll tell you something. I don't believe the fire was your fault.'

'How could you know anything about it?'

'Because I saw you holding two torches, and there was a third torch on the floor.'

'Do you mean you think someone else's torch caused the fire?'

'I don't know, but I think the Viscount of Castelbon is feeling more secure, now that Yvain is dead.'

Louis looked at the young duchess, wondering at the implications of what she'd said.

The old duke glanced over at the couple on the window seat. 'What are you two talking about?'

'Nothing, husband. Go back to your manuscript.'

Sun streamed through the colored glass in the windows, setting the young duchess's hair alight with a myriad of hues. To Louis, at that moment, she was beautiful.

'That's all I can tell you,' she said. 'There is no way to prove anything, and you mustn't try. It would only make people think worse of you than they do now.'

'I understand,' Louis said. Then, with tears in his eyes, he took his leave of her. On the way out, he bowed to his uncle, who was so engrossed in his manuscript he hardly noticed.

TWENTY-THREE

Age of lies, fraught with pride and envy.

Eustache Deschamps (c. 1340–1404), *Ballade 31*

Alips knew that Brother Michel's warning was meant to show how dangerous it was to suspect any member of the royal family other than the king's brother of causing the fire. Nevertheless, she was convinced the Duchess of Burgundy was behind the tragedy. The duke himself would have little to gain if the king died, he had so much power already, but the duchess would have other reasons. The woman showed nothing but contempt for the king now that he was ill. It was obvious she considered the demented monarch and his suffering an affront to her dignity. Alips thought the duchess's treatment of the queen proved that the evil-intentioned woman knew the king was doomed, and she would soon have the upper hand at the court.

She discounted the king's other uncle, the Duke of Berry. He was interested in nothing but money and possessions. And young men. It was no secret that the pudgy duke had several male lovers on whom he lavished money and jewels. She had to laugh. No wonder he hadn't bothered to warn the king that his constable was about to be attacked; he had too many other things on his mind.

The only other possibility was Louis's wife, Valentina Visconti. But she admired Valentina, who was kind and gentle, despite all the horrible things the Duchess of Burgundy said about her. She knew Valentina came from a family of tyrants. Her father was a murderer and a despot. Nevertheless, his court in Milan was a center of learning and respect for the arts. Valentina was a woman of culture and refinement, and Alips just couldn't suspect her of wanting to harm anyone.

No. It had to be the Duchess of Burgundy.

She sat in the room where she slept, near the queen's chambers, and tried to remember when she'd first encountered the treacherous woman. It must have been eight years earlier, when she'd first come to the Hôtel Saint-Pol. She remembered that time vividly. The queen's residence had been overwhelming, with many huge rooms, each more lavishly decorated than the next. There were elaborately embroidered tapestries that completely covered the walls, colorful carpets so thick she could hardly stand upright on them, ceilings decorated with inlaid scrolls and leaves and golden fleurs-de-lis, windows filtering light through glittering red, blue, and green glass. When she set out to explore, she walked and walked until she came to the entrance courtyard, where a stone lion glared at her from the top of a pillar in the center of a fountain. The tall *portier* who stood at the door saw her looking up. He smiled and said, 'You should go and see the real lions.'

She shuddered. She knew the king and queen kept many animals, but she hadn't heard anything about lions.

'They won't hurt you unless you frighten them. They're old and fat. Their stockade is on the other side of the orchards. Don't mind the lion-keeper's assistant. She's a bit odd, but she won't hurt you.'

He seemed a strange sort of guard, prattling on like that.

'I know who you are,' he said, and she was immediately suspicious. Perhaps Catherine de Fastavarin had been talking to him, and they'd decided to feed her to the lions. She started to back away.

'Are you afraid?' he asked.

'Should I be?'

'Of course not. Let me take you back to the queen.'

He picked her up and carried her through the maze of corridors and passageways to the queen's chambers. 'My name is Simon,' he said. 'I'm always out there if you need me.'

After that, she'd often sought Simon out, and from him she'd learned about everyone at the court: the king and his family, the courtiers, and the people who worked there: the officials who managed the queen's money, the secretaries, physicians, apothecaries, herbalists, astrologers, priests, sergeants-at-arms, *huissiers*, stewards, valets, butlers, footmen, doorkeepers, housekeepers, porters, cupbearers, seamstresses, washer-women, candle-makers, gardeners, and barbers. And the *grand maître d'Hôtel*, who was in charge of them all. Simon told her which ones to befriend and which ones to avoid. One of the people he took special care to warn her about was the Duchess of Burgundy. She soon saw why.

Shortly after her arrival, the king arranged a grand fête, a magnifi-cent affair that included a sumptuous banquet. At first she'd been reluctant to go, because she'd learned that the cooks had prepared a giant pie shell stuffed with live doves that would fly out when the crust was cut open, and she knew there'd been talk of using her rather than doves for this purpose. Simon said this was often done with court dwarfs, and he intimated that Catherine de Fastavarin had put the cooks up to it. Fortunately, the scheme came to nothing when the queen found out about it.

After the banquet, she'd clambered up the steep steps to the musicians' balcony and peered down at the floor below. Now that the feast was over, the tables were covered with overturned goblets, puddles of wine, and globs of gravy; and under the tables, scrawny dogs gnawed on bones and snarled at grimy children who'd wandered in from the street. The nobility milled about in multicolored gowns and robes, wearing jewels that sparkled like a thousand suns, while commoners stood in shadowy corners and gaped at them. The queen, in a gown of vermilion silk embroidered with gold, her hair arranged under a diamond-studded circlet that threw off flashes of light when-ever she turned her head, stood with the king's uncles, their wives, and several noblemen. The Duke and Duchess of Burgundy, wearing robes covered with rubies and diamonds, towered over her, keeping their eyes on the king. Then a small boy approached. He held out a gift for the king: a little horse made of sticks that he'd made himself. The duchess stepped up to him, took the horse, and waved him away. A short while later, Alips saw her toss the horse into a corner to be swept up with the trash left from the banquet.

The rotund Duke of Berry, homely in spite of a scarlet robe even more lavishly bejeweled than his brother's, paid little attention to either the king or the queen. Instead, he stroked the buttocks of a coarse-looking man beside him. He obviously didn't think anyone noticed, but the Duchess of Burgundy did, and she made signs to the king's brother, who was standing nearby, so he would be sure to see.

The king disported himself like a child, darting in and out among the guests, speaking to some, slapping others on the back, always in motion with his peculiar lurching gait. He leapt into the center of the room, where acrobats, tumblers, and jugglers performed, and clapped loudly for attention. A clown held out a large metal ring for a small black dog to jump through, and the king grabbed it. He swung it high over his head and roared with glee as the little dog tried in vain to reach it. The watching crowd laughed and applauded. The queen laughed too, but her eyes were troubled. This was long before the king's first fit of madness, but Alips knew that even then the queen was aware that there was something amiss with her husband. The Duchess of Burgundy knew it, too. She'd touched the queen's arm, pointed to the king, and grimaced.

No one knew more about events at the court than the ugly little poet Eustache Deschamps, who was always around, commenting on everyone's misfortunes, including his own, and writing about the perils of life at the palace. He was bitter and disillusioned and, because of his acid tongue, heartily disliked by many people. She herself had once been the object of that sharp tongue when he'd fallen under the spell of Catherine de Fastavarin's malicious talk. He'd sought her out so he could say, 'I know about you dwarfs. You bring bad luck. Misshapen limbs, misshapen minds.'

'Speak for yourself,' she'd retorted.

The little man had looked at her with surprise, and then started to laugh. After that, they'd become friends, and she'd learned much from him. Now she decided to seek his help, because of all the people at the court, he was the most likely to know about the Duchess of Burgundy's devious ways. She'd seen him in one of the palace orchards the day before, and since it was another warm day, she thought she might find him there again.

In the gardens, where there were a few early snowdrops and crocuses, it was almost like spring. She walked past a bare plot that would soon be fragrant with lavender, rosemary, and other sweet-smelling herbs, wandered through a rose garden where prickly stems tore at her dress, and entered an orchard. There, instead of the poet, she found the king and his brother sitting on a bench under the leafless branches of a cherry tree.

And the Duchess of Burgundy, on the other side of a hedge, watching them.

One of the gardeners had left a wheelbarrow on a path. Alips crouched behind it and stayed perfectly still, observing the scene. The king sat slumped against Louis, nervously biting his fingernails and clutching his breast as though he felt a great pain there. Louis had his arm around his brother, not speaking, but moving his lips as if in silent prayer. She felt desperately sorry for them, the monarch who feared he would at any moment suffer another attack of madness, and his brother, suffering because he believed he'd caused the deaths of four of his brother's friends.

The duchess, who had a cruel smile on her lips, showed no such sympathy. She seemed to cast an evil shadow over the brothers. *Surely this is the shadow the queen feels*, Alips thought. *The duchess couldn't have hurled the flaming torch at the king herself.* She smiled as she pictured the big woman trying to clamber up the steps to the musicians' balcony in her long *houppelande* and voluminous hairdo. No, she wouldn't have done it by herself. She must have bribed someone else to do it.

If only she could find out who that other person was before the shadow overtook the lives of everyone at the court.

TWENTY-FOUR

As for chambermaids and house servants, dear sister, have them chosen by Dame Agnes the beguine.

From a book of moral and practical advice
for a young wife, Paris, 1393

Ever since Klara's arrival, Christine's children had been quarrelsome and difficult. Now Christine was shocked to find that she herself, never the most patient person in the world, was growing increasingly short-tempered. The morning after she'd worked late and found herself alone in the queen's chambers, she decided to stay home and rest, but that was impossible because of all the squabbling going on downstairs. She went down and ordered everyone but Klara to go outside. She took the girl by the shoulders and made her sit down on a bench.

'This can't continue, Klara. You are a guest here. We don't have to keep you, you know. We can just take you back to your house and let you fend for yourself. Surely there are plenty of servants there who will make sure you don't starve, even though that's what you deserve.'

'I don't care, just as long as that woman, the beguine, isn't there.'

Georgette, who stood nearby, trying to untangle the strings of her apron, said, 'What would she do by herself? She didn't learn anything from the book her husband wrote for her.'

'Maybe it's time she did,' Christine said. She turned to her mother. 'Why don't you teach her how to cook something? Georgette can learn, too. Why not show her how to make another of your onion tarts?'

'As long as I don't have to chop the onions,' Georgette said.

Francesca went into the pantry and returned with flour, oil, and onions. 'I'll let you make the dough, Georgette. But *I'll* put it into the pan and put the pan into the fire.' She went to a shelf, got down her treasured tart pan, and set it carefully on the table.

'I know what to do,' Georgette said. 'I've watched you often enough.'

'Then you can show Klara,' Francesca said.

Georgette got a bowl and started to mix the dough, while Francesca chopped the onions. When some pieces of onion fell to the floor, Georgette said, 'You're always mad at me when that happens.'

'I suppose I shouldn't be,' Francesca said, laughing and wiping her watering eyes.

Klara wasn't interested in the onion tart. When Goblin wandered over, smelled the onions, and turned up his nose, she picked him up and buried her nose in his white coat.

Christine said, 'We have to find your husband, Klara. Surely you must have some idea where he is.'

'I don't,' Klara said.

'Well, think. Who would know? What about the beguine, Agnes?'

'I don't know anything about her,' Klara sniffed.

'Not even her last name?'

'I don't even know where she came from.'

'She lives at the beguinage on the rue de l'Ave-Maria,' Francesca said.

'That's not far from here,' Christine said. 'I'm going to see her. Do you want to come with me, Klara?'

Klara turned away, tears in her eyes.

'Did she treat you so badly?' Francesca asked.

'She liked my brother better than me. Willem and I used to be good friends, until she came. Then he would hardly talk to me anymore. And she didn't let me have my way with the servants. She was more interested in telling me to say my prayers and think of my sins. Just like Martin.'

'Your husband wrote about lots of other things,' Christine said. 'What about all those recipes?'

'Who needs them?' Klara said.

'You do,' Francesca said. 'And you need all the other instructions your husband gives you about caring for him and his household.'

Christine knew that her mother would soon be telling Klara what a woman's goal in life should be, and she didn't want to hear it.

'I'm going to find Agnes,' she said, and she left the house.

The community where the beguines lived was not far from the Hôtel Saint-Pol; Christine had passed it many times. Such beguinages existed all over Europe, particularly in Flanders, and the women who lived in them were dedicated to lives of chastity and good works. But they were not actual nuns; they were allowed to keep private property, and they could leave their communities at any time. Christine understood how it had happened that Martin du Bois had engaged Agnes to look after his young wife, for beguines often went outside the beguinages to work, and many of them were housekeepers and teachers of children in other people's homes.

The beguinage was enclosed by walls, and it consisted of numerous houses where individual beguines lived, a hospital, a chapel, and a school for children. Christine took a deep breath when she entered because she was apprehensive about meeting the grand mistress, who laid down the rules of the community and maintained discipline. The woman was coming toward her down a long hallway, and as she looked at her, she couldn't help wondering why the beguines wore such unattractive clothes – wide, shapeless habits that completely hid their bodies and made them the object of ridicule by people in the street. But she had little time to think about this. The grand mistress descended on her with a frown that indicated visitors were not welcome.

'I'm looking for someone named Agnes,' Christine said quickly.

The grand mistress looked her up and down before she said, 'There is only one person with that name here. Come with me.'

The woman strode through a courtyard, past small cottages where some of the wealthier sisters lived and into a large communal area where the poorer beguines lived together. Four of these women sat talking together at a long table. In their shapeless habits and big white veils that nearly hid their faces, they all looked alike.

The grand mistress went up to one who seemed broader than the others and said, 'This lady has come to see you, Agnes.' She turned and walked away.

Christine looked around the room, which was bare except for the table at which the beguines sat, and a large fireplace. A yellow cat lying by the fireplace raised his head and looked at her, yawned, and went back to sleep.

Agnes motioned to a place on the bench beside her, and said, 'I suppose you're here about Klara.' Her voice was deep and gruff.

'Yes. My mother felt sorry for her, and she brought her to our house. Now we need to find her husband so she can go back where she belongs. Do you know where he is?'

'No.'

'Klara can't stay with us. She's upsetting my children.'

Agnes smiled slightly. 'I can imagine.'

The three other women at the table didn't seem to be paying attention to their conversation, but Christine leaned close to the woman before she asked in a low voice, 'How long have you worked for Martin du Bois?'

'Several years.'

'Who took care of Klara and Willem before Martin du Bois hired you?'

'My impression is that they were pretty much on their own.'

'Martin must be a kind man to have brought them away from Courtrai and to care for them as though they were his own children.'

'He is a kind man, that much is true.'

Christine noticed that Agnes spoke with a slight accent, and she asked, 'Where are you from? You don't speak like a Parisian.'

'Paris is my home now.'

Christine waited for her to say something more, but she was silent. The three other women got up and walked away. The yellow cat followed them. A log shifted in the fireplace with a loud crackling noise that echoed in the empty room.

'Surely you can tell me something that will help me find out whether Martin du Bois is dead or alive. And where I can find him if he still lives.'

'I don't know anything.'

'What about the boy, Willem?'

Agnes looked away.

Christine realized she would get nowhere with the woman. 'Thank you for your help, Agnes,' she said, although she'd gotten no help at all. Agnes merely sat in her ugly beguine habit and stared at her impassively.

Christine walked away, more disturbed than before, because she knew the beguine was hiding something.

TWENTY-FIVE

The old lion reseth woodly on men, and only grunteth on women, and reseth seldom on children, except in great hunger.

Bartholomaeus Anglicus, thirteenth century

She left the beguinage and turned down the rue de l'Ave-Maria, where she saw Marion and Klara coming toward her.

Klara stepped back, but Marion pulled her forward. 'I hoped we'd find you here,' she said. 'I went to your house, and your mother told me where you were. She didn't object when I said I wanted to take Klara out for a while. In fact, she seemed pleased.'

'I can imagine.' Christine couldn't help smiling. 'Where are you going?'

'To visit Loyse and the lions.'

'I suppose you think I should be watching your mother make tarts,' Klara said to Christine.

'It wouldn't hurt you to learn something from my mother,' Christine said.

'Enough of this,' Marion said. She took Christine's hand on one side and Klara's on the other and pulled them down the street toward the palace gardens. A group of richly dressed courtiers, out enjoying the sunshine, stared at them as they passed. The feathers in their beaver hats bobbed up and down as they put their heads together and made rude comments.

Klara heard what they said, and she looked at the ground, embarrassed. Marion stood tall and told Klara to do the same. 'You're just as good as they are,' she said. 'Don't pay any attention.'

Christine had to laugh. She'd been depressed about her meeting with Agnes, but Marion made her feel better. She said to Klara, 'I've been to see your beguine. I can understand why you aren't happy with her.'

Klara looked at her in surprise. 'What did she tell you?'

'Nothing. That's just the problem.'

'She doesn't know where Martin is?'

'That's what she says.'

They'd entered the cherry orchard, and Klara walked through it quickly, hurried to the lions' stockade, and peered through the palings. Loyse appeared and opened the gate. Christine stood aghast. 'What's going on, Marion?'

'You don't have to be afraid. Those lions won't hurt anyone. Not unless they're provoked.'

Christine was astonished to see Klara walk right into the stockade with Loyse. 'You don't need to go in if you don't want to,' Marion said.

'I don't,' Christine said.

'That's all right. We'll stay out here. I have something to tell you.' Loyse had left the gate to the lions' stockade open, and she stepped over and closed it.

Christine laughed. 'Surely you're not afraid those old lions will get out. You assured me a while ago that they're so fat and lazy they can hardly move. I think you told me they've lost all their teeth.'

'They have their teeth, most of them, anyway. But you don't have to worry; they won't eat you unless you provoke them.'

'I suppose that's reassuring.' Christine went to the gate and checked to make sure it was firmly closed. 'What were you going to tell me? Have you found out where Martin du Bois is?'

'Not exactly. But I know where he isn't.'

'What do you mean?'

'Did you know he has a house in the country? Klara told me. It's near La Courtille. I went there to see if I could find him.'

'You went there? It's a long walk!'

'I didn't walk. I borrowed a horse.'

Christine put her hand over her mouth so Marion wouldn't see her laughing. Marion did see, of course.

'What's so funny? Riding's not difficult, you know.'

'I'm not laughing at you. I'm picturing the expressions on the faces of the people in the street.'

'I have to admit, everyone looked surprised.'

'I see you got back in one piece. Did you learn anything?'

'Not much. He wasn't there, of course, and no one could tell me where he was. But I found out that he'd borrowed some clothes from one of his workers. Which means . . .'

'He's disguised himself. If he's still alive, that is.'

'The other interesting thing I learned is that Henri Le Picart got there to ask about him before I did.'

'The swine!'

'That's what I said, too. But he didn't get any more information than I did.'

They heard crunching and chewing sounds coming from inside the stockade, and they looked through the palings. Klara and Loyse were feeding the lions. 'Unbelievable,' Christine said.

'Not really. Klara likes your little dog. Why not lions?'

'Does Loyse talk to Klara?' Christine asked.

'Have you ever heard Loyse talk?'

'No.'

'Not even the night you and Michel thought you were going to be eaten by those lions?'

'She drove them back, but I didn't hear her say anything.'

'Of course she didn't say anything.' Marion stamped her foot. 'Don't you see, Lady Christine? Loyse doesn't know how to speak. She's deaf!'

Christine stepped back and put her hand to her head. 'I should have guessed! That's why her mother mistreated her. She thought that because she couldn't hear and didn't speak, she was possessed by demons.'

'Loyse isn't possessed by demons. She isn't stupid, either. In fact, she's very intelligent. But who would know? Everyone treats her as though she were a monster.'

'How did you find this out?'

'I have friends who work near here, on the rue de Pute-y-Muce. I used to see Loyse's mother, Blanche, coming to visit her. She wasn't as cruel to Loyse as you think. She just didn't know what to do with her.'

'Does Loyse know her mother is dead?'

'How could she? But I know she wonders where she is.'

'How do you know that since she can't speak?'

'She used a stick to draw something in the sand. It looked like a tall woman. Then she pointed to the picture and back to herself. I knew she meant herself and her mother. She wanted to know why her mother hadn't come to see her.'

'And you had no way of telling her what happened to Blanche.'

'No. And I don't think I want to tell her.'

'She has to find out sometime.'

Loyse and Klara came out of the lions' stockade. Loyse's face was, as usual, smeared with dirt, and her hair was unkempt; next to Klara she looked like a beggar.

'We can't let the poor girl go on like this,' Christine said.

'You're the smart one, Lady Christine. Think of something to do about it.'

Christine bowed her head. All sorts of considerations ran through her mind, foremost of which was her relationship with Alips. She'd never paid much attention to the dwarf before. What about all the other people the queen cared for: the fools, the mute, the minstrel, the Saracen? The queen treated them all with respect, often seeming to care for them more than she cared for her ladies-in-waiting.

Loyse had shut the gate, and she and Klara were standing in front of it, looking at something Loyse had drawn in the sand. It was an arrow, pointing toward the stockade.

'See that?' Marion asked. 'She's letting Klara know she wants her to come again. She's very clever. It's not right for her to spend her life in a lions' den.'

'No, it isn't. I think I know what to do,' Christine said.

TWENTY-SIX

At great courts it is often best to play dumb. Don't say what you think, just flatter others and beware of intrigues. Humor, dissimulate, and endure, but don't linger.

Eustache Deschamps (c. 1340–1404), *Ballade 208*

Christine had a plan, and she was eager to try it out; so early the next morning she went into the hall and started to get ready to go to the palace. Francesca came in and saw her. 'It is a cold day, *Cristina*. Why do you not stay home?'

'You know I can't do that.' Christine picked up her brown cloak. Then she threw it down. A mouse ran across her foot.

Francesca gave a horrified cry. She seized the cloak and examined it all over, paying no attention to her daughter, who stood tapping her foot as she waited impatiently to put it on. Finally, she gave a sigh of relief and said, '*Grazie a Dio!* There are no holes.'

'Even if there were, this is an old cloak. You've patched it before, and I'm sure you could do it again.'

'It is not that,' Francesca said. 'Holes don't matter. But what if the mouse had chewed on it? That would be a sign that something very bad would happen to you today.'

Christine hurried out the door.

Her mother had been right about one thing. It was a cold day. She pulled the cloak around her tightly as she walked toward the palace, where she found Simon and Renaut huddled together at the entrance to the queen's residence. The great gallery was chilly in spite of its several large fireplaces, and she was glad to arrive at the queen's chambers, where, in addition to fireplaces, there were braziers filled with hot coals.

The queen sat with Catherine de Villiers, reading aloud from a large book, while the other ladies stood around, discussing the missing playing cards. The women were becoming more and more agitated, distressed because the present for the king had been lost.

The queen looked up and said to them, 'Do not distress your-selves. They will be found.' She pointed to a window seat on the other side of the room where Gracieuse the minstrel sat, playing a slow, sweet melody on her lute. 'Let the music calm you.'

After a maid had taken her cloak, Christine approached the queen. She was curious about the book she was reading, and as she knelt, she tried to see what it was. The queen held it up. It was the story of Tristan and Isolde.

Alips came over. 'I don't like that book. There's a dwarf who does something mean.'

The queen laughed. 'So, you have been listening.'

'I always listen,' Alips said.

'Sit on this cushion and we can talk,' Isabeau said to Christine. Catherine de Villiers and the other ladies-in-waiting drifted away, still arguing.

Christine sat on the big blue cushion that Catherine de Fastavarin had always used, and looked around the room. The queen's fools, Guillaume and Jeannine, twirled each other around in a strange little dance, Collette the mute played hide and seek with the squirrel, the monkey swung from one of the tapestries, the grey-hound rolled on the floor, and Jeannine's mother stood quietly in a corner, watching.

A chambermaid came in with the Saracen girl, who ran to the queen and climbed onto the day bed. Guillaume let go of Jeannine, danced over, and stood in front of her. He made a face and said, 'I won't bite you, but if you bite me, I'll make you cry.'

The little girl stuck her thumb in her mouth and looked puzzled.

'It's a riddle,' Alips said.

'It's an onion,' the queen whispered, and the child clapped her hands.

Guillaume danced back to Jeannine, grabbed her hands, and started to swing her around again.

The queen was occupied with her godchild, and Christine had time to observe the ladies as they stood by the window discussing the missing cards. Jeanne de la Tour seemed genuinely upset; her hands shook uncontrollably. When Madame de Malicorne noticed this, she put her arms around her and eased her down onto the window seat. Catherine de Villiers, still holding the book she and the queen had been reading, sat beside her, put the book down, took her hands in hers, and stroked them, while Marguerite de Germonville spoke to her in an uncharacteristically soft voice. Symonne du Mesnil stood to one side, watching the queen with a frown on her face. *Is she angry with her?* Christine wondered. Symonne saw Christine looking, and turned away. She's so slender, she could almost pass for a boy, Christine thought.

She came out of her reverie when she realized the queen was looking at her, waiting for her to speak. She drew a deep breath and said, 'You know, *Madame*, Blanche the murderess had two daughters. Alix de Clairy was one. Have you ever thought about the other one?'

'I am aware she is with the lions. It has been told to me that she is a very strange person, that she has demons.'

'That is what people say. But it is not true.'

'Then why did her mother not love her?'

'She just didn't know how to care for her. You see, *Madame*, Loyse – that is her name – has always been treated as though she were not in her right mind. But she is merely deaf.'

The queen sat up straight. 'How you have startled me! Is that all that is wrong with her?'

'Yes, that is all. She doesn't talk or respond as others do, because she is deaf. She is actually very intelligent. It is not right that she should have to live in the lions' stockade.'

The queen put her arm around her godchild and smiled at Christine. 'I see that you have something in mind for her.'

'I do, *Madame*.' She hesitated. Alips touched her hand, and she bent down to her. 'Don't worry,' the dwarf whispered. 'She will agree.'

Christine said to the queen, 'I wonder whether you would care for her here.'

The queen looked thoughtful. 'The girl has been with the lions for a long time. Would she not be lost here? And my ladies would not like to be with someone who smells like lions.'

Christine shuddered as she thought of Loyse's unkempt hair and the rags she wore. She would have to ask Francesca to make her presentable. It seemed an impossible task. But she'd come this far; she'd have to try.

'Perhaps I could go to see her in the lions' den,' the queen said.

'*You* won't go into the lions' den, *Madame*,' Alips said. She and the queen burst out laughing.

The ladies gathered round, wondering what the joke was.

The queen said, 'I think it is possible to have the girl here. Bring her to me.' Then she waved her ladies away and said in a low voice, 'But do not forget, it is more important that you find out who is trying to kill the king.'

Christine nodded, made her obeisance, retrieved her cloak, and went out into the hallway. Alips followed her. 'I'm sure it's the Duchess of Burgundy,' she whispered.

'Be careful what you say. Remember Brother Michel's warning. Someone may be listening.' Christine went back to the door of the queen's room and peered in. Most of the ladies still stood by the window, but Symonne du Mesnil had gone over to the queen's day bed and was playing a game with the Saracen girl; the child put her hands over her eyes and tried to guess how many fingers Symonne held up.

'What do you know about Symonne, other than the fact that she drinks too much wine?' Christine asked Alips.

'Not much yet. I told you, she's new here.'

'Was she with the queen at the masquerade?'

'I didn't notice, so much was happening.'

Christine said, 'We have a problem, Alips. If the person we're looking for is a member of the court, how can we, as commoners, accuse him? We need help.'

'Brother Michel helped you when you were trying to save Alix de Clairy. Why is he not helping you now?'

'I'm not sure.'

'Do you know that poet who's always here at the court?'

'You mean Eustache Deschamps. He was a friend of my father's. I know him, too. I showed him some poems I'd written. He liked them and said he'd help me learn more about composing verse. Why do you ask?'

'We could get him to help us.'

'Unfortunately, he's away, on a mission for the king's brother.'

Loud sounds came from the queen's room. Symonne and the Saracen girl were playing a clapping game. The girl giggled. The queen drew the little girl close and hugged her.

Christine said to Alips, 'In any case, Henri Le Picart is helping us.' Then she remembered that she hadn't seen Henri since the day she and Marion had gone to talk to Bernart le Brun's wife. Sudden anger overwhelmed her. Not only had the man disappeared; she realized that she rather missed him.

TWENTY-SEVEN

Tell the woman who sells you milk that you don't want it if it is watered. They often augment their milk this way, and if it has water in it, or if it is not fresh, it will go sour.

From a book of moral and practical advice
for a young wife, Paris, 1393

Francesca had asked the children to help Georgette prepare for dinner. Marie and Jean were calmly setting up the trestle table, but Thomas and Klara ware having a tug of war with the knives and spoons.

'I said I'd do it,' Klara cried. 'I don't need any help.'

'You need all the help you can get,' Thomas smirked. 'You're stupid. Why don't you go back to your husband?'

Klara threw down the knives and spoons, which clattered onto the floor. Startled by the noise, Goblin began to race around nipping at everyone's ankles. Georgette laughed, and Francesca threw up her hands in despair.

Finally, Georgette ordered everyone to sit down. She picked up the knives and spoons, dusted them off on her apron, and put them on the table. Then she brought bowls of soup and there was peace for a while, until Francesca said, 'This soup was made from one of your recipes, Klara.'

'They aren't *my* recipes.' Klara got up from the table and left the room.

After the meal, Christine found Klara in her room looking through the pages of her husband's manuscript. 'I'm trying to find the soup recipe,' she said.

'I know where it is,' Christine said. She took out the page. 'Your husband gives you some good advice here. He tells you not to buy watered milk. Did you know that the women who sell milk often cheat their customers that way?'

'No. I'd give them a piece of my mind.'

'You see? You could be a good housekeeper if you wanted to be.'

'But I don't.'

Georgette had come into the room with a pile of logs for the fire, and she'd heard all this. 'She'd rather go to see the lions,' she said.

'That's a good idea,' Christine said. 'Get your cloak, Klara.'

Out in the street, they were met with a blast of cold air. 'Hurry,' Klara said. 'It's warm in the lions' stockade.'

'We have to stop somewhere else before we go there.'

Klara looked disappointed, and she dragged her feet. But when they came to the beguinage, she took Christine's arm and tried to hurry her past.

'What's wrong?' Christine asked.

'Marion said that's where Agnes lives. What if she comes out?'

'What if she does? You don't have to be afraid of her. Why do you dislike her so much?'

'Everything was fine until she came. I thought she would be nice to me if I did everything she asked me to. I even promised to read Martin's book. But she only liked my brother.'

A man selling crispy waffles approached. 'Buy one for the pretty little miss,' he cried. With a grand gesture, he bowed to Klara and offered one of his wares. Christine handed him a denier.

'Thank you,' Klara said as she munched the sugary cake. 'Why don't you have one, too?'

Christine handed the vendor another denier.

'My mother says I'm always eating,' she said as she devoured the waffle. 'I don't deny it. But I disagree with her when she says that means I should enjoy cooking.' Too late, she realized what she'd said, and she added hastily, 'That doesn't mean *you* shouldn't enjoy cooking, Klara.'

Klara started to laugh. 'So you aren't perfect after all.'

'I admit I don't like housekeeping. My mother thinks that's all a woman is good for. My father thought otherwise. He taught me to read and write, and now that I have to support my family, I'm grateful. I do the job of a man, and I believe any woman is capable of this.'

'Martin taught me to read and write, too,' Klara said. 'But I don't think that means much if I have to stay home and do nothing but cook and sew and obey all the rules he wrote about in his book.'

'Perhaps he didn't mean exactly that.'

They were approaching a small house near the palace gardens. 'We have to go there before we visit the lions,' Christine said.

A man with a red face and a big mustache answered her knock on the door. 'Do I know you?' he asked, his mustache bouncing up and down as he spoke.

'You probably don't remember me,' Christine said. 'I was only a child when my family lived at the palace. But you might remember my father, the old king's astrologer.'

The man's face became even redder and he exclaimed excitedly, 'I certainly do remember him! He'd come to see the lions, and he'd ask questions about them. He was interested in everything.' He squinted at Christine. 'I think you came with him sometimes. You've changed a lot.'

Christine laughed. 'Of course I have. I was only a child then. I was always afraid to go near the lions.'

She turned to Klara. 'This is Gilet, the lion-keeper. Loyse helps him.' Then she turned to Gilet and said, 'This is Klara. She isn't the least bit afraid of the lions.'

Gilet made a slight bow in Klara's direction, and Klara made a little curtsy.

Christine said to Gilet, 'I have a favor to ask. I'm concerned about Loyse, living with animals. It's not right. She's an intelligent young woman, and I want to take her away.'

'Where? What else can she do?'

'Do you realize she's deaf?'

'I know. Everyone thinks she's demented, but I've never believed it.'

Christine said, 'I've talked with the queen, and she's willing to have her at the palace. There's another woman in the queen's entourage who's deaf. I think Loyse would be happy there, too.'

'I've gotten used to having Loyse around,' Gilet said. 'My wife thinks I'm too old to do the work alone, but that's not true. I'm just lazy. It's nice to have someone to help.'

'I could do that,' Klara piped up.

Christine looked at her in surprise. 'You?'

'I could, you know. You were just telling me women can do anything.' She frowned. 'Perhaps you were just saying that. Perhaps you really want me to be like your mother, happy with the housework.'

Christine laughed and said, 'Come with us, Gilet. We'll go to the lions, and Klara will show you how she gets along with them.'

At the stockade, Loyse appeared and went in with Klara and Gilet. Christine followed, keeping well behind, and watched as Klara approached each of the lions in turn, talking in a low voice.

'One of the reasons Loyse works so well with them is that she doesn't speak,' Gilet said. 'These lions are old and so accustomed to humans, they aren't really dangerous; but they can get agitated if someone talks to them in a loud voice. I see that Klara understands that.'

'I can feed them, too, just like Loyse does,' Klara said, and she went to a large trough and pulled out some red meat. Christine looked away as the lions gathered around her and took the meat gently from her hands.

Gilet was smiling. 'We can give her a try.'

'I hope you don't think you're going to live here, Klara,' Christine said.

'Of course she won't,' Gilet said. 'I'll be close by. And the lions can be by themselves at night.'

Klara looked disappointed, but Christine put her arm around her and said, 'I'm sure you wouldn't want to miss my mother's good meals.'

'Or your rude children.'

Gilet interrupted. 'How are you going to make Loyse understand what's happening when you take her away?'

'I'm not sure,' Christine said. 'But I have an idea. We'll come back soon and see if it works.'

TWENTY-EIGHT

Perfect disciples seldom speak, even for good, holy, or edifying conversation, for it is written: If you speak much, you will not escape sin.

Saint Benedict's Rule *for Monasteries*, sixth century

As Christine and Klara walked down the street to Christine's house, they found Brother Michel hurrying toward them, battling a strong wind that sent his black habit swirling around him. Christine told Klara to go in and help Francesca.

'I'm worried about Alips,' the monk said. 'She's still asking questions, and she's going to get into trouble.' The wind had set his cowl askew, and he pulled it back over his head.

'She's just curious. Nobody takes her seriously,' Christine lied.

'I do. Even innocent curiosity can be misinterpreted.'

The wind blew Christine's cloak open. 'It's cold out here,' she said. 'Come inside.'

Francesca was happy to see the monk. She wanted to know what was happening at the palace.

'These are terrible times there, terrible,' Michel said. 'Since the king is ill, the rivalry between the dukes of Burgundy and Orléans has become truly dangerous. They both vie for power, and no one knows where it will end.'

'But the Duke of Orléans is regent,' Francesca said. 'He controls everything, doesn't he?'

'It should be so,' the monk said. 'But the Duke of Burgundy challenges him.'

The children came in and crowded around the monk.

'And then there's the Duke of Burgundy's son, Jean,' Michel continued. 'The hatred he and the king's brother have for each other seems to have no bounds.'

'But they're cousins,' Marie said. 'It's not right.'

'They have always despised each other,' Michel said.

Christine pictured the two men. Jean was ugly and ungraceful, with heavy-lidded eyes and a long, thin nose that ended in a point, like the beak of a bird. His lips were always pursed, which gave him a perpetually dissatisfied expression. Louis, on the other hand, was handsome and elegant, pleasing to everyone, and irresistible to women. It was even rumored that among his many conquests was Jean's own wife; supposedly Louis had a portrait of her in a secret gallery where he kept paintings of the women he'd seduced. Christine could understand Jean's resentment. Like all men with money and power, he had many liaisons, but it was certainly not because of his looks and personality.

Suddenly, Christine knew what Michel was afraid of and why he wanted to discourage anyone from trying to find out whether someone other than the king's brother was responsible for the fire. It was the dissention between the Duke of Burgundy, his son, Jean, and the Duke of Orléans. Michel was afraid the Burgundian faction, perhaps even Jean himself, had something to do with the fire. If that were the case and people found out about it, there could be real disruption at the court. Since Louis accepted responsibility, Michel probably thought it would be better to let well enough alone. That was why he was acting so strangely.

The children had started to remind the monk again about his promise to take them to his abbey. 'Maybe I'll stay there and become a monk,' Thomas said.

'Then you won't be able to go to Italy with your grandmother.'

'Don't encourage him, Michel,' Christine said.

He laughed. 'I'd better leave now.'

Christine followed him into the hall and said, 'I need your help.

He faced her angrily. 'Do I have to tell you again? Stay out of affairs at the court!'

'It's something else.'

He fingered the prayer beads that hung from his belt. 'I fear trouble every time you ask for my help.'

'I don't know that you'd call it trouble. It has to do with Loyse, the lion-keeper's assistant. The girl is not possessed, as many people think. She's deaf. That's why she doesn't speak. Marion found out.'

'How does Marion know Loyse?'

'Marion knows everyone at the palace. She befriended her.'

'Surely it is not wise to let Marion influence the poor girl!'

Christine stamped her foot. 'You've always thought the worst of Marion. I'll tell you something: she's making her living selling her embroidery now. She thinks I don't know, so don't tell her I told you.'

'*Laus Deo!* Now if we could only get her to wear respectable clothes.'

'I wouldn't want her to change her ways that much!'

'But if what you say is true, there is a great injustice here. If Loyse acts the way she does because she's deaf, she should not have to live with wild beasts.'

'That's what I want to talk to you about. I've asked the queen to care for her at the palace.'

'God forbid!'

'Let me explain. Isabeau has her official entourage of ladies-in-waiting, all chosen from the nobility. She is kind to them, as a queen should be. But I think she cares more for her dwarf and her fools and her mute. I think she would love Loyse, too.'

'That's ridiculous. How could you take such a disheveled, dirty girl into the palace?'

'I've already spoken to the queen about it, and she's agreed.'

'I don't believe this, Christine. Such a plan will never work. What will happen when the ladies-in-waiting see her? And how long do you think the girl will be able to stay there once the Duchess of Burgundy finds out?'

'They won't see Loyse the way she is now. I'll bring her home and make sure she's bathed and neatly dressed before I take her to the palace.'

'And what does your mother say about it?'

'I haven't told her yet.'

'I don't want to be here when you do.'

'First I have to get Loyse away from the lions. I've spoken to Gilet, the king's lion-keeper, and he's agreed.'

'I thought he needed an assistant.'

'He admitted he's just gotten lazy. In any case, Klara has volunteered to help him, once Loyse is gone.'

Michel looked as though he would faint. He said, meekly, 'After this, I'll believe anything of you, Christine.'

'The problem is, how do we explain to Loyse what's happening?' Christine asked. 'We don't know what she thinks, we don't even know whether she's aware her mother is dead. Marion communicates with her on a very simple level, but this is complicated. That's where you come in, Michel. You communicate with the brothers at the abbey with signs. Couldn't you do that with Loyse?'

Michel shook his head. 'We do communicate that way some of the time. But the hand signs and gestures we use have to do with our life at the monastery: worship, food, and the everyday necessities. How could I use them to tell her she's going to leave the lions and live with the queen?'

'I'm sure you can figure something out.'

Francesca came in. 'What are you two doing out here?'

'Nothing. I'm merely asking Michel to help me solve a problem. And he's agreed, haven't you, Michel?'

Michel shuffled his feet.

'Meet me here tomorrow morning,' Christine said.

TWENTY-NINE

Some bodies are not as perfect as others. There may be physical imperfection, weak limbs, or some other defect, but Nature makes up for it with something even better.

Christine de Pizan,
Le Livre de la Cité des Dames, 1404–1405

E arly the next morning, Michel arrived, looking very unhappy. Even one of Francesca's freshly made rissoles didn't cheer him. 'What's wrong?' Francesca wanted to know. 'What mischief are you getting up to now, *Cristina*?'

'Nothing. We just thought it would be nice to take Klara to see the lions.'

Then Marion appeared. 'Now I know there is something going on,' Francesca said, and she stormed up the stairs.

'Never mind her,' Christine said. 'Come on, Klara. It's time to take Loyse away from the lions.'

'Does that mean I can stay with them instead?' Klara asked.

'Soon,' Christine said. 'For now, just remember to be quiet and calm. Remember what Gilet said about not getting the lions excited.'

'She'll behave,' Marion said. 'Let's go. I can't wait to see what you have in mind.'

Out in the street, people stared at the monk in his solemn black habit accompanied by a tall prostitute in a crimson cloak, a lady in a plain brown cloak, and a young woman who fairly skipped along beside them, talking excitedly. As they passed the beguinage on the rue de l'Ave-Maria, Klara said to Marion, 'I wish Agnes would come out. I'd tell her I don't have to do any more housework because I'm going to be a lion-keeper.'

Michel heard, and he said to Christine, 'I hope you know what you are doing.'

They went to the door of Gilet's house and found him waiting for them. 'I had a feeling you'd be here today,' he said. 'Loyse doesn't know anything about this, of course.' He looked at Marion. 'I've seen you with her.'

'And this is Brother Michel,' Christine said. 'He's going to help us.'

Gilet looked at the monk dubiously. 'Do you know anything about lions?'

Michel shook his head.

'He will know how to communicate with Loyse, though,' Christine said.

Loyse emerged from the lions' stockade as soon as they approached. She looked encouragingly at her visitors, and indicated that she wanted them to go into the stockade with her. Marion held out her hand to signify that they would stay outside. Then Christine motioned to Michel, who stepped up to Loyse and made a sign of blessing. Immediately, Loyse crossed herself. Then Michel did some curious things with his hands. Loyse laughed soundlessly and made some strange gestures with her own hands.

'What's going on, Michel?' Christine asked.

'She knows some rudimentary signs.'

'That means you can talk to her!' Marion exclaimed.

'Not exactly,' Michel said. 'Those were just the signs we brothers use in our everyday life, like how to ask for bread, or find out where our shoes are. It's amazing, though. She must have spent some time in a convent; that's the only place she could have learned this.'

Christine thought back to the day she'd learned about Loyse's birth from the midwife who'd delivered her. Vaguely, she remembered something about Loyse's mother having sent the child away for a while, but she couldn't think where.

She asked Michel, 'Can you make her understand what we're here for?'

'She's obviously very intelligent. She's learned how to use her good mind to make up for her affliction. We should be able to communicate.'

'I've been able to do it,' Marion piped up. 'You're smarter than I am, so you should be able to do it, too.'

Michel wiggled his fingers at her. Then he turned to Loyse and made some hand motions. At first she didn't understand. But after a while it became obvious that she did.

'Does she know where we're taking her?' Christine asked.

'She knows we're taking her away. I've been able to make her understand that it's going to be all right. She doesn't know we're taking her to your house first, or about your mother. Perhaps it's just as well.'

'Can I stay here with the lions?' Klara asked.

'Not today,' Christine said. 'We'll come back soon, and Gilet will show you what to do.'

Klara looked disappointed, but she didn't object. Loyse indicated that she wanted to go back into the stockade. Klara went with her.

'Don't you want to go with them, Michel?' Marion asked.

Michel coughed. 'I think not.'

'Does Loyse know that Klara is going to help Gilet now?' Christine asked.

'I think she understands that the lions will be well treated when she's gone.'

Loyse and Klara emerged from the stockade. Loyse looked long-ingly back at the lions, who had followed her to the entrance, but she didn't try to go back. 'Good luck,' Gilet called after them as they went out into the orchard.

Now Christine had to consider how to deal with her mother. She looked at Loyse, her disheveled hair and the tattered rags that passed for clothes, and she was certain that as soon as Francesca saw her, she would explode in a fit of anger. On the other hand, she remembered that Francesca had brought Klara home without consulting her first.

Francesca wasn't there. 'She went to the market,' Georgette said, looking not at Christine but at Loyse. Christine expected her to recoil from the ragged stranger, but she didn't. Instead she said, 'I know who this is.'

'You've seen her before?' Christine asked.

'Sometimes I go to look at the king's lions. Many people do. Everyone thinks this girl is possessed, but I've never thought so. She seems to love the lions. Why have you brought her here?'

'She's going to stay with us for a while.'

'What will your mother say?'

Loyse was looking around the kitchen with awe. Marion had her arm around her, as though she expected she might try to run away, but Christine could see there was no likelihood of that. Loyse was entranced.

Just then the children ran in, followed by Goblin. Christine pushed them back into the hall. 'We have a guest,' she told them. 'You may have heard of her. The things you've heard are wrong.'

'Who is it?' they all cried at once.

'It's the lion-keeper's assistant. People say she's possessed, but it's not true.'

'But she never speaks. There's something wrong with her,' Thomas said.

'She's deaf. And since she's never heard anyone speak, she's never learned how. Now listen to me. Her name is Loyse, and she is our guest. You must be kind to her.'

'Is she going to live with us?' Jean asked. 'What will grand'maman say?'

'Loyse will stay with us for a little while, until she gets accustomed to living somewhere other than the lions' stockade. Then I'm going to take her to the queen.'

'The queen! What will she do with her?'

'The queen is kind to all sorts of people. Remember, I told you about the dwarf, the fool, the Spanish minstrel, the mute?'

'Can we go there too?' Thomas cried.

'Perhaps someday. Not now. First come into the kitchen and meet our guest.'

Klara stood protectively near Loyse, seemingly to ward off any attacks by the children. But they merely stood staring at the disheveled girl, until Christine spoke. 'This is Loyse. If you speak to her, she won't hear you, but you can make her welcome in other ways.'

Jean was the first to respond. He approached Loyse with a smile on his face and bowed slightly. Thomas followed and did the same thing, while Marie and Lisabetta curtsied. Even Goblin was subdued, although he sniffed the air. 'He smells the lions,' Thomas whispered to Jean.

Klara looked as though she were about to cry. *She thinks Loyse is hers, and she doesn't want to share her*, Christine mused. She said, 'I know she's your friend, Klara, but you can't have her all to yourself. Cheer up. You can go with us when we take her to the queen.'

'When?'

'After my mother gets home and makes her presentable.'

Marion laughed. 'What makes you think your mother is going to agree to do that?'

'Agree to what?' asked Francesca, who was standing in the doorway holding a large loaf of bread. She hadn't yet noticed Loyse because all the children were standing around her. Michel went to her. 'Don't be alarmed. We've brought Loyse, the lion-keeper's helper.'

'She *was* the lion-keeper's helper. Now she's going to be a companion for the queen,' said Marion.

Francesca seemed so stupefied that Christine put her arms around her to keep her from fainting.

'I know what you've heard about her, Mama. But she's not possessed. She doesn't speak because she's deaf.'

Michel made some mysterious signs to Loyse. The girl smiled at Francesca and held out her arms.

'I've made her understand that you are Christine's mother,' Michel said.

Francesca hesitated, and then she stepped up to Loyse and enfolded her in her arms. 'Poor little woman,' she said. She turned to Christine. 'But why is she here?'

'It's a long story. The important thing is that the queen wants to see her, and we have to make her presentable first.'

Francesca lowered herself onto a bench and fanned herself with the loaf of bread. 'And you expect me to take care of that?'

'Well, it's what you're good at.'

Francesca studied Loyse. 'I think a bath house would be best, but they wouldn't let her in. Go and get the tub, Georgette.'

Georgette dragged the big wooden tub into the middle of the room and went out to get water. While the water was heating over the kitchen fire, Francesca shooed everyone out except Georgette, Christine, and Marion. Loyse looked apprehensive when Klara left, but she didn't object when Francesca undressed her and helped her into the tub. The warm water seemed to soothe her.

'You see, she isn't a stranger to all of this,' Marion said. 'Her mother didn't treat her as badly as everyone thought.'

'This is probably the first bath she's had in a long time,' Francesca said, as she poured water over Loyse's hair and rubbed soap in. Loyse put her hands over her face to keep the soap out of her eyes and gave a soundless laugh of pleasure.

'I think the lion-keeper's wife took her to their house and gave her a bath once in a while,' Marion said. 'I know she brought her meals.'

Francesca and Marion helped Loyse out of the tub, and Georgette dried her hair. Klara peered timidly around the kitchen door. 'Can I come in?' she asked. She held up one of her dresses and announced, 'We're the same size.'

'So you are,' Christine said as she lifted the dress over Loyse's head. Then Francesca combed and braided her long auburn hair. There was a collective gasp of surprise: Loyse was beautiful.

'If we gave her a starched linen headdress, she could pass for one of the queen's ladies,' Christine said.

'Does she know she's going to the queen?' Klara asked.

'Not yet,' Christine said. 'But soon.'

'How soon?' Francesca wanted to know. 'If she stays here, where is she going to sleep? I've already got Klara in my room, *Cristina*, and you need your room for your work. We can't put the children out of their beds.'

'I hadn't thought of that,' Christine said.

Marie had crept into the room. She'd overheard the conversation, and she said, 'She's been sleeping with the lions, so she won't mind sleeping on the floor.'

'We could fix her a bed in front of the fire,' Georgette said.

'So we could,' Francesca said.

The other children came in. 'I'll help,' said Jean. 'Me, too,' said Thomas. 'And me,' chimed in Lisabetta.

Christine smiled at them all. 'It won't be for long. I'll be taking her to the queen soon.'

'Don't forget, you promised to take me, too,' Klara said.

THIRTY

Those who chatter incessantly are like mill clappers, never silent.

From a book of moral and practical advice
for a young wife, Paris, 1393

Marion left Christine's house musing about Klara. It had been a good idea to take her to see the king's lions, but things had gone too far; Klara thought she was going to stay with them forever. She decided it was time to try again to find the girl's missing husband.

But how? Her trip to Martin du Bois's house in La Courtille had yielded only the fact that Martin had borrowed clothes from one of the workers on his farm. That meant he could lose himself among all the hundreds of laborers on the streets of Paris. To make matters worse, she didn't even know what the man looked like, except for Klara's description of him as 'old.'

But Marion was never one to give up. *I'll ask the people around the water trough at the entrance to the Grand Pont*, she decided. Dressed in her crimson cloak, with a gold belt hidden beneath and the beads in her hair flashing in the sunlight, she hurried to the trough and started asking whether any old men in farmer's clothes had appeared recently.

'If the clothes are ragged, there are lots of people around here who look like that,' said a disheveled man with bandaged hands. All the other beggars looked down at their clothes and laughed.

'This man is very old,' Marion said. 'He probably has white hair and lots of wrinkles.'

'That's not much of a description,' said an old beggar who also had white hair and a lot of wrinkles.

'Has he done something wrong?' an old woman leaning on a crutch asked.

'Perhaps the sergeants from the Châtelet are after him,' suggested a thief with a patch over one eye. This led to much speculation about people who had recently been arrested, as well as about those who were on the run and the crimes they were said to have committed. Everyone seemed to know someone who was in the Châtelet. A beggar who wore dirty bandages over his eyes so he would appear to be blind said he had a friend who'd been taken there for nothing more than having fallen down drunk in the street. One of the thieves announced proudly that he'd just been released, and a fat prostitute with locks of black hair that looked like snakes chimed in to say she never worried about getting arrested because she had friends who could always get her out. But an old reprobate who rolled along with one leg attached to a little cart said he knew for a fact this was impossible. 'You'll die in there,' he announced, and this led to a great deal of talk about the miserable conditions in the dreaded prison.

A tall man in a shabby tunic and high, muddy boots stepped up to Marion and said, 'I want to talk to you.' He took her arm and led her away from the crowd, through the narrow streets around the

Châtelet to the church of Saint-Jacques-la-Boucherie. Against a wall of the church were many wooden booths where scribes worked. One of these booths was empty; the man led her into it and gently pushed her down onto a bench in front of a little desk.

'I don't mean to frighten you,' he said. 'But so much useless talk irritates me.'

'It would take more than you to frighten me,' Marion said. 'I need to find someone who's disappeared, and the only way to do that is to ask questions.'

'You weren't getting any helpful answers. It was a lot of useless prattle. In any case, you shouldn't go around asking about people you don't even know.'

Marion bristled. 'You have no right telling me what to do. Who are you, anyway?'

The man laughed. 'You're right. I shouldn't be telling you what to do. But I'm afraid you're going to get yourself into trouble. You and your friends, babbling about things you shouldn't be discussing. Why are you trying to find this man?'

'He suddenly disappeared, leaving his young wife. It's time he came back.'

'Why?'

'Because she's been taken in by the family of a friend of mine, and she's making their lives miserable.'

'Is she a very unpleasant young lady?'

'Not really. It's just that she needs to grow up.'

'Perhaps there is a good reason why her husband went away.'

Marion stood up and went to the entrance of the booth to see whether anyone was standing there listening. But she saw no one. She wondered whether she should worry about being alone with this strange man. Did he know she was a prostitute? Probably. But he was treating her with respect.

'What's your name?' the man asked.

'Marion.'

'Well, Marion, it seems to me this young lady is lucky to have a friend like you to watch over her until her husband gets back.'

Marion felt herself blushing. 'I do what I can,' she said. 'But the girl needs a husband to teach her how to behave. She doesn't know how to get along with anyone. In fact, she's made friends with the king's lions, and she seems to get along with them better than with people.'

The man started to laugh. 'Indeed! The king's lions! She must be quite an unusual young lady.'

'She's not so unusual. She's just unhappy and confused.'

'Why is that?'

'Her husband is much older than she is. The way she talks about him, he's probably at death's door.'

'Well, if that's all you know about this man, I don't see how you are going to find him.'

'You're probably right.'

The man got up from the bench, gave Marion a little bow, and walked away. Marion sat for a moment, thinking, and then she jumped up and ran out of the booth.

'Come back,' she cried. 'I know who you are!'

Martin du Bois didn't turn around. He just kept walking and was quickly swallowed up in the crowd of people on the rue Saint-Jacques-la-Boucherie.

THIRTY-ONE

Many young and beautiful women have loved their old, ugly husbands.

Christine de Pizan,
Le Livre de la Cité des Dames, 1404–1405

Christine knew that if Alips's suspicions about the Duchess of Burgundy were correct, they would need help. So the day after she brought Loyse home, she went to talk to the Duchess of Berry.

She found the duke and his wife in the same room at the Hôtel de Nesle as before, but this time in the company of a large man with a prominent nose and long grey hair. The duke sat at his desk, and the man stood before him, carefully placing on the desk, one by one, a series of playing cards. The Duke bent over them, engrossed. The duchess sat on a window seat on the other side of the room, her blond hair tinted red, green, and blue by the rays of sun passing through the stained glass behind her. She motioned to Christine, indicating that she should come to her. As Christine passed the duke and his visitor, she paused to look at the playing cards. They were like the ones she'd seen at the palace, except that instead of pictures of war implements, these had castles.

'The duke heard about some playing cards the queen ordered for the king, and he had to have some for himself,' the duchess said. She was holding the little dog, and she threw a small ball for it to chase. The dog bounced off her lap and ran after it, bumping against the legs of the duke's guest. The man laughed. His long grey hair fell over his face as he picked up the ball and threw it across the room.

'That's the man who painted the cards,' the duchess said. 'He was good enough to deliver them to the duke himself.'

'I saw the queen's cards,' Christine said. 'Did you know they have disappeared?'

'I've heard. I'm sure they will be found.' The dog brought her the ball, and she lifted him onto her lap and fondled his ears. 'Did you want to talk to the duke? If so, you may have a long wait; he needs time to admire his new treasures.'

'Actually, it's you I came to see.'

'I remember your last visit here. You were trying to find a missing husband. Have you had any success?'

'Unfortunately not.'

'Tell me more about this young woman. You said she is sixteen.'

'She was fifteen when she married. Her husband is much older, and she seems to resent that,' Christine said cautiously, remembering the duchess had been only twelve when the Duke of Berry married her.

The duchess looked over at her husband and smiled. 'There are worse things in life than having a husband who is old.'

Old and not very attractive, Christine thought. Yet the duchess seemed genuinely fond of him. She pushed these thoughts away and said, 'Actually, I came because I want to talk to you about the conversation we had the other day concerning the fire at the palace. You told me you saw a lighted torch lying on the floor, and you thought it was meant for Yvain de Foix. Do you still think that?'

'I've since learned that the Viscount of Castelbon secured the inheritance left by the Count of Foix long before the fire. My husband has assured me there was no way the king would have transferred it to Yvain. So there would have been no need for the viscount to have tried to kill Yvain. But I know what I saw.'

'I didn't tell you everything when I was here before,' Christine said. 'The torch you saw lying on the floor was thrown from the musicians' balcony. It was intended for the king, not Yvain.'

'Are you sure?'

'Yes. I can't tell you how I know, but I'm sure. Whoever threw it meant for the king to go up in flames. The queen thinks so, too. She has asked me to find out who it was.'

'Are you here because you think I can help?'

'Yes. You know your way about the court even better than the queen, who still considers herself a stranger there.'

'I can't imagine that anyone I know would want to kill the king.'

'Many people believe someone has put a spell on him. Someone might take the next step and try to kill him.'

'But who? There are so many people around him. How could we ever determine which one it is?'

'That is true. But there are some who might gain more than others if the king were to die.'

The duchess looked discomfited. 'Surely you aren't thinking that one of the king's uncles climbed up onto the musicians' balcony and threw a lighted torch at him! Or ordered someone else to do it!'

Christine blanched and looked over at the duke, who was still studying his new playing cards.

The duchess smiled. 'I can assure you, my husband is not interested in gaining more power; all he wants is to be left alone with his beautiful manuscripts and jewels and castles.'

What an extraordinary young woman, Christine thought.

'And anyway,' the duchess continued, 'the king's uncles would have nothing to gain. The dauphin is next in line to be king.'

Christine started to say something, but the duchess interrupted her.

'As for the king's brother, I refuse to believe he had anything to do with the fire.'

'What about the Duchess of Burgundy?'

The duchess set the little dog on the floor, took Christine's hand, and said, 'I realize that since the queen has asked you to do this, you must pursue it, no matter where it takes you. But I really can't entertain the thought that any members of the court would try to kill the king. It doesn't make sense. It's too dangerous.'

'The queen feels it's someone very close to her. It could be some unimportant person who held a grudge or acted out of spite. But it could also be someone of much higher status.'

The duchess thought for a moment, and then she said, 'I, too, want to know who threw the lighted torch. I know now that it was not meant for Yvain, but it killed him, nevertheless, and I want the person who did it brought to justice. I will talk to my husband discreetly about this and see if I can find out anything.'

The white dog bounded over to the duke's visitor, who picked him up and startled everyone by exclaiming in a loud voice, 'The Duke of Orléans's wife has a dog that looks just like this little fellow!'

The Duchess of Berry laughed and called out to the man, 'Now my husband won't rest until he sees that dog. He thinks there are no other dogs in the world that can compare with his.'

'Perhaps he should compare playing cards, too,' the man said, looking at the duke, who was too engrossed in studying the pictures on his new playthings to pay attention to the conversation. The duke looked up, however, when the man said, 'The Duchess of Orléans wants a set of playing cards like yours. Only, on hers, she wants a picture of a viper devouring a human.' He laughed, and the booming sound reverberated around the room. 'That's the Visconti coat of arms, fitting for the "vipers of Milan."'

'I have never understood how Valentina could come from such a family,' Christine said to the duchess.

The duchess laughed. 'The Duchess of Burgundy says she's a sorceress.'

The duke was engrossed in his cards again, and the illuminator stepped closer to Christine and the duchess and said, 'Just like her father, the murderous Lord of Milan! Actually, I've heard *he's* the one who's bewitching the king.'

'How could he do that?' Christine asked.

'Easy. He makes a wax figure of the king and sticks pins into it.' He laughed and went back to the duke.

'What nonsense,' Christine said.

'I think so, too,' the duchess said. 'But when I was at the palace the other day, I heard the Duchess of Burgundy telling people a malicious story about Valentina. She said she has a magic mirror, and when she looks into it, the spirits of the dead appear and reveal terrible secrets, like how to make the most deadly poisons. The duchess says she will use these poisons to kill the king.'

The illuminator was beside them again. 'There's a rumor, you know, that on the day Valentina left Italy, her father's parting words were, "The next time I see you, you'll be the Queen of France."'

Christine wondered. The rumors were absurd, but what if there really was something to them? Valentina was slender and lithe, and, in the right clothes, could pass for a boy. Like Symonne du Mesnil, she would have had no trouble climbing up to the musicians' balcony.

She turned to the duchess and asked, 'Was Valentina with you on the dais the night of the marriage ball?'

'I didn't see her there,' the duchess replied.

THIRTY-TWO

Because I have tender and loving compassion for you, who were torn away from your relations and the country where you were born and who for a long time have had neither father nor mother nor any other of your relatives near you to whom you could turn for advice and help in your private needs, except for myself alone, I have many times imagined that I might myself come across some easy general course of study . . . and it seems to me that this can be accomplished by a general instruction that I will write for you.

From a book of moral and practical advice
for a young wife, Paris, 1393

Christine left the Hôtel de Nesle deep in thought. She walked slowly toward home, ignoring the cries of the vendors on the Grand Pont and the pleas of the beggars around the water trough near the Châtelet. All through the streets the noises of the city rang in her ears, and at the place de Grève they became unbearable. Two wine criers vied for attention, their faces red from exertion as they tried to out-shout each other. Crowds of laborers hoping to find work proclaimed their individual merits. A group of laughing, whooping boys pushed their way through the crowd, bumping into women out doing their marketing and overturning their baskets. Onions and cabbages rolled on the ground, and the air rang with curses as the women chased after them. Stray dogs ran around barking. Christine put her hands over her ears and hurried up the rue Saint-Antoine to her quiet street.

Things were not quiet at her house. As soon as she got there, she was met by Francesca, who hurried out of the kitchen and announced, 'Your friend Marion was here. She was very excited about something, but she would not tell me what it was.'

'Did she say when she'd be back?'

'No. She just rushed off.' Francesca ran back into the kitchen, where things were in an uproar. Georgette had let a pot hang too close to the logs in the fireplace, and the soup had started to burn. In her haste to remove the pot, she'd spilled soup onto the floor. Marie was trying to mop it up, but Goblin, smelling something good to eat, kept getting in the way.

'Set the table, Klara,' Georgette ordered.

'Bet she can't do it,' Thomas cried. Klara went to get some spoons, but instead of carrying them to the table, she waved them at the boy, and dropped them.

'You'd better read that book your husband wrote,' Thomas taunted. 'Maybe you'll learn how to do things right.'

'I don't need his instructions. You made me drop them, *enfant pourri.*'

Jean laughed, picked up the spoons, and threw them onto the table. Klara looked as though she were about to cry.

Francesca stamped her foot and ordered everyone to be quiet.

Loyse, her hair arranged in long braids into which Francesca had woven bright red and blue ribbons, sat before the fire, watching everything. She didn't seem to mind that she couldn't hear the conversation. Francesca went to her, smoothed her forehead, and said to Christine, 'She wasn't brought up to live in a lions' den. At some point in her life, she must have lived in a proper household where she was treated with respect.'

'She's actually more at home here than Klara, who was brought up in a well-to-do man's home,' Christine said. She looked at Klara and added, 'A man who had the foresight to write a book of instructions for her, so she would know how to care for him and for his household.'

Goblin bounded over to Loyse, who picked him up and hugged

him. Klara made no move to take the dog away. 'Perhaps she's learned something about sharing, at least,' Christine said.

'Perhaps,' Francesca said. Then she drew Christine out into the hall, away from the children. 'You haven't told me what is going on at the palace. I suspect that visit from Marion has something to do with it.'

'There is nothing for you to concern yourself with, Mama.'

Francesca threw up her hands. 'How many times have I told you, you should not be involved in what goes on at the palace. There is evil there. The king's mind is gone. More terrible things are sure to happen.'

That's true, if we don't find out who is trying to kill him, Christine thought.

'The king's uncles and his brother will all murder each other, and then where will we be?' Francesca continued.

'You're talking about things you know nothing about.'

'I know well enough you are putting yourself, and all of us, in danger. I do not think we are safe even in this house. Do you know someone has been prowling around outside, hiding in the shadows?'

'What are you saying? How do you know this?'

'We have all seen him, or felt his presence, at least. We are frightened.'

'Why didn't you tell me before? Do you have any idea who it is?'

'No. We have always lived quietly here, until you started involving yourself in affairs of the court.'

'You must tell me the next time you see this prowler!'

'I do not see him. I just know he is there.'

Christine felt chilled. She hadn't considered the possibility that she was putting her family in danger. She gave her mother a hug and went into the kitchen.

The children sat at the table waiting for supper. 'What were you two talking about?' Jean wanted to know.

'Your grandmother tells me you think someone is prowling around the house.'

'He goes into the shadows when we come out,' Marie said. 'We've never actually seen him.'

'I'm not afraid,' Thomas said.

'I am,' said Lisabetta, and she started to cry.

Loyse, who couldn't understand what they were talking about, looked alarmed. Klara just stared at the floor.

Georgette stood in the doorway. 'I've told my mother about this prowler, and she says I shouldn't work here anymore.'

'Oh, Georgette,' Francesca cried. 'I am sure this has nothing to do with you.'

Christine could see that her mother, in spite of all her criticisms of the girl, was very upset. Georgette was slovenly and saucy, but she was the only servant they could afford. And she was not all that bad. Lately, she'd even improved. She was certainly a help with Klara, more patient with her than the rest of them.

'We need you here, Georgette. Don't worry. We'll find out who this prowler is and send him away. As my mother says, it has nothing to do with you.'

At the sudden reassurances from Christine, who had never been particularly sympathetic to her, Georgette started to cry. That set off the rest of them: Jean, struggling to hold back tears and looking embarrassed, Marie and Lisabetta sniffling, and Thomas, for once not making a smart remark, bawling loudly.

Christine realized how little attention she'd been paying to them and their fears. She felt guilty. And very tired.

THIRTY-THREE

The wise princess, like all wise women who value their honor, wants everyone to know that she loves her husband.

Christine de Pizan,
Le Livre des Trois Vertus, 1405

As Christine walked to the palace the next morning, she hoped to buy a meat pasty or a sweet wafer from one of the vendors on the rue Saint-Antoine. But she heard thunder and saw all the vendors scurrying away, eager to avoid the rain. The storm rose quickly. Women out doing their marketing took off their aprons, held them over their heads, and hurried toward home, darting around merchants who were busy gathering up the wares they displayed in front of their shops. A group of beguines strode by and turned down the rue de l'Ave-Maria, their shapeless habits already soggy. Two very wet stray dogs ran after them.

She held the pouch with her writing supplies under her cloak and dashed to the Hôtel Saint-Pol. The rain poured down as she approached the queen's residence.

'Go inside quickly,' Simon said.

Lightning flashed, and Renaut, who'd been trying to catch raindrops with his tongue, laughed and clapped his hands. 'The queen won't like this. She's afraid of storms.' His tawny hair hung in wet ringlets around his face.

Christine made her way to the queen's apartments, worrying that her visit might come to nothing because she'd heard that the queen, who was terrified of thunderstorms, often refused to see anyone until they were over.

Alips was waiting for her. 'I knew you would come.'

'Will she see me?' Christine asked.

'She will. She's fine at the moment. I put an acorn on the window-sill, to prevent the lightning from striking us.'

Christine had to laugh. 'She believes in that old superstition?'

'She learned it from her mother. You probably learned such things from your mother, too.'

Indeed I did, Christine thought.

The queen was sitting calmly on her day bed. 'There is no need to fear the storm,' she said. She and Alips smiled at each other.

Christine looked around, wondering why no one had closed the shutters over the windows. Collette the mute sat watching the flashes of lightning, unaware of the claps of thunder that resounded throughout the queen's chambers. The Saracen girl tried to coax the queen's squirrel out from behind a cushion where it was hiding, while Gracieuse played her lute and sang a song in French about ships in a storm. Jeannine the fool, whose mother was not there that day, held the queen's monkey and covered his ears with her hands.

Guillaume the fool danced over to Christine, bowed to her, took off his cap, and said, 'Cut off the tip of your calf's right ear and throw it into the wind.'

Christine laughed. 'I know that old proverb.'

'That's good,' the fool said. 'Your calf will grow up to be a strong bull.'

'She doesn't have any calves,' Alips said.

'She should bless the sun, the moon, and the stars, and she'll get one. Then she should bless them again, and she'll get another.' He danced away, his bald head glistening in the lightning flashes.

'Where are your ladies, *Madame*?' Christine asked the queen.

'The Duchess of Burgundy sent them away.'

Just then a loud clap of thunder rattled the windows and shook the floor. The queen's greyhound, which had been lying quietly beside the bed, jumped up and began to howl. The queen buried her face in her hands. *Alips's attempts to calm her fears go only so far*, Christine thought.

Guillaume came back, bringing Jeannine, who put the monkey on the floor, and sat down on the bed next to the queen. Guillaume announced, 'Swans' eggs will hatch now.'

'That's one I haven't heard before,' Christine said. 'What does it mean?'

'Thunder and lightning are supposed to crack the shells of swans' eggs,' Alips said.

Guillaume clapped his hands. The monkey jumped up and climbed onto the bed with Jeannine.

Another clap of thunder rocked the room. The queen cried, 'Thunder in February means someone is going to die!'

Christine said, as she always did when her mother repeated this old superstition, 'No one is going to die. That is a foolish belief.'

'The king is safe,' Alips said. 'I just saw him with the Duke of Orléans in the great gallery.'

Guillaume did a few somersaults, but the queen did not look reassured. Then the fool said, 'Listen. There is music in the rain.' He ran to the window where the deaf girl sat and put his ear against the glass. 'It sings on the leaves. It dances on the roofs.' He went to Gracieuse and pulled her over to the queen. The minstrel sat on one of the big cushions and sang about raindrops that come on a gentle west wind, bringing violets and primroses and all the flowers of spring. Guillaume smiled and nodded. Jeannine rocked the monkey in her arms.

The queen tried to smile, but she couldn't conceal her unease about the king. It was obvious that Charles meant more to her than anything else in the world, and she was not afraid to let everyone know it. *To what lengths would she go to keep him safe?* Christine wondered. *Should a wife give up everything for her husband?* Her mother certainly thought so, as did Martin du Bois, who'd written a book exhorting his wife to obey and serve her husband, no matter what. She felt sympathy for Klara, who chaffed under these commands.

Christine became aware that the queen was looking at her. 'What are you thinking about?' Isabeau asked.

'Only the thunder,' Christine lied. 'Why do you fear it so?'

'Something my mother told me.' Isabeau sat up straight on the bed. 'I must rid myself of these superstitions.'

That she should, Christine thought. *Superstitions will not serve her well.*

The queen was making an effort to control herself. She waved Gracieuse and the fools away and said to Christine, 'I am sure you will find the person who casts a shadow over me and threatens the king.'

'I will continue to do what I can,' Christine said, and she went into the room where she did her copying. Alips followed her. 'She's counting on you. There is little she can do by herself. Especially with the Duchess of Burgundy watching her so closely.'

As she said this, the duchess stalked in and stood over the queen with her hands on her hips. Before she could say anything, Isabeau called out, 'Come back here, Guillaume.' The fool pranced over and asked the duchess, 'Shall I speak now?' The duchess stamped her foot and said, 'I *will* have you hanged.'

'No, you will not,' Isabeau cried. 'You can dismiss my ladies, but you will not harm my fool!'

The duchess sneered at Guillaume and left the room.

Catherine de Villiers came in with the manuscript and laid it on Christine's desk. 'The queen is upset,' she said. 'I will read to her. That will calm her.'

'I hope it's not the book with the mean dwarf,' Alips said.

Catherine glared at her. 'If you don't like it, you don't have to listen.'

'I listen to everything,' Alips said.

THIRTY-FOUR

King Charles had a valet de chambre *of whom he was very fond because of his good character. This valet surpassed everyone, and he read aloud better than all the others, with the appropriate intonations. The man, Gilles Malet, chevalier and* maître d'hôtel, *was very intelligent, wise, and respected, and he was enriched by the king. One day one of Gilles Malet's sons was holding a knife while he was running, and he fell on the knife and died. In spite of his great grief, the father came to the king and read to him at length as usual, with the customary countenance and expression. When the king, who was attentive to everything, learned later about the child's death, he esteemed this man even more and said, 'If he did not have such a strong character, he would not have been able to conceal his mourning so well.'*

Christine de Pizan, *Livre des faits et bonnes moeurs du sage roi Charles V,* 1404

C hristine was too distracted to concentrate. After she'd made a mistake in her copying, and spent a long time scraping away the error, she decided it was time to leave.

The thunderstorm had abated, and she walked slowly away from the palace, sloshing through puddles, her head down, not looking where she was going, so lost in thought that instead of turning down the street that led to her house she continued down the rue Saint-Antoine. When she realized where she was, she decided that since she was halfway there, she'd continue on to the royal library at the Louvre and talk to the librarian, her friend, Gilles Malet. He might be able to tell her something about Martin du Bois since he had known the old Duchess of Orléans and had been involved in her search for someone to copy the housekeeping manual.

Gilles, who'd been librarian for the king's father and now served

Charles the Sixth, knew Henri Le Picart, too, because in addition to all his other accomplishments, Henri was a scribe, and he often did his work at the library. The duchess had first asked Henri to make the copy of Martin du Bois's manuscript, but Henri had said he wasn't interested in anything having to do with housework and morals. He and Gilles had then advised the duchess to give the work to Christine.

She'd had difficulties with Gilles lately. He held conventional ideas about women, and when she'd said she intended to help Alix de Clairy, he'd tried to stop her. In his way of thinking, no woman would ever get involved with an accused murderess. He'd become especially incensed when she'd announced that she would go into the prison and visit Alix. She hoped he wouldn't get angry now, when she told him that she was looking into the mysterious disappearance of Martin du Bois.

She walked down the rue Saint-Germain-l'Auxerrois, cringing as she passed the Châtelet, and came to the Louvre, the palace where the library was housed in a tower. She crossed a moat, went up a spiral staircase, and found Gilles, a tall, lean man with bushy eyebrows, pacing up and down with a stack of books in his arms. When he saw her, he threw the books down on his desk and sat down behind them, as if to hide.

Christine couldn't resist smiling; Gilles was embarrassed.

'I understand why you're surprised to see me, Gilles.'

'I didn't think you would be coming here any time soon, after the way I treated you a few weeks ago. I have to admit, I was wrong about Alix de Clairy.'

'Do you still think I shouldn't have pursued what I knew was right, just because I'm a woman?'

Gilles hesitated, then frowned. 'It isn't proper for a woman to be involved in such things. To think that you went into the prison! And then you almost lost your life because you decided to go after the murderess yourself! No, Christine, I didn't think it was seemly at the time, and I never will.'

She resisted the temptation to lash out at her friend and said calmly, 'I want to discuss something else with you, Gilles.'

Gilles peered over the books and wiggled his bushy eyebrows at her.

'There's no need to be wary. I'm simply trying to find out why someone I think you know, Martin du Bois, has disappeared, and whether you know where he has gone.'

'I don't know Martin very well, but I am aware that he has disappeared. I have no idea where he is. Why do you ask?'

'My mother was worried about his wife, so she brought her home to stay with us.'

'How like your mother. I've always found her to be a sympathetic soul.'

She looked around the room, remembering the days when her father had brought her there to look at the books. Now that the king was ill and paid little attention to the library, his uncles had helped themselves to the finer volumes, and there were many empty spaces on the shelves. She knew that Gilles was distraught about this, and about the fact that everything was falling into disrepair. She could see for herself the cracks in the painted floor tiles and the holes in the ceiling where pieces of inlaid wood had fallen away. She was almost as distressed about this as Gilles, because the library seemed like a second home to her.

She'd not been listening to Gilles, who was still talking about her mother. 'You should listen to her,' he was saying. 'She knows that women have a place, and that is with the housework.'

'You knew my father, Gilles, and you know he didn't agree with my mother about that. He wanted me to learn more than how to cook and sew. He felt that a woman could learn just as well as a man, and he wanted me to have as good an education as my brothers. Étienne thought so, too.'

Gilles slammed his hand down onto his desk. 'Learning is one thing, Christine. Chasing after murderers is another. Your father brought you here to teach you about books, not criminals.'

Christine decided it was time to leave. Gilles didn't know where Martin du Bois was, and he was making her angry. But as she turned to go, she noticed that one of the books on Gilles's desk was an illuminated *Life of Saint Catherine*. She picked it up and said, 'I'm copying a *Life of Saint Catherine* for the queen. I hope that when the illuminators get through with it, it will be just as beautiful as this.'

Gilles went to a shelf, took down another book, and handed it to Christine, 'A woman helped illuminate this one. She was such an accomplished artist that she was able to assist her father in his work. That's the kind of thing with which you should be concerning yourself.'

Christine put the book down on the desk, started for the door, and was nearly swept off her feet by a large man with long grey hair who burst into the room calling loudly for Gilles. She recognized him as the illuminator she'd seen at the Hôtel de Nesle the day before, delivering a set of playing cards to the Duke of Berry. He wore a big black cloak, and when he threw it open, it nearly swept the books off Gilles's desk. Gilles ran over and put out his hands as if to stop the man from going farther into the room.

'Wait, Jacquemin,' he said. 'I'm glad to see you, but books are delicate.'

The man laughed. 'I know that. Let me see the one on top of the pile. It looks as though it has a lot of gold.'

'It does,' Gilles said as he handed him the book. 'You should know. You did the gilding.'

Gilles turned to Christine. 'This is Jacquemin. He is the one who will add the illuminations to the *Life of Saint Catherine* you are copying for the queen.'

Christine looked at the big man and wondered how he could do such delicate work. She was reassured when she saw him put the book gently back on the desk.

Gilles suddenly became animated. He said, 'Christine is just the person you are looking for, Jacquemin. She's a scribe.' He went to a shelf and took down a small volume. 'You wanted a copy of this, and she can do it for you.'

Jacquemin took the book from Gilles and handed it to Christine. 'I need this for my work. It's a book of instructions for manuscript painters. I'd be grateful if you would take it home and copy it for me.'

Christine looked through the book quickly and saw that it contained detailed recipes for mixing various kinds of paints, instructions for preparing parchment, and other things of interest to manuscript illuminators. Gilles was looking at her intently, to get her reaction. In truth, she was delighted to have the work, but she didn't want him to know. She didn't want him to think she was willing to stay at home and concentrate on activities he thought were safe for women.

'I will compensate you well,' Jacquemin said. 'When you have finished, bring it to me at my shop on the rue des Rosiers; anyone there can tell you where it is.'

Christine nodded. Gilles was smiling and rubbing his hands together. *Let him think what he likes*, she said to herself. She put the book in a small sack she always carried in case she needed to buy something for her mother at the market, left the library, went quickly down the spiral staircase, crossed the moat, and stepped into the street, where she nearly collided with a man in a torn brown jerkin. He turned away before she could reprimand him for not watching where he was going.

As she walked up the street, she couldn't help feeling that the man was following her. She arrived at the water trough at the entrance to the Grand Pont and was trying to escape from the beggars who approached her with outstretched hands when she thought she saw him again. She hurried to the church of Saint-Jacques-la-Boucherie, darted in, sank down onto a bench at the back of the empty nave, and looked around the church, breathing deeply.

The sun had come out, and light streamed in through the colored glass windows, touching the statues adorning the pillars. They seemed to be watching her: Saint Catherine of Alexandria holding a spiked wheel, Saint Dorothy carrying a basket of roses, Saint Barbara clutching the tower in which she'd been imprisoned by her father. She winced when she looked at a figure holding pair of pincers with a tooth in them. Saint Apollonia had been tortured by having all her teeth pulled out, and this was the saint to whom Francesca prayed whenever she had a toothache. Saint Mary of Egypt, a reformed prostitute with long hair covering her naked body, was smiling; she was pleased because it seemed that Christine had finally persuaded Marion to change her profession.

Someone slid onto the bench next to her. The man in the torn brown jerkin and muddy boots said, 'You've been looking for me. Here I am. I'm Martin du Bois.'

THIRTY-FIVE

I've been to Flanders twice in the winter and twice in the summer, first when the king defeated the Flemish at Roosebeke . . . I have lots of complaints about that country. On the road I was covered with a mantle of disgusting mud. My horse and I sank into it up to our necks, and we were there for a long time, with all my baggage. When we came out of it, we were black as ashes.

Eustache Deschamps (c. 1340–1404), *Ballade 17*

Christine stared at the man. She'd pictured Klara's husband as old and decrepit, but Martin du Bois, though certainly past middle age, was far from infirm. He was a large, robust man with a full head of dark-brown hair that showed only a trace of white, and a weathered but still handsome face. Not a man to be scorned by his wife because he was too old, he seemed more virile than many younger men she knew.

She found her voice. 'If you've known I've been looking for you, why have you waited to come to me?'

'I need your help. I've learned you are someone I can trust.'

Christine thought it should be the other way around. Could *she* trust *him*? After all, he'd disappeared the night of the fire at the palace, and he seemed to have known the king's life was in danger. He'd left his young wife without a word, and he'd done nothing to reassure the young woman that he was still alive.

'We have a lot to talk about, Martin du Bois,' she said.

He stood up and strode up the nave of the church, peered into each of the chapels, and walked around every column. When he had assured himself that no one was hiding in the shadows, he came back and sat on the bench again.

Christine asked, 'Do you know your wife is at my house?'

'I do.'

Christine couldn't help thinking of Henri Le Picart. Had Martin been talking to him? She was exasperated with Henri; the irritating little man always left her guessing.

'Klara doesn't tell us much about you, but we know you brought her and her brother back from Courtrai.'

'I was there with the Duke of Berry.'

'Did you take part in the sack?'

'No. But I saw everything.'

Christine shuddered, remembering the reports she'd heard of the massacre. 'What justification was there for the slaughter of all those innocent people?'

'There's no way to justify it. But I can understand how it happened. It was winter, there were fierce winds, blinding rains, bitter cold. When our horses weren't sliding around on the ice, they were mired in mud, often up to their necks. After the victory at Roosebeke, the soldiers were so wretched that by the time they reached Courtrai, their lust for revenge against the Flemish was out of control.'

'And so they committed unspeakable acts of brutality!'

'I know. I didn't take part in it. I was just one of the duke's secretaries.'

'How did you find Klara and Willem?'

'I saw them weeping and calling for their parents. I just swept them up and carried them away.'

'Did you give any thought to what you would do with them when you got back to Paris?'

'I thought only of caring for two children who'd lost their parents. I was married long ago, when I was young. My wife died in childbirth, and I'd lived by myself for many years. It pleased me to think I would no longer be alone.'

He shifted uneasily on the bench and sat for a moment with his head bowed. When he looked up, he had tears in his eyes.

'It didn't work out well; Willem hated me, and all the French, for what was done to his parents. And now Klara seems to resent me, too. I discovered she has some cousins here in France, and I thought I should take her to live with them. But after I met them, I decided they were not the kind of people who would have a good influence on her. And heaven knows, she needs some good influences. I've done everything I could to bring her up properly, even teaching her to read and write. But as she's grown older, she's become more difficult. I thought marriage would help, but it hasn't.'

Christine said, 'I talked to your beguine. She didn't seem sorry to be away from Klara.'

Martin inhaled deeply. 'I thought Agnes would be good for Klara. She'd heard I was raising two children on my own, and she came to my house and asked me to hire her so she could help.'

'I went to see her, to find out whether she knew where you had gone. She was very secretive about herself.'

'I don't know much about her, either. She may have come from the north; she spoke Flemish with Willem. I had hoped she would set a good example for Klara, but Klara never liked her. After Willem ran away, things got worse.'

'Do you know where he is?'

He got up from the bench, went to the door of the church, and looked out. Then he came back and sat next to Christine again. 'Willem means to kill me,' he said in a low voice.

A cloud passed over the sun, and the church grew dark. Christine shivered. 'How do you know this?'

'He left signs.' He shifted on the bench. 'The soldiers leaving Courtrai took the golden spurs the Flemish had hung in their church. Willem knew I had two of those spurs, and when he ran away a few years ago, he took them with him.'

'One of these spurs was found at the palace, after the fire.'

'I know. That was one sign.'

Christine's head was reeling. 'The fire was started by someone who threw a lighted torch from the musicians' balcony. Are you telling me it was Willem?'

'Exactly. But how did you know the torch came from the balcony?'

'A friend of mine saw someone throw it, though she doesn't know who it was.'

'It was Willem. He left a second spur, too.'

'When my mother and I took Klara to your house to get some of her clothes, we saw one in a coffer with her jewelry. Was that it?'

'Yes. Willem put it there. He knew I'd find it because I like to leave gifts for Klara in the coffer so she'll be surprised when she opens it. And I did find it, when I left a ring for her, on the night of the fire. The golden spurs are his way of letting me know he's still planning to kill me. And the king.'

'Does Klara know all this? Does she know where Willem is?'

'I have no idea what Klara knows. But she's younger than Willem and doesn't have as much hatred in her heart as he does.'

'I gather you have been aware for some time that the king's life is in danger. Klara said she heard you mutter something about the king the night you disappeared.'

'I didn't think Klara ever paid any attention to what I say.'

'Is that why you wrote a book of instructions for her?'

'How do you know about that?'

'You lent it to the Duchess of Orléans, and she gave me the job of making a copy for the queen's ladies.'

'I didn't know that was what she intended to do with it.'

'That's one of the reasons I've been looking for you; I want to return it to you. Also, I'd like to return your wife; she's causing chaos in my house.'

'Klara can be difficult.'

'And you thought a book of instructions would be helpful. Unfortunately, Klara doesn't seem very interested in what you wrote for her.'

'I know.' Martin shook his head sadly. 'Perhaps I am too old and set in my ways. I tend to go on about the importance of observing all the rules.'

'There certainly are a lot of rules in your manuscript. What makes you think a young woman would have the patience for all that?'

'There is no reason why Klara can't take a little time to read what I wrote for her!'

Christine could understand now why Klara would resent this man. She herself might sympathize with him, but young Klara would merely see him as a stern father figure. As for Willem, he wasn't a boy who would ever stop resenting a man who'd been with the army that slaughtered his parents and destroyed his city. She said, 'Are you sure Willem is the one who's trying to kill the king?'

'I'm absolutely sure. That's why I've come to you, to tell you he's the person you're looking for. You have to find him.'

'What does he look like?'

'Willem is only eighteen, but he looks much older. When I first saw him, he was a fine-looking little boy, but after I brought him to Paris, he changed. His hair turned white, he stooped, and his face became lined with signs of anger and hate. Sometimes when I looked at him, I'd think I was looking at an old man. The only thing that remains of his youth are his eyes, which are blue and as cold as ice.'

Martin took a deep breath. 'Willem is not in his right mind. He has already tried to kill me several times.'

'What did he do?'

'The first time, he told me it would be fun to have a mock duel. Only for him, it wasn't play. He stabbed me and I nearly bled to death. I was fool enough to think it was an accident. But then he tried to poison me. He took some of the wolfsbane I use to kill mice and put it in my food. He wasn't very careful about it; I could tell something was wrong. Then he set fire to my study while I was working there. I'd fallen asleep at my desk, and he hoped the fire would get to me before I woke up. Fortunately, I wasn't fully asleep, and I was able to put out the flames before they could do much damage.'

'My mother and I took Klara to your house to get some of her clothes. I saw blood stains on the floor of your study. And the charred floor.'

'Then you know how dangerous the boy is, and why I left. Klara is safer without me around. He could have burned the house down, with her in it. I didn't tell her I was going because it would have frightened her.'

'Where do you think he is?'

'At the palace. I'm sure he's disguised himself; he was always clever at doing that. The golden spurs are his way of letting me know he's still planning to kill the king. And me.'

'Does Henri Le Picart know all this?'

'Henri knows everything.' He smiled. 'He's told me all about you.'

'I thought so.' Christine was full of rage at Henri. 'If he knows so much, why isn't he helping us find Willem?'

'He is helping. You just don't understand his methods.'

THIRTY-SIX

To make a green color for writing, mix good vinegar with sour honey. Put the mixture in a vessel, and set the vessel in very warm dung. Leave it there for twelve days, and it will make a good green.

Jehan le Begue, *Experimenta de Coloribus*, 1431

When Christine got home, she avoided her mother, dashed up the stairs to her room, sat at her desk, and tried to regain her composure.

Martin du Bois had finally revealed himself, but there was no way she could return Klara to a man who was hiding to save his life. He hadn't even told her where she could find him again. And the one person who could help her, Henri Le Picart, seemed to have abandoned her.

The situation was becoming increasingly disquieting. Not only did she have to fear danger at the court, now she had to worry about what Klara might do. Did the girl know where her brother was? Was she somehow in contact with him? She thought of the prowler her mother and the children sensed near their house. Was her family in danger? She went back downstairs, determined to confront the girl. But she wasn't there.

'Where's Klara?' she asked her mother.

'I let Georgette take her and Loyse to see the lions.'

'Do you think that's wise?'

'I do not see any harm in it. Klara has been begging to be allowed to go and help the lion-keeper. She'll be all right, especially since Loyse is with her.'

Christine went back to her room and sat at her desk. After a while, she picked up the book of instructions for painters that Gilles Malet's friend Jacquemin had given her to copy. She leafed through it and slowly became engrossed. She'd always wondered how manuscript illuminators achieved their vibrant colors, and here was a book that told them what to do. When Jean appeared at the door, she beckoned for him to come over and look at the book with her. Soon he, too, was lost in the intricate recipes. Some of the colors were made from everyday substances such as rue, parsley, egg yolk, ground-up stones, even urine and dung, which made Jean laugh. Some recipes were outlandish, such as the one stating that if you put bulls' brains in a vase and left them there for three weeks, they would turn into gold worms that could be used for gilding. 'Don't believe that one,' she told her son.

They studied recipes that used mysterious chemical substances with strange names to achieve lustrous colors. Jean was fascinated with gold, a color that could be made with real gold, or with an imitation gold obtained from a poisonous stone. 'That sounds dangerous,' he exclaimed.

After a while, Christine's worries took over again. She looked at her son. 'I've been meaning to ask you, Jean, what have you observed about Klara?'

'I don't like her.'

'I know that. But don't you think she's become more agreeable lately? Especially since Loyse has been here?'

'Perhaps. But she's still awful.'

'Do you ever really talk to her?'

'Once I did. I asked her about her family in Courtrai, and she started to cry. Then I asked about her brother, and she became very quiet.'

'Do you think she knows where her brother is?'

'I don't know. She might.'

'Do you think it's her brother prowling around the house?'

Jean pushed a lock of his brown hair away from his eyes. 'Whoever it is hides in the shadows whenever we come out. We're all frightened, but we didn't want to tell you, you have so much on your mind.'

Christine reached over and hugged her son. 'I'm so sorry, Jean. You shouldn't have to feel like that. In the future, don't keep anything from me, especially anything that frightens you.'

'But what are you going to do about Klara? She can't stay here forever. She's making us unhappy.'

Christine thought of what she'd learned from Martin du Bois. Jean didn't know about Willem's threat to kill the king, and she wasn't about to tell him. But she knew she had to find Willem and stop his evil plan, for her family as well as for the queen. She needed Martin to be safe so he could go back to his house and she could return Klara to him and bring peace to her own family.

Marie and Thomas and Lisabetta appeared at the door. Christine motioned to them, and they gathered around her.

'I know you're frightened. I don't think you have to worry; the prowler is not here for you. But you mustn't go out unless I'm with you. Or your grandmother, or Georgette.'

'Georgette,' Thomas scoffed. 'What could she do to protect us?'

'Haven't you noticed how Georgette has changed? Your grand-mother and I have begun to rely on her.'

'It's true,' Marie said. 'She knows how to deal with Klara.'

'So maybe she'll get Klara to let us have Goblin back,' Thomas said.

Christine smiled at her younger son. But she couldn't let his comment pass. She said, 'Try to be more understanding of Klara. She's had a hard life.'

'I don't think her life is so hard,' Marie said. 'She has a husband who cares about her and wrote a book for her. He even got a beguine to help her. She doesn't have to do much work.'

'She doesn't have to do any work at all,' Thomas snickered.

'That's enough,' Christine said. 'This isn't helping us solve our problem.' *Fortunately*, she thought, *they don't know what the real problem is.*

They heard Francesca talking to someone at the door, and suddenly Marion ran up the stairs and into the room. She went to Christine and whispered in her ear, 'I've seen him.'

'Go downstairs and play,' Christine said to the children. 'Don't go outside unless your grandmother is with you.'

Marion waited impatiently until they'd gone. Then she said, 'I didn't know who he was, and he didn't tell me.'

'Who are you talking about?'

'Martin du Bois. He said I shouldn't go around asking about someone I don't even know. I didn't realize he was talking about himself. It wasn't until after he left that I guessed it was him.' She started to laugh. 'You won't believe it when I tell you what he looks like. Klara certainly had us fooled.'

'I know. I've seen him, too.'

'Where?'

'He followed me into the church of Saint-Jacques-la-Boucherie. He told *me* who he was. He said he needs my help.'

'Help doing what?'

'Help finding Klara's brother, Willem. He's the one who's trying to kill the king.'

'Is he sure?'

'Absolutely. He told me Willem hates the king for what he did in Courtrai. He hates Martin, too. That's why Martin went into hiding. He has to make sure he gets to Willem before Willem gets to him.'

'Do you think Klara's seen her brother?'

'I wouldn't be surprised. We have to suspect them both. But there's one good thing about this. The queen's dwarf is convinced the murderer is the Duchess of Burgundy. That's a dangerous thought. Now we don't have to worry about it.'

'I don't know about that. Perhaps the duchess is in league with the boy.'

Christine thought for a moment. 'That could be. Someone seems to be helping him. Otherwise, how would he have known there would be a masquerade and the king would be in a flammable costume? It was supposed to be a secret.'

'He could have heard about it from someone at the palace. Or from someone in the street, like I did. I heard Huguet de Guisay boasting about it.'

'So that's how you knew! I thought perhaps you had sources of information at the palace. Some of the guards, for example.'

'People always think things like that about prostitutes.'

Christine looked at Marion, took a deep breath, and asked, 'Do you still make your living as a prostitute, Marion?'

Marion laughed. 'Not really. But don't tell Brother Michel. It's so much fun to argue with him.'

Christine smiled. 'I'll miss hearing you two taunt each other.'

'But that isn't important now,' Marion said. 'We have to find Willem. Does Martin have any idea where he is?'

'No. And Martin will have to hide until the boy is found.'

'How can we possibly find him? He could be anywhere in Paris.'

'I don't think so. Martin thinks he's hiding somewhere at the palace. And the queen feels it. I'm sure she's right.'

THIRTY-SEVEN

*The Duke of Orléans is comely in every way; handsome, with
a pleasing and good-natured manner, magnificent in his rich
and beautiful attire.*

Christine de Pizan, *Livre des faits et
bonnes moeurs du sage roi Charles V*, 1404

Alips walked away from the queen's chambers, too preoccupied to look where she was going, until she came to a
passageway that overlooked the hall where the tragic ball
had been held and saw the Duke of Orléans wandering around in
the great space below. Curious, she went down some stairs into a
corridor next to the hall and peered cautiously around the door.
She could hear the duke muttering something to himself, and she
ventured closer.

'I don't see how it's possible,' she heard him say. His face was
covered with tears. She stepped a bit closer and stumbled. The duke
turned. At first he didn't see her, then he looked down.

'Who are you? What are you doing here?'

Alips fell to her knees. 'I don't mean any harm, *Monseigneur*.
Perhaps you have never seen me before. I'm the queen's dwarf,
Alips.'

'I've heard about you. People tell me you have strange powers.'

Alips was frightened. Was the duke going to accuse her of being
a witch? Did he think she had a hand in causing the king's madness?

Louis motioned for her to rise. He no longer looked angry,
but he was studying her intently. 'What do you know about me?'
he asked.

She mumbled something about how she knew he was the king's
brother.

'That's not what I meant,' the duke said. 'I'm asking whether
you know that everyone hates me because I caused the fire that
killed four men and could have killed the king?'

'I know people think you caused the fire, *Monseigneur*. But I know you did not.'

Louis started to laugh. 'Of course, you would say that. You are just like everyone else, trying to curry favor with me. But you won't succeed, my little friend. Get out of my sight!'

Alips stood as tall as she could and looked up at the duke, meeting his eyes. 'I am, indeed, little. And you're right to call me your friend, because I know it wasn't your torch that started the fire.'

'How could you know such a thing?'

'I know why you're here, looking at the floor. You're trying to understand how it could have been your fault. I'll tell you again, it wasn't.'

'If only I could believe you.' The duke's eyes filled with tears.

'You must believe me, *Monseigneur*.'

'It had to have been my torch. No one told me there was going to be a masquerade, or that my brother and his friends were going to be in costumes covered with pitch. But just because I was ignorant, that does not make me less guilty.'

'But you aren't guilty, *Monseigneur*.'

Louis was crying now, and Alips was heartsick to see it. She knew that this handsome, elegant man, so different from his brother, had two sides. He was greedy, spending wildly of his own vast fortune and plundering more from the royal treasury; he was arrogant; he seduced many women; and he was hungry for power. But she also knew that he was exceptionally pious, a man of contradictions. It pained her to see him suffer.

She said, 'I know you are going to try to make amends for the fire by having a new chapel built at the Celestine priory. That is a fine thing to do. But it will not assuage the guilt you feel. The only thing that will do that is for you to believe what I tell you. The fire was not your fault.'

Louis was weeping so hard now she feared he would make himself sick. She took his hand in hers, a soft hand that she knew had caressed countless women, and she felt the attraction all those women felt for him. Seemingly without thinking, he touched her hair, and a thrill ran thought her body. But she knew this was not for her, a woman certainly, but nevertheless, a dwarf. She moved away and stood looking at him.

'*Monseigneur*,' she said. 'Look up at the musicians' balcony.'

'The musicians can't have had anything to do with it. I know them all.'

'But there was someone else there that night. I was up there, too, and I saw him throw a torch.'

The duke looked Alips up and down, and she felt herself withdrawing into her small body, ashamed of it. She knew what he was thinking.

'You can't imagine how someone as short as I am could get up there. That's because you cannot put yourself in anyone else's shoes. We little people have ways of accomplishing what we want. Stop thinking only of yourself.'

The duke had a strange look on his face. She knew that if she'd gone too far she would pay for it. But instead of lashing out at her, he crumpled and fell to the floor, weeping.

Alips was dumbfounded. At first she just stood there, not knowing what to do. *Perhaps I should leave so he can forget I saw him in his moment of weakness*, she thought. She started to walk away. Then she returned. She watched the sobbing duke for a moment. Then she sat down on the floor beside him and stroked his head.

'Now will you listen to me?' she said when he became calmer. 'It was not your torch that set those men on fire.'

'If the musicians saw someone throw a torch, they would have told me about it.'

'Perhaps they didn't see. But someone threw a torch, and I saw him do it.'

'Then you must know who it was.'

'I don't. He was in the shadows, and he ran away. I can drag myself up those steep stairs, but to chase someone down them is beyond me.'

Louis smiled.

'Yes, I know you're picturing it. How I waddled over to the stairs, hitched up my skirt, and pulled myself up, step by difficult step, my behind sticking out. A comical sight, I'm sure.'

'Now who's feeling sorry for herself?' the duke asked, and they both started to laugh. *This is the way men and women get to know each other*, Alips thought. *But it's not for me.* She remembered what Eustache Deschamps had said to her, equating misshapen limbs with misshapen minds. *There are a lot of misshapen minds around here*, she thought. *My limbs may not be normal, but my mind is perfectly good. I don't feel sorry for myself at all.*

The duke had risen from the floor. 'If it wasn't one of the musicians, who could it have been?'

'Do you know that the vielle player, Bernart le Brun, is dead?'

'I hadn't heard anything about it.'

'He was poisoned. It was because he saw the person who threw the torch.'

The duke flew into a rage. 'The other musicians must have seen him, too. They're deceiving me!'

Alips felt powerless to calm him, but she had to try. 'You don't know that. You can't condemn them!'

But the duke wouldn't be calmed. He dashed out of the hall, threatening all kinds of horrible punishments for the musicians.

The duke and his squire, who'd been waiting outside the palace, rode to the rue Saint-Martin, urging their horses at full speed through the crowds. People stared at Louis, resplendent in a gold-trimmed crimson doublet, silver hose, and a beaver hat with a large peacock feather. The stares were not friendly.

Louis knew where to find the musicians. He strode through the tavern to the table where Denisot the trumpeter sat with Thibault the piper and Philippot the bagpipe-player. 'Who threw the torch from your balcony?' he shouted.

They knew what he was talking about, and they were terrified.

'None of us had anything to do with it, *Monseigneur*,' said Denisot in a voice so shaky and thin, the duke could hardly hear him.

Louis slapped his hand on the table. 'Don't play innocent with me. I *will* know who threw the torch!'

'Bernart le Brun probably knew,' Denisot said. 'But he's dead.'

Louis sank down onto the bench at the table, whereupon Thibault and Philippot jumped up and started to leave. Louis shouted, 'Stop!' and they sat back down again. All three musicians shook with fear. The duke could have them all arrested and beheaded, no matter how much they protested their innocence, no matter that he had known them all for a long time and had no reason to think they had committed such a horrible crime. But the duke did something none of them could have anticipated: he put his head down on the table and began to cry.

The musicians were stunned. They knew he was arrogant and vain, they knew he consorted with magicians and sorcerers, they knew he imposed horrific taxes on the people to finance his appetite for riches and women. But they had never seen his other side: This great prince was capable of great suffering.

All the other patrons of the tavern turned to look at the richly costumed duke, who was emitting great sobs that shook the table. No one dared try to comfort him. When Louis finally raised his head, the tavern was empty.

THIRTY-EIGHT

A ruler who wants to win the hearts of his subjects must be gentle and kind to them.

Christine de Pizan,
Le Livre des Trois Vertus, 1405

'I'm going to take Loyse to the queen,' Christine told her mother. Francesca looked at Loyse, who was sitting quietly by the fireplace, and smiled. 'The queen will love her,' she said.

There was a knock at the door, and when Christine went to answer it, she found Marion, come to take Klara to the lions' stockade.

Then Michel appeared, rubbing his hands together nervously.

He's going to tell me he's worried about Alips, Christine thought. But before he could do that, he saw Marion's gold belt. 'Shameful,' he said.

'Call off your monk friend,' Marion said.

Christine took them into the kitchen. The older children were at school, and Lisabetta, Loyse, and Klara were watching Georgette make dough for a tart, instructed by Francesca. When Klara saw Michel, she went to Francesca and asked politely whether she could chop the onions.

'This isn't an onion tart,' Georgette said. 'Do you want to peel some garlic?'

Klara turned up her nose, but she didn't object.

'That young woman has changed since she's been here,' Michel said.

'It seems that way,' Francesca said.

Christine looked at Klara and wondered whether it was really true. Klara did seem less angry, even with the children. But Christine couldn't forget that she might be in communication with her brother. She didn't trust the girl.

'I'm going to take Loyse to the queen,' Christine said.

'I don't think that's a good idea,' Michel said.

'I think it's a fine idea,' Marion said. 'When do we go, Lady Christine?'

'I didn't say I was taking you. But you and Michel can help. You have to tell her what we're doing. I can communicate with her a little, but not that much.'

'She'll understand about the queen,' Michel said. He went to Loyse and made some signs.

'You promised you'd take me, too,' Klara said.

'You can come as far as the palace courtyard.'

Klara flounced up the stairs. Soon she came back down, carrying her best gown. She handed it to Loyse.

They made a strange procession as they marched toward the palace. A group of street urchins trailed along behind them, making faces and mocking them. Several old women with market baskets shied away from Marion, but others smiled when they saw Michel.

'It's supposed to be good luck to meet a Benedictine monk in the morning,' Christine said to Klara.

'Do you believe that?' Klara asked.

'I don't,' Marion said.

At the entrance to the queen's residence, Simon stared at Loyse. 'That looks like the girl who takes care of the lions.'

'It is. Pretty, isn't she?' Christine said.

'It can't be! That girl is demented.'

'She's not demented. She's deaf.'

Simon put his hand to his head. 'To think she's been living with the lions.' He put his arm around Renaut. 'Do you know who this is?'

Renaut shook his head.

'You can tell him later,' Christine said. 'Loyse and I are going to the queen.'

Klara was staring at Renaut with a puzzled look on her face. Marion took her arm and led her away. Michel followed. Out in the street he said to Marion, 'You might get to meet the queen yourself if you'd put on some respectable clothes.'

'Mind your own business, *teste de boeuf*,' Marion said as she marched down the street, dragging Klara with her.

Christine and Loyse walked slowly through the great gallery. The girl ran her hands over the heads of carved wooden lions on arms of chairs standing against the walls, and paused to admire a tapestry where lions, bears, dragons, and a unicorn stood on a carpet of flowers. The tapestry swayed in a breeze that came into the gallery through an open door, and she put her hands out, as though she feared it might come tumbling down. Christine pointed to the heavy metal hooks that attached the tapestry to the moldings under the ceiling, and Loyse nodded to show she understood. The sergeants-at-arms stood silently at their posts, smiling to each other. Some of them looked as though they knew who Loyse was, and Christine suspected that Marion had been talking to them.

When they reached the queen's chambers, they paused at the door and saw that the queen was attended by several of her ladies-in-waiting and the Duchess of Burgundy. The duchess frowned when she saw them and stepped forward to ward them off. 'The queen doesn't want to see you,' she said.

The queen rose and stamped her foot. 'Let them come to me.'

'But, *Madame*, you must not let these people invade your privacy. It is not befitting for a queen,' the duchess said.

'I shall see them! Now!'

The duchess waved to the ladies-in-waiting, who cowered behind her. 'Leave us,' she commanded, and they all crept out of the room. Then she turned to the queen and said, 'I am in command here, now that the king is ill.'

The queen sank back on her pillows with an air of hopelessness. Suddenly her greyhound bounded up to the duchess, nearly knocking her off her feet. She let out a little scream and tried to swat the dog away. Christine looked around, expecting to find Alips laughing from the other side of the room. But Alips wasn't there.

The queen smothered a smile, put out her arm, and grabbed the dog's collar. The duchess called for her attendant and left, grumbling about all the improper things going on in the queen's chambers. Before she went out the door, she turned and said to the queen, 'Be assured, I shall speak to my husband about this.'

Christine approached the day bed and knelt. 'I've brought the deaf girl, *Madame*.'

'Let her come to me.'

Christine went to Loyse, took her by the shoulders, guided her to the queen, and indicated that she should kneel. Isabeau looked at the girl, smiled, and said to Christine, 'You have not told me that she is beautiful.' She touched Loyse's arm, motioned for her to rise, and patted the bed to show that she should sit beside her. She made several hand gestures that Loyse seemed to understand. 'This I do with Collette,' she said.

Christine moved away, to the corner of the room where Gracieuse played her lute and sang a song praising the queen for her kindness to everyone. Collette sat looking at her and smiling, as though she could hear. The fools, Jeannine and Guillaume, locked arms and swayed in time to the music. Jeannine's mother looked at the floor.

The queen beckoned to Collette. Soon the two deaf girls were sitting on the day bed with the queen, making gestures to each other. The queen seemed to understand. She made some gestures of her own, and they all smiled.

Christine wondered where Alips was. She needed to talk to her, to tell her what she'd learned from Martin du Bois.

The room seemed incomplete without her.

THIRTY-NINE

Cookes with theire newe conceytes, choppynge, stampynge,
and gryndynge,
Many new curies alle day they ar contryvynge and fyndynge.

John Russell, *Boke of Nurture*, fifteenth century

Alips had decided that whomever the Duchess of Burgundy had enlisted to throw the torch from the musicians' balcony must be someone new to the palace. She went out to ask Simon about people who'd been hired recently. The *portier* leaned against the side of the entrance door and tried to think.

'There's a new boy helping the hounds' keeper,' he said. Alips knew about him because she often visited the dogs – big mastiffs that looked so fierce, most people kept away. She liked to stick her arm through the bars of their kennel and stroke their noses, which made the hounds' keeper angry. 'Those aren't pets,' he always shouted at her. She'd been there recently, and she'd talked to the new boy, who seemed so mild-mannered and polite she was sure he couldn't be a murderer.

'Then there's our new sergeant-at-arms,' Simon said. 'You wouldn't want to tangle with him.' Alips agreed; the man was huge, and he looked very strong. He also looked very stupid. She didn't think he had the wits to carry out a dangerous scheme.

An extra helper had been hired to work with the chief gardener as he prepared the palace gardens for spring. Alips had seen him in the herb garden, energetically turning the soil. She went out to talk to him and learned that he was only fourteen, and so timid and shy, she couldn't suspect him.

'And, of course, there are all those doctors who keep coming and going, each with a different remedy to make the king better,' Simon said when she returned.

None of their remedies have killed the king so far, Alips thought. *There's always the chance that one of them will; but even if I found out about it, there would be nothing I could do.*

Simon mentioned several other people, and she sought them out, observed them carefully, and ruled them out as suspects.

She went back to Simon to see if he could think of anyone else.

'You're certainly inquisitive,' he said.

Alips laughed. 'You know I like to find out about everyone and know what they're doing.'

'Is that why you're always hiding behind things?' Renaut asked.

'I'm not hiding, *dandin*. It's just that I'm so short.'

'That's enough, Renaut,' Simon said.

'He doesn't mean any harm,' Alips said.

'I just remembered, there are three new kitchen boys,' Simon said. 'They're ordinary boys, but they think they're important because they're working at the palace. I've known one of them since he was a child.'

The kitchen would be the perfect place to prepare something to kill the king, she thought. She decided to go there right away.

Simon added, 'There's a new master cook, too. The old one has just retired.'

That makes the kitchen even more interesting, Alips thought as she hurried to it. But she was sorry to hear that the old master cook had left. He'd always let her have a taste of what he was preparing, and it was always delicious. He was well known for his talents and had even written a cookbook.

The palace kitchen was immense. It had to be, because meals were prepared there every day for the royal family and all the hundreds of people who worked at the Hôtel Saint-Pol. Within the vast space were four fireplaces, one blazing in each corner, the light reflecting fitfully on the paved floor. Even in the cold of winter, the doors were kept open to give the cooks and their helpers some relief from the heat. Nine pillars were needed to support the ceiling; they stood like sentries as the master cook and the lesser cooks and a multitude of helpers bustled around them – boys running in with pails of water to splash into vats where the dish-washers worked with their arms submerged up to their elbows; wood-choppers stumbling in with fuel for the fires; spit-turners rubbing hot fat from their faces; knife-sharpeners nursing cut fingers; floor-sweepers pushing piles of dirt and crumbs into corners. Stray dogs wandered in and out, and a cat slept before one of the fireplaces, unaware that a mouse was running across the feet of one of the cooks.

Alips looked around for the new kitchen boys. One of them was collecting ashes from the fire for the dish-washers to use as they scoured the pots and pans. He was thin and so tall he couldn't possibly have been the torch-thrower, whom she remembered as being of average height. Another boy, who had one leg shorter than the other, hobbled around with such a limp that he couldn't have escaped quickly down the stairs from the musicians' balcony. The third new helper sat in a corner, pretending to sharpen a knife, but actually taking a nap. She thought he was probably the one Simon had known since he was a child. He was obviously not a murderer.

As she walked around the room, she noticed the master cook looking at her. 'You'd better watch out; he doesn't like people sticking their fingers into his pots,' one of the pot-washers called out, barely making himself heard above all the noise of the cooks squabbling and the assistants shouting at each other.

'You know I'd never do that,' Alips said, laughing because that was exactly what the old master cook had let her do.

There were other buildings near the kitchen, places where wine was bottled, sauces prepared, butter churned, fruit made into jams, poultry killed and plucked. Alips went into each of them and asked questions. As she did so, she could see the master cook watching her through the open doors of the kitchen.

'You'd better go. He doesn't like people snooping around,' the sauce-maker said.

She stared back at the master cook, who stamped his foot. She laughed, waved to him, and started back to the palace, wondering about the man. *Surely a cook wouldn't meddle with poisons*, she thought. Everything the king ate or drank was tasted before it got to his table, and even at that, after he'd had his first attack of madness, the first people to be suspected were the people who'd prepared and served his food and wine.

She felt very discouraged. She'd set herself an impossible task, and she was failing. She went back to Simon. The *portier* said, 'I forgot to tell you, there's a new *portier* at the king's residence. He used to work for the Duke of Berry. He might have some interesting gossip for you.' He winked.

Alips hurried to the king's residence. The new *portier* seemed to take his job very seriously, questioning at length everyone who went in or out the door. She stood watching, trying to decide how to approach him when Brother Michel appeared at her side.

'You must stop this, Alips,' he said, and he walked away.

She was hurt. Brother Michel had seemed so friendly. Now he was admonishing her. *He's afraid of something*, she thought. She sat down on a low wall and watched the new *portier* for a while. After she'd seen him roar at some small boys who got too close, pelt a stray dog with stones, and shake his mace at a ragged man who'd come to beg, she decided she'd wait until another day to talk to him.

FORTY

Concerning worldly prudence, the first teaching has to do with the love and faith you owe your husband and how you should behave with him.

Christine de Pizan,
Le Livre des Trois Vertus, 1405

'When will we get to meet the queen?' Klara asked Marion as they walked away from the palace.

'*You* will, someday,' Marion said. '*Me?* Probably never.'

As they passed the king's residence, a stout man in a rose-pink cloak embroidered with golden fleurs-de-lis bounced up to the entrance on a grey horse. Beside him on a white palfrey rode a graceful young woman in a dark-green *houppelande*.

'That's the Duke of Berry,' Marion said.

'The duke who married the young girl?'

'The very one. And that's his wife.'

'He's ugly!'

'Does your husband look like that?'

'No.'

'Don't you miss him, just a little bit?'

Klara bit her lip. 'A little, perhaps.'

'You owe him some consideration. Why do you always speak as though you dislike him?'

'I don't dislike him. It's just that he's too old.'

Klara watched the duke getting down from his horse, assisted by a handsome page. 'How could anyone love that ugly old man?'

'His wife does.'

They turned down the rue Saint-Antoine, where Marion in her crimson cloak looked like an exotic bird in the midst of all the women out doing their marketing in plain black or brown cloaks. An old crone stopped and stared at her. '*Idiote*,' Marion said.

Klara giggled as she watched the woman scuttle away. She became downcast again when she realized that Marion was talking to her.

'Your husband is far from ugly, Klara. In fact, he's quite handsome.'

'You don't know anything about him!'

'But I do. I've met him.'

Klara stopped short, and a man walking behind her carrying a crate of chickens bumped into her. He dropped the crate, the door flew open, and chickens fluttered out.

'*Merde*,' the man cried, shaking his fist at Klara. Marion grabbed a chicken and handed it to him. He stuffed it into the crate, slammed the door shut, and hurried off to find the others, which had flown off in all directions.

Klara seemed in a trance. Marion took her arm and shook it. 'Don't you want to know how I met him?'

'Did he tell you why he went away?'

'He's looking for your brother.'

'Why?'

'I think you know, Klara.'

Klara hung her head. 'Willem hates Martin. He talks about it all the time.'

'Do you hate Martin, too?'

'Not like that. Willem wants to kill him. He's already tried.'

'What did he do?'

'He dressed up like a knight with a big sword and challenged Martin to a duel. Martin thought it was in fun because Willem was always putting on disguises and pretending to be someone else. But this wasn't a game. Willem actually stuck his sword right into Martin's neck. Martin bled a lot, but he didn't die.'

'Were you and your brother very close?'

'We used to be, before the beguine came. She and Willem were always whispering together. They didn't pay any attention to me.'

'But you had Martin. Didn't that make up for Willem?'

'Not really.' Klara stopped to look at some embroidered purses displayed in front of a shop. 'Did you make any of these?' she asked.

Marion picked up one of the purses and examined it. 'I can do better. But you aren't paying attention to what I'm saying. I'm trying to make you see how you should behave toward your husband. Once he finds your brother, he'll come and get you. And when he does, you should tell him you missed him.'

'I miss his house, and I'll be glad not to sleep with Christine's mother any more. She snores. And the children are rude.'

'That's beside the point. But as long as you brought it up, let me tell you something about Christine and her family. If you can stop thinking about yourself long enough to listen.'

Klara looked as though she would cry. Marion gave her a hug and asked, 'Did you know that Christine's father was an astrologer who was so famous that the king's father brought him here from Italy just so he could have him as his special adviser? Or that Christine's husband was one of the royal secretaries?'

'Is that why Christine is welcome at the court?'

'Of course. Everyone there has great respect for her.'

An old woman approached Marion and said, 'You'll be arrested for wearing that gold belt.'

Marion shook her fist at her. 'I assure you I won't, *punaise*.' Then she asked Klara, 'Did you know that Christine saved a woman from burning at the stake?'

'Really? Who was the woman? Have I seen her?'

'You know her sister. And you've just seen her nephew.'

'What are you talking about?'

'That boy with the *portier* is her nephew. Loyse is her sister.'

Klara stared at Marion, who said, 'The woman who was condemned to die at the stake was Loyse's twin sister.'

'Where is she now?'

'She's gone away. She's a fine lady.'

'How can that be? Loyse isn't a fine lady.'

'No, she isn't. Do you know about the old superstition that if a woman has twins, she must have lain with two different men?'

Klara started to laugh.

'It's funny, until it causes a tragedy. Loyse had a twin, and because her mother was terrified her husband would think she'd slept with another man, she gave the twin away. That twin got to live with a wealthy lord and his wife. The other baby – that's Loyse – didn't fare so well. Her mother resented her because she wasn't like other children. Everyone thought she was demented.'

'Did her mother believe that, too?'

'I don't think she did. But she was an ignorant woman, and she didn't know how to care for her.'

'What has this to do with Christine?'

'No one knew all this, until Christine found out. She almost got killed because of what she'd learned.'

'I don't know much of anything, do I?' Klara said sadly. A pasty-seller approached and held out his basket, but she shook her head.

'Not hungry?' Marion asked. 'I am.' She bought two of the vendor's wares. 'I'll save one, in case you want it later.'

Klara asked, 'Is Loyse's sister coming back?'

'I don't think so. Loyse doesn't know anything about her.'

'That's sad. They could have grown up together.'

'Like you and Willem?'

'Yes. Before the beguine came.'

'Do you know where Willem is now, Klara?'

Klara met Marion's gaze and shouted, 'No. I don't. And I don't care. I hate him!'

FORTY-ONE

I know a learned woman named Anastasia who paints the borders of manuscripts and the backgrounds of miniatures so skillfully that she has no equal in all of Paris.

Christine de Pizan,
Le Livre de la Cité des Dames, 1404–1405

Once she saw that Loyse was comfortable with the queen, Christine decided to go home. As she left the palace, she asked Simon if he knew where Alips was.

'She's roaming around outside somewhere,' the *portier* said. 'She wants to meet anyone who's new here. You know how she is, always curious about people.'

Christine was worried. She hadn't had a chance to tell Alips that she'd learned who the murderer was and that he'd disguised himself. She went out to the gardens, but she knew the chances of finding the dwarf were slim; the palace grounds were extensive, and Alips could be anywhere. After she'd walked by the kitchens and didn't see her, she decided to leave and come back first thing the next day. *As long as she doesn't know what she's looking for, she's probably safe*, she reasoned. Nevertheless, she asked Simon to tell her not to ask so many questions.

Outside the king's residence, she encountered the Duke of Berry and his wife, accompanied by a large group of retainers. When the duke saw her, he stopped and leaned down from his horse. Christine smothered a smile as his rose-pink cloak flew open to show his pudgy body in a richly embroidered tunic much too tight for him.

'I have something to tell you,' the duke said. 'Perhaps it would be better if I got down.' He signaled to a page, who helped him as he slowly descended. Long before he reached the ground, the young duchess had dismounted gracefully and approached Christine.

'Have you found out who threw the lighted torch at the dancers?'

Christine shook her head. 'No, *Madame.*'

'I've talked to my husband about it. He's convinced the Duke of Orléans did it, but accidentally. He tries to convince his nephew to stop blaming himself.'

'I believe that one day soon the duke's conscience will be clear,' Christine said.

'And what about the missing husband you've been looking for?'

The duke was now standing on the ground beside his wife, adjusting his cloak. 'That is what I wanted to talk to you about, Christine. I remembered something that may be of help.'

She looked at him expectantly.

'When you came to the Hôtel de Nesle the other day, there was a man there who brought me playing cards.'

'I remember, *Monseigneur.* I met him later at the royal library. He gave me a book of illuminator's instructions to copy.'

'Well, I have known Jacquemin for years. He told me recently that he had an assistant, a young boy, a sort of apprentice, who disappeared. This put me in mind of someone else who disappeared, the man you were asking about, Martin du Bois, and I remembered then that Martin had worked as one of my secretaries. I once asked him to accompany Jacquemin on a trip to my château in Lusignan, to deliver some valuable manuscripts.'

'Do you think there is any connection between Martin du Bois and this assistant?' Christine asked.

'I have no idea, other than the fact that they have both disappeared. I do know that Jacquemin is very anxious to find the boy. He stole some valuable paints.'

'Perhaps I should visit Jacquemin,' Christine said, thinking it unlikely the missing assistant would really be Willem. *But I can't overlook anything*, she said to herself.

The duke suddenly seemed to lose interest. He was staring at a young page who had just come out of the palace. The boy wore tight hose, and his buttocks swayed as he walked down the street.

'*Monseigneur?*'

'Oh, yes. You said you should visit Jacquemin. Why not do so? His shop is on the rue des Rosiers.'

'Thank you, *Monseigneur.*' Christine made her obeisance quickly and turned to go. The young duchess caught her arm.

'I hope you will bring the missing man's young wife to see me sometime. I would like to meet her.'

What an appealing young woman the old duke married, Christine thought. It really would be good for Klara to meet her. But she was unsure of Klara, so perhaps it would be unwise. She smiled and nodded, hoping the duchess would take that as an affirmation, curtsied quickly, and left.

She hurried down the rue Saint-Antoine to the rue des Rosiers and asked a woman who stood in front of a belt-maker's shop where to find the illuminator. But before she could answer, Jacquemin himself came out of the shop next door and emptied a pail of water into the gutter that ran down the middle of the street. When the big man saw her, he greeted her with his booming laugh, ushered her into his studio, made her sit down on a bench, and announced proudly that this was where he did his work. It was an intriguing place: pots of paint, mortars and pestles, brushes of all sizes and shapes, burnishing tools, and partly finished manuscript pages covered every surface. She thought perhaps she should have become a manuscript painter instead of a copyist.

Jacquemin had several young assistants. One boy was energetically grinding red paint in a big mortar, turning himself red in the process. Another was beating out sheets of gold, while a third rubbed a piece of parchment with powdered pumice, preparing it for painting. Jacquemin also had a female assistant, a woman absorbed in her work on a brightly colored illumination.

'Are you surprised to see her here?' Jacquemin asked.

'Not at all. I know there are women in this profession.'

'She does very good work. Come and see.'

The woman was painting intricate scrolls and leaves around a picture of Saint Margaret holding her dragon. Cleverly mixed in with the foliage were other dragons, as well as lions, bears, and little men who looked like dwarfs. Christine thought of Alips and wished she could see them.

Jacquemin asked Christine, 'How is my book coming along?'

'I haven't had time to work on it. I have other things on my mind. That's why I've come to see you. The Duke of Berry tells me you had a young assistant who disappeared.'

'That rascal! I tried to teach him my craft, but he never learned. I kept him on because he didn't mind cleaning the shop and running errands. Then he ran away, taking some of my paints. If I ever get my hands on him . . .'

He was interrupted by an outburst from the woman, who looked up from her painting and said, 'I hope I never see that one again.'

'What was his name?' Christine asked.

'He said his name was Pierre,' Jacquemin said. 'I don't believe it.'

'How long had he been with you?'

'Several years. When he first came, he seemed honest enough. Then he changed. I can't say I'm sorry he's gone.'

'I'm delighted,' the woman chimed in. 'Now I can work in peace. He was no good; I can tell you that.'

Christine thought she looked quite able to protect herself from any man's advances. Another woman might have been easy prey.

'Can you describe him?' she asked.

'He wasn't much to look at,' the woman said. 'I don't know why he thought he was so attractive.'

Jacquemin said, 'He looked much older than he was, mostly because his hair was turning white. But he was nondescript, except for his eyes. They were a most unusual blue, and cold as ice.'

It was Willem, Christine thought.

FORTY-TWO

There was a time when it was a pleasure to visit the court and admire acts of courage firsthand and learn how to be virtuous from the excellent men who governed France. But things changed quickly, and it became better to be shrewd and have one foot in the court and the other elsewhere. Today it makes more sense to have both feet as far from the court as possible.

Eustache Deschamps (c. 1340–1404), *Ballade 1104*

A lips went back to Simon, who said, 'Your friend Christine was here, asking for you. She said I should tell you not to go around asking questions. Brother Michel is worried, too. He says the court is a dangerous place, and you should be careful.'

Alips laughed. 'I'm just interested in people. It's fun to overhear their conversations. Especially people who are new here.'

Renaut piped up, 'Always hiding behind the furniture. That's what Brother Michel said.'

Several courtiers came into the courtyard. Renaut ran to greet them. 'We're looking for new people,' he said.

The courtiers laughed. 'That's the *portier's* job,' said a tall man in a bright blue fur-lined cape.

Simon stepped aside to let them pass into the palace, and then he said to Alips, 'It is not wise for you to be talking like this in front of the boy.'

'I've seen someone new,' Renaut said. 'I've seen him sneaking around.'

'Who?' Simon asked. 'How could he get past the door without my knowing about it?'

'I don't know, but I've seen him. He'll be right in front of me, and then he disappears.'

'You're imagining things,' Simon said.

Renaut looked downcast. 'You believe me, don't you, Alips?'

'I'm afraid I do.'

Simon shifted his mace from one hand to the other. 'I've always said, people come and go too freely here.'

Just then the door opened, and Colin stepped out. He greeted Simon, ruffled Renaut's tawny hair, and said to Alips, 'The queen doesn't know where you are. You'd better go to her.'

She went to the queen's chambers, sat on the floor with the greyhound, and pondered. Her investigations had come to nothing. She'd been so sure the person who'd thrown the torch must be someone new at the palace. Now she wondered. Might it not be someone who'd been there all along, someone who seemed innocent, but who harbored evil intentions no one suspected?

She looked around the room. While she'd been out, Christine had brought the deaf girl, and everyone was being kind to her. Madame de Malicorne had even brought in the queen's baby for her to admire. Now the girl was on the other side of the room, sitting with Collette. They seemed to be devising gestures they could use to communicate with each other. The two fools pranced around mimicking them, making everyone laugh.

No one needed to have worried that the girl would be out of place at the palace, Alips thought. *She's already right at home.*

The queen was resting, and Catherine de Villiers was reading to her. Alips got up, went to the queen's day bed, perched on one of the big cushions, and looked around the room.

Marguerite de Germonville stood in front of the goldfinches' green and white cage. She'd opened the door and put her hand inside so she could entice the birds to sit on her finger. Jeanne de la Tour, looking very small and fragile next to Marguerite, cautioned her not to let the birds fly out. 'Don't worry,' Marguerite said in her loud voice, 'I have little birds of my own. The queen has given me two silver cages for them.'

Symonne du Mesnil sat on a window seat with Madame de Malicorne, who was reprimanding her for napping in the room where Christine did her copying. 'There's no harm in lying down for a bit,' Symonne said. She turned away and began to scold the queen's monkey, which was scampering up and down the tapestry on the wall beside her.

Alips had made it her business to learn everything about the queen's ladies, and she considered them all now. She knew that Marguerite's husband was a carver for the queen and that Jeanne de la Tour, who was in charge of the queen's jewels, came from a family that had been at the court for many years. Catherine de Villiers had originally been a lady-in-waiting for the king's mother, and Madame de Malicorne was so trustworthy that the queen had given her control over everything having to do with the royal children. The one lady she didn't know anything about was Symonne, who'd been brought to the queen by the Duchess of Burgundy and seemed to be the only person the duchess didn't scowl at.

Gracieuse played her lute and sang about a horse because she knew that the queen had just given Madame de Malicorne a new bay palfrey. The *huissier*'s daughters were there that day, looking prettier than ever, and they joined hands and trotted around the minstrel. Collette and Loyse were still conversing with their mysterious hand gestures. Guillaume the fool had told Jeannine the fool a joke. Alips couldn't hear what it was, but it must not have been funny because Jeannine wasn't laughing. Jeannine's mother looked away.

She felt discouraged, and very tired. She slouched on the cushion, and her eyes started to close as she listened to Catherine's soft voice droning on and on, reading from the book about the mean dwarf. All of a sudden, she came to a passage that gave Alips a start, and the dwarf was wide awake. She thought she knew who was planning to kill the king.

She sat up straight and looked around the room again. She was sure she was right. But she couldn't tell the queen, not yet. It would be too dangerous. She got up quietly and left the room.

She didn't know that cold blue eyes watched her every move.

*   *   *

She went out into the palace gardens and walked along the paths, lost in thought. After the recent rains, more snowdrops and crocuses had appeared, and the gardeners were busy preparing for the spring planting; the sound of spades biting into the soil rang in her ears. She could hear the dogs barking in their kennels and the caged birds chirping along with the wild birds perched in the bare branches of the trees in the orchards. In the distance, one of the king's lions roared.

She started to laugh. It all seemed so simple. Why hadn't she thought of it before? She walked quickly back to the palace. Christine would be coming tomorrow, and then they would decide what to do.

'Did you meet anyone?' Renaut asked at the entrance to the palace.

'You'll find out soon,' she said, and she went in, leaving Simon scratching his head.

There were no guards in the great hall, but she could hear them calling in the distance. *The queen's monkey must have run away again*, she thought as she entered the corridor leading to the queen's chambers. She walked along slowly, admiring the tapestries lining the walls and searching, as she always did, for any small beings that might be dwarfs among the lords, ladies, knights, and mythical figures embroidered there.

Footsteps sounded behind her. Someone spoke her name. She turned to see who it was. She said, 'But I thought . . .'

He looked surprised. Then his expression changed to malice. 'You were wrong,' he said.

FORTY-THREE

Like most women, your mother wanted to keep you busy with spinning and the silly things girls do.

Christine de Pizan,
Le Livre de la Cité des Dames, 1404–1405

The next morning when Christine went downstairs, she found the children sitting calmly at the table, with Goblin lying quietly at their feet.

'What's gotten into them?' she asked Francesca.

'Klara is not here. She is still in bed.'

'Let her sleep. It's so peaceful here without her,' Christine said.

'She should come down and learn to make what Georgette is preparing.'

'What is it?' Christine asked Georgette, who was grinding something with a mortar and pestle.

'Spices for one of your mother's soups,' the girl said.

'*Zanzarelli!*' Thomas shouted. 'Can we have saffron in it?'

'Yes, Thomas.' Christine laughed. 'We can buy saffron now.'

Francesca said, 'If Klara won't read the book her husband wrote for her, at least she could learn something about cooking from me. You never wanted to do that, *Cristina.*'

'You know I hate cooking.'

'You are a bad influence on Klara.'

Christine groaned.

Francesca went on with her complaint. 'What will her husband say when he finds out you have encouraged her to live with lions rather than learn how to be a good wife?'

'Helping with the lions is good for her.'

'I hope she stays with them,' Thomas said.

'Me, too,' said Jean. 'When are you going to find her husband?'

'I have found him. Or, at least, he found me.'

'*Mio Dio!*' Francesca exclaimed. She sat down heavily on a bench. Georgette stopped her grinding. Marie, who was holding Goblin, squeezed the dog so hard he yelped.

'Where? What did he say? Why did he go away?' Everyone talked at once.

'He came up to me in the street.'

'When's he coming back to get Klara?' Thomas asked.

'*Basta, Tommaso!*' Francesca said. 'What did he say to you, *Cristina*?'

'He said he went away because Klara's brother, Willem, is trying to kill him.'

'Surely not!' Francesca exclaimed.

'Willem wants revenge for what happened in Courtrai.'

'Was Klara's husband there?' Jean asked.

'Yes. He says he didn't have anything to do with the killings, and he saved Klara and Willem from being taken away by the soldiers. But Willem doesn't care about that. He only knows he saw his parents being murdered.'

'If he kills Klara's husband, Klara will have to stay with us forever,' Thomas wailed.

'That's one of the reasons why we want to make sure Martin finds him,' Christine said. 'You can all help. We need to find out what Klara knows. You've told me there's someone prowling around the house. It may be Willem. We need to know whether she's spoken with him.'

Francesca said, 'If she's spoken to her brother, I would know about it. She sleeps with me, and I know she doesn't sneak out at night.'

Christine thought about how her mother snored, and she wondered how Klara got any sleep at all.

'But I do know one thing,' Francesca continued. 'Do you remember the golden spur we found with her jewelry, the day we went to her house?'

'Have you seen it since?'

'She has it in the chest where she keeps her clothes. She takes it out every once in a while and looks at it.'

'She's thinking of her brother. And her family, killed by the king's troops,' Georgette said. 'And her country. It's no wonder she's unhappy. The old man who brought her and her brother back to France may be kind, but that wouldn't make up for everything she's suffered.'

'But the sack of Courtrai was eleven years ago,' Jean said.

'Do you think anyone could forget something like that?'

Thomas made a face. But Georgette persisted. 'I'm sure the girl misses her brother.'

'If she misses him, maybe she's figured out where he is,' Christine said.

'Did Martin du Bois tell you what Willem looks like?' Jean asked.

'His description was pretty vague. All he said was that the boy has ice-blue eyes, his hair is turning white, and he looks much older than his age. And he's sure he's disguised himself.'

'I'll bet that even in a disguise, he couldn't fool Klara,' Jean said.

He's right, Christine thought. *As soon as Klara wakes up, I'll take her to the palace.*

Klara was so excited about going to meet the queen, she went upstairs and put on her best gown. The children looked at her and started to giggle. Georgette shushed them. 'You look very pretty,' she said to the girl. 'Let me fix your hair under your headdress.' Christine felt a pang of guilt; she wasn't planning to let Klara stay long with the queen. Her plan was to introduce her and then have Alips take her away, show her around the palace and the grounds, and watch her carefully to see whether she recognized anyone.

She shooed the children out of the kitchen and let Klara preen. Then they put on their cloaks and went out into the street, where they were met with a driving winter rain. On the rue Saint-Antoine, none of the pastry vendors were out crying their wares. A lone horseman galloped toward the palace, a rag-picker pushed a cart laden with soggy clothes, and a lame beggar sought shelter in a doorway; Christine stopped to press a coin into his hand. Then she urged Klara to hurry, and they raced up the street, getting colder and wetter by the minute. When they reached the palace, Klara was in tears. Her cloak was soaked and the trim white headdress Georgette had so carefully arranged was askew. Her hair formed damp ringlets around her face.

'Never mind,' Christine said. 'I'm as wet as you are. The queen won't mind.' They ran to the entrance to the queen's residence, where Christine expected to be welcomed with a hearty laugh when Simon saw how bedraggled they were.

But Simon wasn't laughing.

'Is something wrong?' Christine asked when she saw his somber face.

'I'm afraid there is,' the *portier* said. 'Alips has disappeared.'

Christine gasped. 'Come on, Klara,' she said. She grabbed the girl's hand and pulled her into the palace.

'Who's Alips?' Klara asked breathlessly as they rushed through the great gallery.

'The queen's dwarf,' Christine called back over her shoulder. 'The queen loves her.'

Christine left Klara standing at the door to Isabeau's chambers and ran to the queen, who wailed, 'Alips is gone.' She'd been crying; her eyes were red, and her nose was running.

'I was afraid this would happen, *Madame*. She's been asking too many questions.'

Christine was so distraught, she hadn't noticed the Duchess of Burgundy standing nearby. The woman asked, 'Why are you so concerned about the dwarf? Everyone knows dwarfs bring bad luck. You should be glad she's gone.'

The queen's greyhound stood quivering on the other side of the room. Suddenly, he sprang toward the duchess. She stepped back and nearly fell. One of her ladies, who was standing nearby, caught her and steadied her.

The queen stood up and took hold of the dog's collar. She looked toward the doorway and saw Klara. 'Who is that?' she asked.

'That is my friend, Klara, *Madame*. I brought her to meet you. But we were caught in the rain, and with all that has happened, perhaps it would be best to wait for another day.'

The queen just smiled and motioned to Klara that she should enter. Klara tiptoed over and knelt.

'Why do you have all these misfits around you?' the duchess raged at the queen. 'It's not fitting.' Christine felt her face get hot. She hadn't known the duchess considered her a misfit.

'They are very welcome here,' the queen said to Klara. She told her to rise, and called to one of her chambermaids. 'Take their wet cloaks and make them dry.'

By this time, Klara had adjusted her headdress and pushed the damp strands of her hair under it. She stood before the queen, her eyes shining.

'Klara's husband has gone away for a while,' Christine said. 'She's staying with me until he comes back.'

'I miss him so much,' Klara said. She put a hand to her eye and pretended to wipe away a tear.

Christine, astonished, stared at her and thought, *She should get along very well here at the court.* She looked around the room. Gracieuse wasn't playing her lute. Loyse, who hadn't yet noticed Klara, sat on the floor with Collette, not gesturing. Guillaume stood with Jeannine, for once not saying a word. The queen's ladies stood in a tight little group, wordlessly scrutinizing Klara. Jeannine's mother stood behind them, looking at the floor. *Everyone is too quiet*, she thought. *Nothing was as it should be, without Alips.*

The queen was doing her best to made Klara feel at home. She told her to sit on one of the big cushions, and she asked questions about her husband. Klara kept up her act, talking about how good her husband was to her. *If she keeps on like this, she'll talk herself into caring for him,* Christine mused.

The Duchess of Burgundy stood with her hands on her hips and looked down her nose at Klara, who didn't seem to notice. After a while Klara looked around and saw Loyse. She gave a little cry of delight, jumped up, rushed over, and threw her arms around her.

The Duchess of Burgundy stamped her foot. 'This is shameful.' She sat down on one of the big pillows and glowered at the queen. The lady who attended her came over and reminded her that the duke was waiting for her outside. The duchess said to the queen, 'We will discuss all the indecent things going on here later.' Her attendant helped her up, and they marched out.

The queen sat slumped on the day bed. She said, 'The person who tries to kill the king must have taken Alips. He has found out she was looking for him. She may be dead.'

'I'm afraid that is so,' Christine said.

'For the king, there is now more danger than before,' the queen said. 'And for you, too. What are we going to do?'

'We're going to continue trying to find this person. I know now that he is here at the palace.'

'Do you feel his shadow, as I do?'

'Not exactly, but I know he's here. I just don't know where.'

'So there is great danger.'

'Yes. You must make sure that every precaution is taken to protect the king. Have him closely guarded at all times.'

'That I have done. I have given orders to some of my own sergeants-at-arms that they must join those around the king.'

'Now that Alips isn't here, I'll need someone else to help,' Christine said, thinking of Marion.

'Do whatever you can. Oh! We must save Charles,' the queen cried.

'We will, *Madame*,' Christine said, trying to sound hopeful. She glanced over at Klara and saw that she was surrounded by the queen's entourage, happy to be the center of attention. Collette and Loyse made welcoming gestures, Gracieuse smiled at her, and Guillaume and Jeannine made mock-bows. Even the monkey seemed glad; he sat at her feet and made soft babbling noises.

The queen's ladies stood nearby, watching. Klara, obviously considering ladies-in-waiting more important than mutes and fools, went over and tried to start a conversation with them. All of a sudden, she moved away and hurried across the room to Christine.

'I want to go home now,' she said, and she started to cry.

FORTY-FOUR

*We have lots of beguines in their wide garments; what they do
under them, I can't tell you.*

Rutebeuf, *La Chanson des ordres*, thirteenth century

Marion was pleased that Klara was getting along well with the lions. But she was still worried that the girl would want to stay with them instead of going home with her husband, if the man ever came back to get her.

She mused about this as she walked from the house where she rented a room toward the Grand Pont, greeting acquaintances, resplendent in her crimson cloak and beaded red hair. Perhaps I'll meet Martin du Bois, she thought. I'll give him a piece of my mind for fooling me the way he did. No wonder Klara resents him. He's probably one of those people who think women should do nothing but cook and sew, like Christine's mother.

But it wasn't Martin du Bois she met. Instead, as she passed the house where Henri Le Picart lived, a gloomy place with carvings of dragons and serpents on the door, she saw Henri himself, standing in the street. *Where's he been all this time?* she asked herself. *He certainly hasn't been helping us.* She bristled as she remembered the day he'd told her and Christine they'd have to find the person who wanted to kill the king all by themselves.

Henri was looking intently at something. At first she thought it was the corpse swinging from the gallows at the intersection of the rue Saint-Honoré and the rue de l'Arbre Sec. But then he walked past the gallows and down the rue de l'Arbre Sec toward the church of Saint-Germain-l'Auxerrois. She followed him, ducking into doorways whenever she thought he might turn around. He went up the rue Saint-Germain-l'Auxerrois. Then he stopped and stared intently ahead. Near the Châtelet stood a beguine. Marion was surprised. Beguines rarely ventured into that part of the city. They were distrusted by many people, partly because no one could decide whether they were nuns or just women who wore ugly costumes so people wouldn't bother them. Among the reprobates around the water trough they were the subject of many cruel jests. She thought of the beguine Klara disliked so much, and she wondered whether Agnes resembled this one, shapeless in her voluminous habit.

The beguine was waiting for someone, and soon a person in a large black cloak, so covered up that Marion could hardly tell whether it was a man or a woman, appeared. The two talked. Henri crept closer and Marion snuck up behind him. The beguine and her companion spoke so softly, she couldn't make out the words. Henri, on the other hand, seemed to hear everything. He had a self-satisfied look on his face, as though he were thinking, 'I knew it.' Marion crept behind a vendor's cart and watched as the beguine and the figure in the black cloak walked away in opposite directions.

The beguine went up the rue Saint-Germain-l'Auxerrois toward the Châtelet. Henri followed her, not even trying to conceal himself. Marion, on the other hand, kept in the shadows of the tall buildings as she crept cautiously after him. Once, he seemed about to turn around, and she had to hurry into a narrow alleyway. She was sure he hadn't seen her, but her efforts to conceal herself made her lose sight of him as she neared the Châtelet. Exasperated, she went to the water trough at the entrance to the Grand Pont. Several of her friends were there: a beggar who wrapped his arms in dirty bandages so he'd look as though he had no hands, another rascal who feigned blindness, and a boy who played on people's sympathy by pretending to cry because his mother had drowned.

'Did a beguine just go by here?' she asked the 'motherless' boy.

'Yes. I wonder if she had anything interesting under that big frock.'

Not likely, Marion thought.

'There was a man following her,' the boy said.

'Which way did they go?'

'Let me think.' The boy man rubbed his chin. Suddenly he shook his head as though to dispel the cobwebs and said, 'I remember now. Over to Saint-Jacques-la-Boucherie.'

Marion hurried to the church, pushing her way through the crowds of people around the butchers' and tanners' shops and holding her nose because of the smell. She saw Henri hurrying up the rue de Vannerie, and ahead of him was the beguine. She pushed aside several old women coming out of the church and went after them.

They passed the place de Grève and turned up the rue Saint-Antoine. *He's following her back to the beguinage*, Marion thought. *What's he going to do when they get there?*

Suddenly, a group of mounted horsemen came down the rue Saint-Antoine and passed so close to her that she stumbled and fell. She got up, shook her fist at them, and swore loudly. Henri and the beguine were gone.

FORTY-FIVE

Why is it that so many different men, including learned ones, say or write in their treatises such wicked and disparaging things about women?

Christine de Pizan,
Le Livre de la Cité des Dames, 1404–1405

A t home, Klara ran up to Francesca's room and shut the door. She didn't appear for dinner.

'What is wrong with her?' Francesca wanted to know.

'Who cares?' Thomas asked.

Georgette went up to talk to her, then came back down and said the girl wouldn't tell her anything.

'Perhaps meeting the queen was too much for her,' Christine said. 'Or perhaps one of the queen's ladies said something that upset her. I'm going back to the palace to find out what happened.'

It was raining again, and she hurried down the street, hoping to reach the palace before she was completely soaked. As she turned the corner onto the rue Saint-Antoine, she was startled to see Henri Le Picart coming toward her.

'Ah, Christine. I'm glad you're here.'

She clenched her fists. 'Where have you been?'

'I've been finding out about Agnes the beguine.'

'I can't imagine you've discovered much. I went to see her at her beguinage and discovered nothing. She would hardly talk to me.'

She tried to step past Henri so she could continue on, but he blocked her way and said, '*I*, on the other hand, have discovered everything. Come with me.' He took her hand and dragged her up the street.

He walked so fast, and the street was so slippery, she could hardly stay on her feet. She couldn't imagine where he was taking her, and she was frightened. Since they were still on the rue Saint-Antoine, she thought, with relief, that perhaps they were going to the palace. But all of a sudden, he pulled her into the courtyard of a large mansion. She tried to hold back, but his grip was strong. The rain was coming down hard, and no one was about.

'The owners have gone away,' Henri said as he drew her along a muddy path to a deserted garden where rivulets of rain water streamed through the empty plots. The air was heavy with the dank odor of wet soil, and somewhere a lone bird chirruped a mournful song. Henri sloshed through the muck, pulling her behind him, until they came to a dilapidated wattle fence surrounding a group of overgrown apple trees. There was an opening in the fence, and Henri pulled her through it. Then he let go of her hand so quickly, she almost fell.

'There,' he said, pointing to the ground.

Breathing hard and trying to catch her breath, Christine looked down and saw a heap of sodden dark cloth.

'I'm afraid I hit her too hard,' Henri said.

It was Agnes. Her face was covered with blood and she seemed to be scarcely breathing.

Speechless, Christine gazed at the woman.

'I saw her near the Châtelet,' Henri said. 'She met someone there and gave him something. I wanted to find out what it was, so I followed her. She realized I was behind her, and she ducked in here, thinking she could hide.'

'What did you do to her?'

'There are ways of making someone reveal what you want to know.'

Christine knew he would never tell her what those ways were. 'Did you find out what she gave the other person?'

'No. Unfortunately, I was too rough with her, and now she can't talk. But before that, she told me a lot. When you went to see her at the beguinage, did you ask where she came from?'

'I did, but all she'd say was that she lives in Paris now.'

'She came from Courtrai. She was a member of the beguinage there.'

Agnes moaned and tried to sit up. Henri pushed her back down.

'After we destroyed her beguinage and her city, she vowed revenge.

Her plan was to come here, insinuate herself into the house of a Frenchman, and kill him as well as the king.'

'But why Martin du Bois?'

'She'd known Klara and Willem's family in Courtrai.'

'Vowing revenge and killing people doesn't seem like something a member of a religious community would do.'

'The beguines are not your ordinary sisters. They come and go as they please, and they don't take the same kinds of vows regular nuns do. Most of them are as devout as the members of any religious order, but not all. Agnes had been an illuminator's apprentice. It was only after her husband died that she went to live with the beguines. She may have been devout to begin with, but the massacre in her city caused her to take leave of her senses.'

Agnes moaned again. 'Shouldn't we call for the sergeants from the Châtelet?' Christine asked. 'We can't leave her here!'

'It's what she deserves. She's the one who's been plotting with Willem to kill the king. But the sergeants wouldn't believe that. There's no proof. People dislike the beguines, but not many would think they are capable of that kind of evil.'

'But if we find Willem and uncover their plot, won't they believe us then?'

'Perhaps. Perhaps not. But you're right to say that we can't leave her here. We'll have to get her back to the beguinage.'

Henri pulled Agnes to her feet. She slumped against him, but he made her stand upright. Christine supported her on the other side, and they practically carried her out of the garden. It was raining hard, and no one was on the rue Saint-Antoine or the rue de l'Ave Maria. Together, they got the woman to the door of the beguinage.

'We found her in the street,' Henri said when the grand mistress appeared. 'Someone must have knocked her down.' The woman looked at them suspiciously, but she didn't ask any questions; she just put her arms around Agnes and took her away.

Then Henri said, 'We have to find the boy and stop him.'

'But even if we do, won't Agnes start some other plot to kill the king, as soon as she recovers?'

'I've made sure she won't do that,' Henri said.

'How?'

'I have my ways. She knows what they are.'

They hurried up the rue Saint-Antoine to the palace. In the court-yard of the queen's residence, Renaut ran to them and laughed when he saw how wet their clothes were. Henri tousled the boy's tawny hair. 'You're just as wet as we are,' he said, as he took the boy's hand and led him back to Simon.

In the great gallery, which was deserted, they sat on a bench. Christine took off her cloak, and Henri removed his black cape. They sat in silence for a while. *Almost as though we're friends*, Christine thought.

But then Henri said, 'I've heard Alips has disappeared. If you women can't do anything right, you shouldn't go running around looking for murderers.'

No. We're not friends. Christine clenched her hands to prevent herself from reaching out and hitting the man. Then he added, 'I'm surprised it's the dwarf who's disappeared. She's more intelligent than the rest of you.'

Christine put her hands behind her back. 'Why do you always insult us?'

'I don't say anything that hasn't been said many times before.'

'That doesn't make it true.'

She remembered Michel telling her that Henri had been brought up in a monastery. *Perhaps that's why he can't get along with women*, she thought.

Henri was looking at her strangely.

'Of course, there may be some exceptions,' he said, adding quickly, 'I've read about them.'

Christine almost laughed. Michel had told her that Henri had hated the monastery and that he'd spent most of his time in the library, learning to be a scribe, and reading. The books had no doubt contained many examples of worthy women.

'Haven't you *ever* met an intelligent woman?'

Henri looked at her intently. 'I knew your father, a long time ago, when you were still a girl.'

She knew he'd been a friend of her father's, though she'd never seen him when she was young because her mother had taken a dislike to him, and she'd made it clear to her husband that the man would not be welcome at their house.

'You don't remember me, do you?' Henri asked.

'All I know is, you helped my father make those tin figures of the Englishmen. Did you really think burying them all around the country would make the English leave France?'

'Why not?'

Christine knew he was an astrologer as well as an alchemist – it was even said he'd discovered the secret of turning base metals into gold. He also knew a great deal about magic. Perhaps he really did believe tin figures had mysterious powers to drive the enemy away. But she couldn't help saying, 'It was a ridiculous idea.'

'No more ridiculous than all those superstitions you women have.'

'Not *all* women. Don't you think that if more women were educated, they'd learn not to believe in superstitions?'

'Learning is wasted on women.'

'Do you think it was wasted on me?'

'You didn't need it. You had a husband to support you.'

'And now I have no husband, and I need that learning. Perhaps you haven't noticed, but I'm a scribe. A good one, too. Perhaps better than you.'

He was looking at her with that peculiar expression again. He said, 'Do you know why I was so anxious to help your father?'

'How would I know? I was just a little girl then.'

'Old enough to be married. Your father was looking for a husband who would be suitable for you.'

'Surely you don't mean . . .'

Henri got up and walked away.

Christine was not as shocked as she might have been. She was getting used to Henri's surprises. Her daughter Marie had once remarked that he was an interesting man. She hated to admit it, but she thought her daughter was right.

FORTY-SIX

The women and ladies of a court ought to love and care for one another like sisters.

Christine de Pizan,
Le Livre des Trois Vertus, 1405

I t was late, so Christine returned home; but the next morning, she was up early, eager to get back to the palace. While she was in the kitchen, getting ready, Marion appeared.

'The queen's dwarf has disappeared,' Christine told her.

'That's bad news. Do you think Klara's brother has anything to do with it?'

'Who else could it have been?'

'That means everyone at the palace is in danger!'

'We have to be careful what we say around Klara,' Christine said. 'I don't know how much she knows.'

Klara appeared. Marion took one look at her long face and whispered to Christine, 'What's wrong with her?'

'She's been like that ever since we came back from the palace yesterday. She seemed happy to meet the queen, and she was delighted to see Loyse again, but then her mood changed. She started to cry, and she asked to go home.'

'What are you two whispering about?' Francesca wanted to know.

'Nothing,' Christine said. 'I'm going to the palace.'

Francesca let out a cry of despair. 'I sneezed while I was putting on my shoes this morning. You know that means something terrible is about to happen!'

'I know nothing of the sort.'

Marion said, 'I'll take care of your daughter.' She took Christine by the hand and pulled her out the door.

On the rue Saint-Antoine, she hesitated. 'Exactly what do you plan to do?' she asked Christine.

'That's the problem. I don't know.'

At the entrance to the queen's residence, Simon saw Christine and shook his head. 'No one has found her,' he said.

'Let my friend Marion come into the palace with me.'

Simon looked at Marion in her crimson cloak and bead-studded hair. 'I know you've been helping Christine. I suppose it will be all right.'

Christine pulled Marion through the door.

When they entered Isabeau's apartments, they found her surrounded by her ladies. She motioned for Christine to approach. Marion followed, and they both knelt.

'This is my friend Marion, *Madame*,' Christine said. 'She helped me save Alix de Clairy.'

'Rise. You are welcome here,' the queen said.

Marion's face glowed with pleasure. *I didn't think she'd be so impressed*, Christine mused.

The Duchess of Burgundy strode into the room, took one look

at Marion, and said, 'This is not to be believed! Do you know that this woman is a prostitute, *Madame*?'

'What does it matter?' the queen asked.

The duchess looked apprehensively at the queen's greyhound, which was lying at the foot of the bed. The dog seemed more nervous than usual, and she stepped as far away from him as she could.

Christine said softly to the queen, 'Marion is here to help us, *Madame*.'

'This is an outrage,' the duchess cried. The dog stood up.

The ladies-in-waiting were staring at Marion. The Duchess of Burgundy stamped her foot. 'Go away,' she cried.

The ladies gasped and moved back. The duchess stamped her foot again, and they scurried over to one of the windows. Shocked and offended, they gathered around Madame de Malicorne, who spoke to them like a mother comforting her children. Jeanne de la Tour started to cry. Catherine de Villiers put her arms around her, and Marguerite de Germonville spoke to her in a voice so low that, for once, Christine couldn't hear what she said. Symonne du Mesnil took Jeanne's trembling hands in hers and led her to the window seat. As Christine watched, she felt very sorry for them. *They are noble ladies*, she thought. *They may argue with each other sometimes; but they aren't used to such hostility, and they deserve better.* She looked at the queen and saw that she had tears in her eyes.

The duchess started to say something more, but the greyhound bared his teeth and growled at her. *It's as though Alips is here, telling him what to do*, Christine thought.

The duchess called for her maid and stormed off.

Christine said, 'I know who took Alips, *Madame*. There is a boy here, in disguise. He started the fire, and he is the one who is plotting to kill the king. He must have learned that Alips is looking for him. We have to find him.'

The queen looked frightened. 'This means the king has more danger than ever. What plan have you for finding this boy?'

'That's the problem. I don't have a plan. That's why I've brought Marion; she knows all the guards and footmen who work at the palace. Perhaps if she asks around, she'll learn something.'

The queen nodded, an anguished look on her face.

'Marion will stay with me and watch everyone,' Christine said, and she went to the room where she did her copying. There she was surprised to see on her desk a leather pouch that looked like the one that had held the missing playing cards. She opened it and looked in. The playing cards were there.

She closed the pouch and started to take it to the queen. Then she hesitated. She opened the pouch again, pulled out a card, and examined it. Then she pulled out a few more, placed them on the desk, and studied them carefully.

'So much gold,' exclaimed Marion, who was looking over her shoulder.

'Too much,' Christine said. The gold that served as background for the implements of war was not as lustrous as the gold she'd seen in manuscript illuminations, and it was so thick that in some places it had peeled off. Jacquemin is one of the finest illuminators in Paris, she thought. He would never have been guilty of such carelessness.

She put the cards back in the pouch and said to Marion, 'These cards were painted by an illuminator named Jacquemin. His shop is not too far from here, on the rue des Rosiers.'

'I know him,' Marion said.

'Willem used to work for him. He stole some paints and ran away. I want you to go and ask Jacquemin what those paints were. Go quickly and come right back.'

Marion hurried to the door. Christine was pleased to see that she remembered to kneel on her way out.

Christine looked into the queen's room. Loyse sat with Collette on a cushioned seat in front of a window. She seemed perfectly at home, and Christine was glad she'd brought her. But the two mutes looked sad, and they weren't gesturing to each other as they usually did. Gracieuse played a mournful tune on her lute, but the goldfinches didn't sing along. Guillaume the fool tickled the monkey, but the monkey didn't make his usual babbling noises. Without Alips there, everyone seemed out of sorts. Jeannine the fool stood next to her mother, ignoring her. The mother, her head covered by her wimple and her face nearly obscured by her gorget, looked at the floor.

Christine slid the pouch with the playing cards under the coverlet on a small day bed that stood on one side of the room and went to the queen. 'Where did Jeannine come from?' she asked.

'Far from here, somewhere in the south of this country. The king found her on one of his journeys and brought her to me as a gift, when we were first married. Her parents are poor, and they were glad to give her away. She has only fourteen years now.' She motioned for Jeannine to come to her. The fool, a thin, rather plain girl, stood before the queen with her head bowed. 'She does not say much,' the queen said. 'But she is really very clever.'

'Will she speak now?' Christine asked.

'That is up to her,' the queen said. The fool remained silent.

'Does her mother visit her often?' Christine asked.

'When she came here some days ago, she had not seen her daughter for many years. Perhaps Jeannine does not recognize her. She was very young when she was taken away.'

Loyse suddenly jumped up from the window seat and gestured to someone who stood at the door to the queen's chambers. Christine turned to look and was amazed to see Klara. She started to go to the girl, but Klara swept past her and knelt before the queen. Christine was horrified. Klara was not supposed to have come by herself; it was not proper. But the queen didn't seem to mind; she smiled at the girl and told her to rise.

Angry at Klara and impatient for Marion to return, Christine went out to talk to Simon. He and Renaut were huddled together, and Renaut was asking over and over again when Alips would be found. When Simon saw Christine, he said, 'The girl you brought yesterday came to find you. She said you forgot her today, you were in such a hurry. I suppose that was because you are so concerned about Alips. I let Colin take her to the queen's chambers.'

'She looked familiar,' Renaut said.

'That's because you saw her yesterday,' Simon said.

'I suppose that's it,' Renaut said.

Christine didn't tell Simon that she hadn't intended to bring Klara to the palace. She went to the center of the courtyard. The fountain had been turned on, and she rinsed her hands in the water in the basin. Then she walked around the courtyard several times, remembering how she'd first met Renaut and how he'd laughed because she'd sworn at the stone lion. She looked up at the lion and thought of the real lions, waiting for Klara to come and feed them. She walked around the courtyard again. She watched several courtiers in big beaver hats stroll in, greet Simon, and enter the palace. She watched several other courtiers come out, tousle Renaut's hair, and amble away. She watched Colin dash out the door, say something to Simon, and run back in. Then she sat down on the edge of the fountain, folded her hands in her lap, and tried to be patient as she waited for Marion.

FORTY-SEVEN

All through Paris you hear them shouting that everyone wants their old rags and worn-out clothes.

Guillaume de la Villeneuve,
Les Crieries de Paris, thirteenth century

Alips thought she was lying on a bed of old clothes in the rag-picker's shack. There was no light, but she was sure it would soon be morning because she thought she heard the cries of the man who hawked his strong eau-de-vie before the sun came up. Soon old Emmelot would wake her. She'd put on a dirty dress, and they'd start out in the dark, going from house to house, knocking on doors, begging for used clothes and linens, enduring the glares of housewives and sleepy servant girls who resented being awakened so early. Then Emmelot would start down the street, hawking what they'd collected, her cries mingling with the cries of the pasty vendors, the water carriers, the wine sellers, the rat-catchers. There was always an old cane seller who would wink at Emmelot and tell her she should buy one of his canes so she could use it to beat the dwarf riding in her cart.

She was glad old Emmelot let her ride in the cart. She could sleep some more. She was very tired, and her head ached.

She burrowed into the pile of old clothes and dreamed of thin soup and crusts of bread, hoping there would be some when they got to the Grand Pont, where Emmelot would stop to greet the beggars, prostitutes, and other wretches who loitered there around the water trough. Horses were drinking from the trough, and she wanted to drink, too, but someone held her back. She thought she smelled sweat and urine. Old Emmelot picked her up, set her in the cart, and they started off again. She shrank deep into the pile of clothes. There had been no soup or bread. And she was so thirsty.

When they got back to Emmelot's shack, they sat outside, sorting through the day's haul. 'Give me something to drink,' she begged, but the old woman merely told her, as she did every day, about her superstitions. They all had to do with water, but she couldn't remember exactly how. Was it bad luck to spill it? Good luck to bathe in it? Bad luck to drink it? All she knew was that she wanted a drink, and Emmelot wouldn't give it to her. She went back to sleep.

The thirst woke her. And the throbbing in her head. Her whole body ached. There must be bruises, she thought, but she couldn't see them, it was so dark. And she was cold. Her dress was ripped and most of her body was uncovered. She felt around, and her hands touched walls that closed in on her. I'm in my coffin, she thought. What does it matter. She went to sleep again, and again it was the thirst that woke her. They were back at the water trough. She clambered out of the cart and started toward it. An old man's hairy arms encircled her and pulled her back. She was terrified. She screamed.

In the queen's chambers, Isabeau reclined on her day bed, talking to Klara, who sat on one of the big cushions. Collette and the fools sprawled on the floor at the foot of the bed, playing with the monkey. Gracieuse sat on a stool in front of one of the tapestries and sang a sad song about a dwarf. The greyhound sat beside her, his head cocked as though he were listening to the music.

The ladies-in-waiting stood talking softly together. Jeannine's mother watched from across the room. Loyse stood next to her, and Klara asked the queen to be excused so she could go and greet her friend.

Suddenly the greyhound jumped up and began to whine, softly at first, then insistently. He raced to the door of the room, slid to a halt when he found it was shut, howled, and began to run around as though possessed. When he came to Gracieuse, he stopped short and stood in front of her, snarling and baring his teeth. The minstrel jumped up and dropped her lute, whereupon the dog, barking and wagging his tail furiously, leapt at the tapestry behind her and began to claw at it, attacking it so fiercely that it swayed and threatened to fall.

A guard came in from the hall. 'What's going on?' he asked.

The queen sprang to her feet and ran to the dog, which bounded away and ran out the now-open door, leaving the tapestry hanging precariously on one of the hooks that attached it to the molding at the top of the wall.

Colin rushed in. 'There's something on the other side of that wall,' he cried.

'Nothing to make a dog act like that,' the guard said.

'You fool!' Colin shouted. 'Don't you know that dogs can hear things we can't?' He raced out of the room. The guard yelled that everyone else should stay where they were and followed him.

In the corridor, the dog was clawing at a large wooden chest.

'That's where the laundresses keep dirty linens,' the guard said.

The lid of the chest was slightly askew. Colin put his ear to the opening and listened. 'She's in there!' he cried. He raised the lid, reached down into the dirty bed clothes, chemises, shirts, and under-garments and lifted Alips out.

FORTY-EIGHT

A color known as orpiment is yellow. It is an artificial color, and it is very poisonous . . . Don't get it in your mouth, for if you do, you will suffer greatly.

Cennino Cennini,
Il libro dell'Arte o Trattato della Pittura, c. 1400

Marion ran into the courtyard. 'Orpiment!' she cried. 'The boy stole orpiment. Jacquemin told me it's used instead of gold. It's less expensive.'

'And very poisonous,' Christine said as she pulled Marion through the door to the palace.

The scene that greeted them when they entered the queen's chambers was one of utter chaos. One of the huge tapestries lay on the floor; the queen's monkey scampered around in a frenzy of screaming and hooting; the goldfinches chattered frantically as they lunged against the walls of their cage, causing it to swing precari-ously on its chain; the fools stood in the middle of the room, laughing hysterically and crying at the same time; and the queen's ladies fluttered like a flock of agitated birds around Loyse, who lay on the floor with blood streaming down her face. Collette knelt at Loyse's side, sobbing silently. In one corner of the room, Gracieuse the minstrel stood bewildered, holding her broken lute.

And even more astonishing, Alips lay on the queen's bed. The queen, her long black hair streaming around her face, stood over her, stroking her forehead with one hand and with the other holding the collar of the whining greyhound.

'Alips was in a chest,' Isabeau said. She patted the greyhound. 'He heard.'

'Is she going to be all right?'

'I know not. She has a blow on the head.'

Christine looked at the dwarf. The little figure lay motionless.

The queen said, 'Colin found her and brought her here. Then Jeannine's mother shoved Loyse out of the way and ran off. Loyse fell and hurt herself.'

'Where is Klara?'

'She ran out with Jeannine's mother.'

Christine knelt beside Loyse, who had an ugly gash on the side of her head. She seemed to be breathing, but she couldn't be sure.

Someone said, 'The doctor is coming.'

Alips moaned and tried to say something. Christine went to her and bent down so she could hear. 'I thought it was Guillaume,' the dwarf rasped. 'It was the mother.'

Christine hurried to the room where she did her copying and lifted the coverlet on the bed. The pouch with the cards was gone. 'What a dunce I've been. I let him get away!'

Marion stood beside her. Thoroughly confused, she asked, 'What are you talking about?'

'Willem disguised himself as Jeannine's mother.'

Marion clapped her hand to her head.

'He took the playing cards,' Christine continued. 'Then he brought them back, with the gold leaf replaced by orpiment, which looks like gold. Orpiment is deadly poison. It contains arsenic.'

'The cards were meant for the king.'

'Of course they were. The king bites his fingernails. After touching the cards, he'd put his fingers in his mouth, and he'd poison himself.'

Christine went to a small fireplace on the other side of the room. In the flames, gold glittered and faded away. Marion came to her side and gasped as she watched the playing cards go up in smoke.

Christine said, 'We have to find him.'

'But he could have gone anywhere!'

'We have to try,' Christine said. She and Marion rushed from the room.

'Did the fool's mother come out this way?' Christine shouted at Simon at the entrance to the palace.

'Yes. A while ago. The girl who came to find you was with her. What has happened?'

'I'll tell you later,' Christine said as she and Marion ran out into the street.

There was no sign of Willem and Klara. Instead, Henri Le Picart strode up to them.

'Willem has run away,' Christine cried.

'Calm yourself.'

'Don't tell me to be calm! We found him!'

'And you let him get away? Why can't you women ever do anything right?'

Christine lashed out at him with her fists. He took hold of her hands to make her stop. She took a deep breath and said, 'Willem disguised himself as the mother of the queen's fool. He stole a set of playing cards the queen intended to give the king and painted them with orpiment.'

'You discovered this?'

'I suppose you don't think a woman is capable of such a thing!'

Henri looked a bit chagrined. Christine even thought he might apologize. But all he said was, 'The king would poison himself. Very clever. Where did the boy get the paint?'

'He stole it from Jacquemin the illuminator.'

'It was the beguine who did the painting.'

Christine had to admit that he was probably right. She remembered Jacquemin saying that the boy had never learned much. Agnes hadn't done a very good job with the paint, either.

Henri said, 'When I saw them together near the Châtelet, she was returning the cards to him.'

'Do you think it was her idea to throw a lighted torch at the king?' Marion asked.

'No doubt,' Henri said. 'She was surely the one who prompted the boy to get entry to the palace.'

'And she probably knew about the masquerade because she heard Huguet de Guisay bragging about it in the street, just like I did,' Marion said.

'But how could they have known that Jeannine's mother was going to visit her?' Christine asked as she wrenched her hands away from Henri's. 'And where is the real mother now?'

'I know,' said Colin, who'd suddenly appeared. 'I'll take you there.'

FORTY-NINE

The work here is very hard, often turning night into day and day into night. The poor sick people have to be kept clean, lifted, laid down, bathed, wiped, given food and drink, carried from one bed to another, covered, set into bathing tubs. Their beds have to be made and remade, their rags have to be cleaned every day in clear water, the cloths they wear on their feet have to be warmed, eight or nine hundred sheets have to be washed in lye and rinsed in clear water every week, wood has to be brought for the fires, the ashes have to be relit, sheets have to be washed in the Seine when there is ice, wind, and rain, spread out in the galleries in the summer, dried by the fire in winter, and folded. The dead have to be wrapped in winding sheets, and there are many other laborious and painful tasks.

Jehan Henry,
Livre de vie active de l'Hôtel-Dieu de Paris, c. 1482

'I'm going to look for Willem,' Henri announced. 'You two go with Colin.'

Will he never stop ordering me around? Christine asked herself as she and Marion ran after the boy. They struggled to keep up as he raced through the courtyard, out into the street, down the rue Saint-Antoine, through the place de Grève, and across the Planche-Mibray to the Île.

'Why is he taking us to the cathedral?' Marion asked breathlessly as they went up the rue Neuve Notre-Dame.

'He isn't,' Christine said. 'He's taking us to the Hôtel Dieu.'

Colin had gone to the main entrance of the hospital, an enormous building that stood on the south side of the parvis of Notre-Dame.

He pulled the chain of a large bell, and a woman in a white habit and a black veil opened the heavy door. Colin spoke to her for a moment, and she motioned that they should all come in. They followed her though a long corridor, at the end of which another woman, wearing a similar white habit and black veil, waited. 'This is Sister Hélène,' Colin said.

They followed the sister into a huge room with many beds and an altar at one end. She led them to a bed with two women in it. One was fat and had a bandaged leg. The other was thin and grey-haired, and she had a large bandage around her head. Colin went to the second woman and said, 'This is Jaquiette, Jeannine the fool's mother.'

The woman looked at her visitors hopefully.

Sister Hélène shook her head. 'All she says is that she wants to go to the queen.'

'How do you know who she is?' Christine asked Colin.

'Because I talked to her once. Don't you recognize her? She's the woman we saw in the cemetery at the church of Saint-Pol.'

'The woman who'd been struck on the head, who'd been lying under a tree all night?'

'Yes.'

Christine was about to question Colin further, but she stopped. She didn't want the boy to say too much in front of the other woman in the bed.

'I keep telling Sister Hélène that Jaquiette is not out of her mind,' Colin said. 'She should go to the queen, so she can see her daughter.'

'He's right,' Christine said to the sister. 'This woman is supposed to be at the palace. Her daughter is the queen's fool.'

Jaquiette started to cry. Sister Hélène stroked her forehead.

'So can she go there now?' Colin asked.

'She was badly hurt, and she should have another day or two to recover,' Sister Hélène said. 'Also, she needs some clothes. She had only her chemise when she came here.'

'The boy who hit her took the rest of her clothes, and he's been wearing them,' Christine said.

The sister looked puzzled. 'It's hard to explain,' Christine said. 'I want to know all about it.'

Christine looked around the room. There were about fifty beds. In each there were two or three patients, and five sisters rushed back and forth caring for them. One was spooning broth into the mouth of an old woman who could barely sit up, another was helping a woman put slippers on so she could go to the privy, another was lifting patients so she could change the sheets where someone had vomited, and another was making the bed of someone who had just died. Christine watched attendants carry the corpse from the room, and she thought about the hard life these sisters had and how little they saw of the outside world. She looked at Sister Hélène's hands, noted that they were red and chapped, and wondered whether she had to help launder the sheets in the cold winter waters of the Seine. She decided that task was probably left to the novices. Nevertheless, Sister Hélène's eyes were rimmed with red, and she looked very tired; she'd obviously been hard at work for many hours. Yet she was looking at her eagerly, wanting to know the story of the poor woman who lay on the bed before them. Christine was not about to reveal everything that was happening at the palace, but she decided to tell her some of it.

The woman with her leg in a cast was listening. Christine smiled at her. 'We mustn't disturb you.'

Sister Hélène adjusted the woman's bedclothes, told Jaquiette she would return soon, and led the visitors to a small chapel. 'We can talk privately here.'

'Jaquiette really is the mother of the queen's fool Jeannine,' Christine said.

'Do tell me how she came to be here in such a condition.' Sister Hélène's eyes sparkled.

'Perhaps Colin is the best one to tell you that.'

The sister looked at Colin. 'It seems you have some explaining to do.'

Colin looked shamefaced. 'It's my fault she got hurt.'

Marion couldn't help interjecting, 'Your big mouth got you into trouble, didn't it?'

'It did.' The boy looked as though he would cry. 'I used to see Willem in the street, and we got to talking, and I started bragging about how I know everything that goes on at the palace. I told him the queen likes me and gives me messages to deliver. I told him about the fool, and how her mother was coming to visit her. Willem wanted to know all about it, so I told him I'd let him know when the mother arrived. When the woman was found lying under the tree, I knew what had happened. He'd hit her and taken her clothes. I had no idea what he was planning to do after that.' He started to cry.

'Didn't you recognize him in the queen's chambers?'

'No. He'd disguised himself so well.'

'You're not as clever as you think you are,' Marion said.

'I think we must forgive Colin,' Sister Hélène said. 'He followed the men who brought her here, and he's been here every day since. He talks to her and tries to get her to remember who she is and where she was going.'

'But she does remember,' Colin wailed. 'It's just that you don't believe her.'

'Well, I believe her now. But what I want to know is, what happened to the boy who stole her clothes?'

'That's what we all want to know,' Christine said. 'He's caused a lot of trouble at the palace, and now he's disappeared. We need to find him, but we don't know where to look.'

'Didn't Jeannine know he wasn't a woman? Didn't she know it wasn't her mother?'

'I'm not sure,' Christine said. 'She seemed to ignore him, but she doesn't talk much, and no one knows what she thinks.'

'Perhaps she was paying more attention than you realize,' Sister Hélène said. 'Ask her whether she knows where the boy went.'

Why didn't I think of that? Christine asked herself. 'You're right,' she said. 'We have to get back to the palace right away.'

'Colin can stay here,' Sister Hélène said. 'I must attend to other patients. Jaquiette will get better faster if she has the boy at her side.' She turned to go, and then said over her shoulder, 'Tell Jeannine her real mother will be joining her soon.'

FIFTY

The lion is cruel and wood when he is wroth, and biteth and grieveth himself for indignation, and gnasheth with his teeth.

Bartholomaeus Anglicus, thirteenth century

Christine and Marion hurried back to the palace. At the entrance to the queen's residence Simon greeted them sadly. 'I'm afraid Loyse is not doing well.'

In the queen's chambers, Alips was sitting in the queen's big high-backed chair, wrapped in a red blanket. She was slumped over and in pain, but she looked up when she realized Christine was standing over her. 'I have a very hard head,' she rasped.

'Can you talk about what happened?' Christine asked.

'Let me sit up.'

A chambermaid who was standing nearby put her arms around the dwarf and lifted her into a comfortable position.

'When did you realize it was the fool's mother?' Christine asked.

'I didn't. I thought it was Guillaume.'

Christine looked over at the fool, who stood next to Jeannine. Jeannine was crying, and he stroked her hand.

'It was that book,' Alips said. 'The one with the mean dwarf. They were reading about a knight who acts like a fool, and I thought of Guillaume. I thought he was in league with the Duchess of Burgundy. I thought they were just pretending to hate each other.'

'The Duchess of Burgundy had nothing to do with this. I'll explain everything later.'

Alips lowered her voice. 'Please don't tell Guillaume I suspected him!'

'Of course I won't. But why did the boy who was pretending to be Jeannine's mother think *he* was the one you suspected?'

'He must have seen me looking around the room, trying to think who was guilty. He knew he was the one, so he assumed I'd found him out.'

Alips put her hand to her head and winced. Christine said, 'He tried to kill you, you know. He left you for dead in that chest.'

'As I said, I have a very hard head. I don't think Loyse does. She's badly hurt.'

Loyse lay on the queen's bed, with the doctor standing over her and one of the queen's maids applying warm poultices. 'There's not much more I can do for her,' the doctor said when Christine approached. 'She may recover if she's kept warm and quiet, but I can't guarantee it.'

'At least she recognizes me,' Christine said as Loyse tried to smile at her.

'And me,' Marion exclaimed. She leaned over, took Loyse in her arms, and said to the doctor, 'All you doctors do is make people worse.'

'Marion!' Christine cried. She was going to tell her to apologize, but the doctor was already out the door, cursing as he went.

Jeannine the fool came to the bed and touched Loyse gently on the cheek. 'A bad person hurt you,' she said.

Remembering what Sister Hélène had advised, Christine asked her, 'Do you know where the bad person went?'

'The lions,' Jeannine said.

'The lions? Why would he go to the lions?' Christine asked.

'We should go and find out,' Marion said. She grabbed Christine's hand and drew her out the door.

It was dusk when they ran out into the palace grounds. A light rain had started to fall, and the paths through the gardens were wet and muddy. Water dripped from the trees and thunder roared in the distance. As they approached the lions' stockade, there were other, more frightening, sounds.

'My God!' Christine cried. 'What are they doing?'

The lions were roaring, and someone was screaming. They raced toward the sounds and were horrified to see the lions surrounding a mangled body on the ground. Spurred on by the scent of the blood pouring from their victim, the lions, no longer the gentle creatures Marion had always claimed were too old to be a danger to anyone, roared and pounced, now wild animals mauling their prey.

Christine and Marion stood, helpless and horrified. Then Gilet appeared. He had a large tree branch, and he used it to drive the lions back. Still growling and snarling, they let the keeper, who spoke to them in a soothing voice, herd them into their stockade.

Christine knelt in the mud beside the figure on the ground. In the fading light, she could see that the women's clothes he wore were nearly all ripped from his body. His face was badly mangled, but the eyes stared at her. They were an icy blue.

'Can you talk?'

Willem made a garbled sound.

'We know what you did. We know you painted the playing cards with orpiment, to poison the king.'

A ghastly grimace appeared on the boy's ravaged face.

Christine's knees hurt so much she had to stand up. Marion knelt in her place and leaned in close to the boy. 'Did you throw the lighted torch at the masqueraders?' she asked. He whispered something. Then he fell back. He was dead.

'What did he tell you, Marion?'

'He said he did it. He said he was only sorry the king didn't die.'

FIFTY-ONE

If you are a married lady, don't object to being obedient to your husband. Sometimes it is not the best thing to be independent.

Christine de Pizan,
Le Livre de la Cité des Dames, 1404–1405

Klara stood at the entrance to the lions' stockade, sobbing. Marion took the girl in her arms. 'Why was Willem here?' she asked.

'I told him he could hide with the lions until it got dark, and then he could run away without anyone seeing him.'

'But why did the lions attack him?'

'Gilet said they would be angry if someone shouted at them, so I did.'

'You deliberately made them attack your brother?'

'I hated him for ignoring me and running away from Martin's house. And he killed Loyse,' the girl said, sobbing louder than before.

'What is she saying?' asked Christine, who hadn't heard because of a loud clap of thunder.

'She says the lions killed her brother because she shouted at them.'

'She *meant* for the lions to attack him?'

'It looks that way. She says she did it because she was angry at him. And she thinks he's killed Loyse.'

'Loyse is badly hurt, but she may not be dead.'

Klara's sobbing grew even louder. Christine took her by the shoulders and shook her gently. 'You must never tell anyone what you did.'

By this time the palace guards had arrived. The rain came down heavily, soaking everyone's clothes and forming puddles at their feet. Christine and Marion wore cloaks, but Klara wore only a dress, drenched and covered with mud. She was shaking uncontrollably.

'We have to get her away from here,' Christine said. She and Marion put their arms around the girl and ushered her along a slippery path through the gardens, lifting her over puddles and water-laden branches that barred their way.

As they emerged into the street, a man enveloped in a huge black cloak rode past on a black horse. He wheeled the horse around and came back. 'What happened?'

'We'll tell you later,' Christine said. 'Right now the most important thing is to get her someplace warm and dry. Take her to my house.'

'I know where it is,' the man said as he leaned down and scooped Klara up onto the saddle in front of him. Cradling her gently in his arms and pulling his voluminous cloak around her, he galloped off.

'I wonder what he was doing here,' Christine said.

'I suspect he has passed by often, ever since I told him Klara was helping take care of the lions,' Marion said.

They hurried down the street, slipping and sliding and plunging through puddles, until they reached Christine's house, where they found Martin du Bois standing outside, waiting for them.

'Your mother is taking care of Klara,' he said.

'Willem is dead,' Christine said. 'The lions killed him.'

'The lions?'

'Those lions are not dangerous if one knows how to treat them. Willem didn't.'

'But why was he in the lions' stockade?'

'Klara took him there.' She couldn't bring herself to tell him why.

Martin was silent for a long time. His eyes were full of tears. 'I tried to do my best for the boy. But it was no use. He hated me, and all of us. I can understand. We did terrible things in Courtrai.'

Christine said, 'Willem admitted that he was responsible for the fire. But we can't prove it, now that he's dead.'

'I want to know the whole story. But not just yet.'

Christine said, 'I haven't even told anyone in my family the whole story. It would only frighten them. Especially my mother. So, come in, but let me do the explaining.'

In the kitchen, Francesca stood at the table, mumbling to herself and doing something with some nuts. She said, 'I gave Klara valerian and put her to bed.' Then she looked up and pointed her finger at the stranger who'd brought Klara home. 'I think I deserve to know who you are and why the girl is in such a state.'

Christine said, 'This is Martin du Bois, Klara's husband.'

Francesca drew a deep breath, put her hand over her heart, and plopped down onto a bench. 'You're supposed to be old and decrepit!'

'Is that what Klara told you?' Martin asked.

Francesca started to laugh. 'She really had us fooled. Have you come to get her? Why is she so upset?'

Christine said, 'Her brother is dead.'

'What happened?'

'She took him to the lions' stockade, and the lions attacked him.'

'I thought those old lions were harmless.'

'Something disturbed them. Don't say too much to Klara about it.'

Marion stood in the doorway, and all the children crept up behind her and tried to peer into the room.

'This is Klara's husband,' Christine said.

'I hope it means that Klara will go back to her own house now,' Jean said.

'Have some compassion. She's had a horrible experience. Her brother has died. You'd be upset, too.'

'Maybe not,' Thomas said. Jean smacked him on the back of his head.

'What is Marion doing here?' Francesca asked. 'I knew you two were putting yourselves in danger again.'

'There's no danger now,' Christine said. 'I'm sure Martin would like to see his wife, so I'm going to take him upstairs.'

In Francesca's room, Klara lay on the bed and Georgette sat beside her, talking to her quietly and smoothing her forehead.

'You can go downstairs now, Georgette,' Christine said. 'We'll take care of Klara.'

When Klara saw Martin, she began to cry.

'I know what happened,' he said. 'I know it wasn't your fault.'

'But it was!'

Christine said, 'No one will think that, Klara. So just keep quiet about it, and everything will be all right.'

'You think I knew what my brother was going to do. But I didn't.'

'You didn't know he's been prowling around the house, looking for you? Or about the poisoned playing cards?'

'What are you talking about?'

'Didn't you wonder why your brother was in the queen's chambers, dressed like a woman?'

'I didn't know he was there, until you took me to meet the queen.'

'So what did you think when you saw him?'

'He was my brother. He did strange things.' She sobbed harder than before. 'But I don't know why he hurt Loyse. She never did anything to him. She didn't deserve to die.'

'She's not dead,' Christine said. 'She's only badly hurt.'

'Who is Loyse?' Martin wanted to know.

'She was the lion-keeper's helper, before Klara came along. She's living at the palace with the queen now.'

'Can I go and see her?' Klara asked.

'First you have to come home with me,' Martin said. 'Do you think you can get up now?'

'Let me stay here and rest for a while.'

Martin and Christine went back downstairs, where the children were crowded around Francesca, who was making walnut preserve. 'I suppose you are going to take the book you wrote for Klara home now,' Francesca said to Martin.

'Perhaps I should let you keep it. Klara isn't interested in it.'

'My daughter has read me a few of your recipes, and I've tried some. They aren't bad if you like a lot of sauces.'

'I know you Italians do things differently.'

'You wrote about this preserve I'm making,' Francesca said. 'I like the way you put holes in the nuts and stuff them with bits of cloves and ginger.'

Klara crept into the kitchen. 'I'm ready to go home now, Martin,' she said.

FIFTY-TWO

Everyone at the court asked for a long time who was respon-
sible for the disaster. When it was finally accepted that it was
the Duke of Orléans, no one dared punish him, because he

was so powerful. But when some wise men reproached him
gently for his thoughtlessness, he promised that in the future
he would make amends for his youthful errors with better
conduct.

The Monk of Saint-Denis,
Chronique du Religieux de Saint-Denis,
contenant le règne de Charles VI de 1380 à 1422

The next morning, Christine hurried to the palace. At the entrance, Simon greeted her with a barrage of questions.

'Do you know about the boy who was killed by the lions? Who was he?'

'That boy was the woman you saw running out of the palace. He'd disguised himself as an old woman and pretended to be the mother of the queen's fool.'

'Then he's the one who nearly killed the deaf girl?'

'Yes. Do you know how she is?'

'They say she'll recover. Tell me more about the boy.'

'He was a mischief-maker.'

To escape further questions, Christine hurried into the palace. In the great gallery, she found Henri Le Picart waiting for her.

'I know you are on your way to see the queen,' he said. 'I must talk to you first.'

'I know how to talk to the queen,' Christine said. 'I don't need your help.'

'But you do. You're going to tell her there really was someone who was trying to kill the king. But you are also going to tell her she must keep it to herself.'

Christine looked at him in surprise. 'Why?'

'The Duke of Orléans suffers because he thinks it was his torch that started the fire. But he would suffer more if people thought he was trying to put the blame on an innocent boy who can't defend himself because he's dead.'

'But we *know* it was Willem who threw the torch. He admitted it to Marion.'

'Who would believe a prostitute?'

'We can prove that he tried to poison the king. He put orpiment on the playing cards.'

'And where are those cards now?'

She remembered. 'Willem threw them into the fire.'

'So you see. No one would believe Louis if he said the boy started the fire. And remember, he did bring lighted torches into the room.'

'But how can we let him continue to punish himself for something he didn't do! And what about Brother Michel? Shouldn't he know the truth so he can put it in his chronicle?'

'Brother Michel will record what everyone believes. The duke will just have to accept the fact that he will always be thought guilty. But his conscience will be clear. That will have to be enough.'

'Who is going to tell him?'

'I am.'

'And what about the musicians who played that night? They suspect the truth.'

'They won't say anything. They're too afraid of being accused themselves.'

'But I must tell the queen everything.'

'Of course. And you will explain to her why she must never tell anyone else.'

'What about Alips and Marion? And the Duchess of Berry? She saw a third torch, too.'

'They will understand, when you explain it to them. The Duchess of Berry is with the queen now. Unfortunately, the Duchess of Burgundy is there too, so you must get her out of the way. She, of all people, must never know.'

Christine could see Henri's reasoning, and, much as she didn't want to, she agreed. She saw him smiling at her, and she remembered their earlier conversation in the great gallery. 'I will do as you advise,' she stammered.

In the queen's chambers, she was relieved to see that Loyse, her head encased in a large bandage, was well enough to sit in the queen's big chair. Alips stood beside her, holding the greyhound by his collar.

The queen sat on her day bed, talking to the duchesses of Berry and Burgundy. Her ladies stood on the other side of the room, murmuring to one another.

'No one knows what is happening,' the queen said. 'Jeannine's mother has hurt Loyse and run away, and the playing cards have disappeared again.'

Christine looked over at Alips. The dwarf nodded and let go of the greyhound's collar. The big dog bounded to the queen's bed, brushing against the Duchess of Burgundy, who gave a startled cry and fell. One of her attendants ran to her, helped her to her feet, and helped her limp from the room. Alips put her hand over her mouth and smothered a laugh.

Christine almost laughed herself, but instead she said to the queen, 'I have much to tell you, *Madame*. Please dismiss your ladies.'

The queen called her ladies and asked them to leave for a while. Sensing that they weren't supposed to be there either, Guillaume, Jeannine, and the rest of the queen's entourage left with them. Then Christine said, 'There is nothing to worry about now, *Madame*. The person who meant to harm the king is dead.'

'This I have felt. Since last night, I do not feel the shadow on me as before.'

'How is this possible?' the Duchess of Berry asked.

Christine recounted all that had happened the day before.

'Then we really do know that the king's brother was not responsible for the fire,' the duchess said.

'Yes. But no one will believe it.' And she told her what Henri Le Picart had said.

'To let Louis suffer for something he didn't do!' the Duchess of Berry exclaimed.

'It would be worse if people thought he was trying to shift the blame onto a boy who is dead and cannot defend himself.'

'The duke suffers so much,' Alips said. 'Who will comfort him?'

Christine had to smile. There were many women who would be ready to comfort Louis. 'We can't worry about that now. The important thing is that there is no longer a boy here hiding in disguise waiting to kill the king. The shadow is lifted.'

At the church of the Celestines, Louis, Duke of Orléans, had set aside his costly clothes, feathered hat, gold rings, and other adornments to don – as he often did when he visited the priory – a plain white robe, in imitation of the austere habit of the monks. He knelt before a statue of the Virgin Mary and wept. In the silence of the empty church he thought he heard her speak.

One of the brothers came in, but quickly left when he heard great sobs echoing through the church and saw the king's brother on his knees. He could not know that the duke was actually rejoicing:

Louis had learned the truth about the fire at the palace, and he was weeping tears of joy. He also realized he owed a great debt to Christine, a woman he'd treated unfairly in the past and who had now saved him from a lifetime of remorse.

The duke accepted the fact that most people would never know the identity of the person who had really set the masqueraders on fire; it would be folly to accuse a boy who was dead and couldn't defend himself. Louis would always be blamed for the tragedy, but he could endure the angry stares and the murmured accusations because he'd been assured that it was not his fault. He had not caused the deaths of the four men who had gone up in flames, and that was all that mattered.

Louis brushed away his tears and stretched out face down on the floor to pray. The light of the afternoon sun streaming through the colored glass in a high window bejeweled the white robe, which glowed emerald green, sapphire blue, and ruby red against the cold grey stones of the church.